The Stone Ma

A Vampire's Reckoning

Book II

V.M.K. Fewings

This book is a work of fiction. References to real people, events, establishments, organizations, or locales are intended only to provide a sense of authenticity and are used fictitiously. All other characters, and all incidents and dialogue are drawn from the author's imagination and are not to be construed as real.

A VAMPIRE'S RECKONING. Copyright © 2011 by V.M.K. Fewings

All rights reserved.

Printed in the United States of America.

No part of this book may be used or reproduced in any manner whatsoever without written permission except in the case of brief quotations embodied in critical articles and reviews.

ISBN: 9780989478465

Cover Designer: Najla Qamber

Cover photo credit:
Shutterstock: Igor Madjinca
&
Depositphotos: TheWalker

For Elizabeth

The Stone Masters Vampire Series

A Vampire's Rise (Book I)

A Vampire's Reckoning (Book II)

A Vampire's Dominion (Book III)

PROLOGUE

JADEON

THE POWERFUL, DISTURBING *images—portraits of memories, a lingering resonance drawing together, fragments of consciousness—at times, I find myself reliving those fateful moments, surrendering to the consuming, agonizing details of June of the year of our Lord 1805.*

I falter in the chill of the night, in the fractured stillness within the great pillars of Stonehenge. Exhausted from my journey, caught up in terror, the darkness engulfs me. But I will not flee, for the promise I have made, I cannot break—my life for that of another. I fear mortality. My apprehension intensifies.

The wait is over.

It is time to wake up.

I want to lead you to safety, distract you, and destroy the clues that lure you into my world. It's too late for that now. This shakes me to the core. It's impossible to turn back the clock, but I still crave peace, still want to gauge this feeling. Reassuringly, my expression does little to reflect such. In fact, all that my presence conveys is the demeanor of a twenty-five year old Englishman, and it easily disguises the enigma of my ageless, chiseled features.

Within those dark Wiltshire woods, hidden from view, I leaned my frame against the trunk of a large tree and stared, memorizing each groove and fissure of Stonehenge.

Scattered thoughts; a multitude of ways to begin.

Unable to stay still for long, I started pacing. Sunrise was only an hour away. A waning moon provided meager light. My gaze darted nervously. These murders had been committed to gain my attention, and it was working.

By my own hand my involvement was set, the consequence of my actions drawing me in. I watched the police exploring the area near the dead girl, positioned face up on the sacrificial stone. Though not foreign to death, I hoped I wouldn't throw up on my tailored Savile Row suit. The mud on my shoes bothered me and the drizzling rain didn't help.

Once apprentice to The Keeper of the Stones, such was the catalyst for all my nightmares. This was not how I envisioned my life unfolding. But I'm getting ahead of myself. It's just that these were the darkest of days. Sharing it with you provides some comfort.

I should not start here.

My aim is to earn your trust, so that you gain insight and are able to comprehend the unfeasible. It's important that this is documented. How ironic that I now reveal what I once strived to keep hidden. Time has proven that it is safer for you to have this knowledge, so that you can prepare.

You want proof. I shall provide it, if you give me an open mind. After all, you have come this far. Therefore, I scribe this for you, in the sanctity of my study, here in St. Michael's Mount in Marazion.

Travel back with me.

The smoke and mirrors of my youth now seem such a brief moment in a long and unordinary life that passed with timeless ease. Those were the years when I knew only innocence. Cornwall, my birthplace, was renowned for its pleasant bays with their golden sands and bleak, sprawling moors.

Heritage made me the lord of a great castle that had been in my family for generations. This immense and towering mansion, grandly structured upon a small island east of Penzance, rests steadfast—as if a part of the very circular island it was built upon. The only access is by foot at low tide, or boat when the sea is in. Once, as a boy, I got caught when the tide turned. It never happened again.

Within these ancient walls, I grew up and took living in such a place for granted. Not so much now. The grand castle had once been a monastery owned by British Royalty during the Reformation, only to be sold again by Queen Elizabeth I to my ancestor, the Earl of Salisbury. The famous ancient vision of the Archangel Michael on the island had even inspired the occasional zealous religious pilgrim. Nevertheless, my father had been reluctant to encourage such an invasion, even one as passive as Christian visitors. He used large hunting dogs to keep the unrelenting observers away and the staff in.

In my mind, I wander the corridors, settling in the Great Hall with its low beams, arched windows, and stone walls, bestowing gothic sconces and ancient relics—typical of an affluent and powerful family of its time. Great tapestries hang fast on the walls—priceless paintings positioned this way and that in order to catch or avoid light. Exquisite Roman rugs strewn over the cold stone floors, and candles light the rooms, casting unfamiliar shadows over everything. During fierce winters, the cold is unrelenting, hence the thick walls and grand hearths within.

The castle's history is as varied as its many rooms—a regal ballroom, which has entertained kings; an armory, which held the weapons used for their battles; lavish bedrooms fitted for visiting dignitaries, a large kitchen, and modest servants' quarters. The rooms facing south overlook the terrace and provide a good view of the gardens below. The castle's imposing towers, once used by loyal castle guards as sentries, look out over the ocean.

Now in the twenty-first century, the posts stand empty. Very often, I like to go up there to breathe in the fresh sea air and admire the view. On occasion, when inspired, I even take my paints and a fresh canvas to capture the dramatic Southern nightscapes. My artistic nature is a good contrast to my athletic pursuits. I am a worthy fencing opponent.

I have traveled, yes, but this is home, where I feel most comfortable; yet still I am unable to shake off the eerie calm of the place. Visitors seldom come here, though when they do, they are excited to take a tour and explore the rare artifacts that have withstood the test of time.

Human nature is appealing when presented in its purest form, but I seem to move in circles that reflect the darkest of realms. By following this venture of self-discovery, I unveiled a supernatural truth. Indulge me again and allow me to wander back, for perhaps soon all I will have will be the memories of my beloved castle.

The library and reading rooms are favorites of mine. Alex, my younger brother of two years, and I received our many and varied lessons within these very tenements, presented by the finest of teachers. We were lectured in the arts, sciences, languages, music, and mastered horsemanship and hunting. My father ensured that we became proficient swordsmen, rounding out our education. Renaissance at its best.

When our lessons were over we spent our time playing, tirelessly investigating each room; but we stayed clear of the servants' quarters for fear of being smacked around the head by the moody cook. We became familiar with the castle's lower chambers, even venturing into its cold, gloomy cellars, bravely exploring the dungeons where criminals had once been held before being condemned and escorted away to suffer their fate. Only rusting shackles are left to convey what horrors these rooms have witnessed. As boys, our imaginations ran wild, though our play never matched the reality of what happened down there.

Although we had the run of the castle, there was but one room to which our father had banned our entrance. We did of course try to turn the huge brass handle of the large imposing door, but alas, it remained locked, its secrets kept hidden within. All we could do was wonder what lay inside such a chamber, until inevitably we became distracted. My fascination with that room was to be my undoing. My present irrevocably dissolves into my past.

PART ONE

I

JADE⊕N
Circa 1789

"IT'S DOWN TO US, ALEX," I warned my younger brother. "We must save the castle. Pirates are scaling the wall. We fight for honor."

At the age of ten years, I often gained great delight in teasing Alex. I held the telescope up to my eye, and from my bedroom window viewed the still waters spreading out beyond the castle. It was late evening, and I watched my younger brother beside me pull on his dress shirt, readying for dinner.

"Jadeon!" He tugged at the telescope. "Let me see."

"Pirates."

Alex grabbed the telescope. He too scanned the horizon, and on seeing nothing but a calm sea, agreed with me.

We both ran out of the room carrying our wooden swords with us, down the dark corridors, past the armory, and out under the stone archway onto the large granite steps leading to the grassy lawn. We made our way down to the rocky reef below, hidden behind the castle walls. The sea crashed against the rocks. The moon reflected off its mutable surface. Here, at the water's edge, we fought with our swords swaying this way and that, taking on the imaginary pirates one by one, using our weapons masterfully.

Each blissful memory blended into innocent days interfused with one another as we shared willingly in everything. I was similar to our father, with his dark complexion and deep brown eyes, tall in stature for one so young, and in temperament intensely serious and passionate. My brother, with his short blond curls and cherubic appearance, had inherited our mother's fairness of skin and her crystal blue eyes. His nature was similar too, quiet and thoughtful, yet spontaneous and vibrant. He looked up to me and relied upon my guidance in all things. Perhaps this dependence was exaggerated because of our father's interminable distance toward us.

Lord William Artimas, our father and master of the castle, always seemed otherwise detained or distracted. He would disappear for weeks at a time on important state affairs, only to return to the castle disquieted and just as aloof. Very often, I would wait by his study on his return, hoping to catch a moment of his time, only to be shooed away by Arthur, his personal secretary. Father would frequently pass us along the corridors without a second glance, his mind so focused on serious matters.

Lord Artimas was an intimidating presence. At six-foot-three, he held an imperious demeanor—a dark and thoughtful face often frowning with the worries of running the large estate and the people who lived there. Despite this, he was a loving father when he had the time, and his attentions, though brief, were of an encouraging nature. He would always appear delighted when we were presented to him on evenings when his commitments would allow, and he reveled in each new skill we had mastered.

Lady Anna Beth Artimas, our doting mother, always seemed without a worry and kept busy with the day-to-day pleasures of the castle, entertaining their friends and visitors. Our mother liked to ensure her sons received an education fit for the lords we would one day become, and a spontaneous visit to our classroom was not unusual. She often pulled us enthusiastically outside to view the blossoming of a new flower or the arrival of a grand ship within view of the castle, only to send us back into the classroom again to continue with our studies.

Lady Artimas's closest ally was Sara De Mercy, the wife of Father Edward De Mercy of the Parish Marazion. The two had grown close as friends while their husbands were engrossed in business, and they could be seen whispering or laughing in corners of the castle, taking a turn around the great hall during banquets, or sitting together at the grand castle dinners. They had found solace in each other's company, and their temperaments suited one another.

The De Mercys had two daughters—a newborn and Catherine, who was a year younger than me. Catherine looked forward to her weekly visits to the castle and enjoyed the short but adventurous boat trip out to the island. She was often placed beside us at gatherings.

She was the image of her mother, possessing her large grey eyes, fair skin, and blond curls cascading down her back.

To us, she appeared angelic, and while at times we were apprehensive she would disturb our robustious play, she was always a worthy advocate. Catherine, not content with running away as a frightened damsel from deadly, make-believe dragons, soon took up her own wooden sword—one of my discarded toys—and fought the imagined serpents as well, much to our delight.

She often took her meals and even her lessons with us. Although this turn of events was most unusual and potentially scandalous, it neither deterred nor prevented the three of us from spending such time together, as our mothers had encouraged. Soon, we were inseparable when Catherine visited the island.

* * * *

By the age of ten, I had developed a deep affection for Catherine, and we rarely played with wooden swords now, but she was often in my presence. Her gentle temperament brought me out of my shell, and it was she who introduced me to astronomy. She would point up at the stars and test my knowledge of the formations. During the long winter nights, we found rooms within the castle in which to hide, and in the summer, we stole out to the water's edge where we would chat well into the morning . . . all so very innocent.

My parents could never figure out why I slept so much during the day.

On a night so similar to the others, I lay under my bed covers and strained to keep my eyes open. I had again arranged to meet Catherine, whose family had enjoyed a late-night dinner as guests of my parents and were staying in the east wing. When the appointed hour arrived, I dressed as quietly as possible, glancing occasionally at my brother who slept soundly beside me. Alex, despite having his own bedroom, often preferred to sleep in my bed, where he found comfort from his fear of the dark. I had grown used to his need and didn't mind at all.

The floorboards creaked, as if cursing my footing. I reached for Alex's still-burning candle from the small rosewood table before heading out to the south terrace. I tiptoed through the shadows, hugging the walls, and made my way down the sweeping staircase into the main hallway toward the exit.

Screams echoed.

I stopped.

They came from a corridor that led away from the foyer. I followed the sobs, proceeding cautiously down the dark, intimidating corridor positioned to the right of the main stairwell. To my horror, a gust of wind blew out the flame from my candle, and for a moment I was thrown into complete blackness.

I hoped Catherine would wait.

My eyes adjusted to the shadowy darkness—again, those female cries—and despite my overwhelming dread, I could not turn back. The noises resonated from the castle's dungeons.

I held my candle in front of me, as though by some miracle it would relight, and fumbled my way down the stairs with my left hand on the cold stone wall, using the torchlight that reflected from the lower chambers. I heard a scuffle from inside the very room my father had strictly forbidden me ever to enter. I considered waking him up but was drawn to the door.

Crouching down, I peered through the keyhole. Numerous candles lit the chamber, allowing a fair view of the men who moved purposefully within. Muffled voices now rhythmically chanted, and over them came a woman's voice.

My hands trembled and I willed them to stop.

I peeked again. A shrill almost knocked me back. Something very bad was happening. A girl begged for mercy. I considered saving her from the monsters that tortured her. Father would know what to do.

I was going in.

I will save you.

A key turned in the lock.

Those inside were coming out.

I sprinted toward the large wooden trunk that was against the far wall, horrified to see Alex had followed me down. Quickly, I shoved him behind the trunk and covered his mouth. Although furious with Alex, the events of the moment took precedence. Together, we watched in fear, startled to see five masked men withdraw from the dark chamber, all dressed in black, their long capes billowing. Forcefully, four of the men dragged a young woman, her disheveled raven hair falling over her face, her eyes blindfolded. She was dressed in a man's clothes.

I covered my ears to block out her screams. Alex wet himself and whimpered.

I grasped his hand.

Her head bobbed up and down as they hauled her away—to my relief, in the opposite direction. I thanked God they headed away from us. For a moment, I feared they would step in the urine and find us. I recognized one of the men. He followed the entourage, walking speedily toward the dungeons. It was Father.

Alex bit down on his hand and I pulled his fingers out of his mouth before he drew blood.

"It's Father," I reassured him.

"Father?" Alex leapt up.

I yanked him down. *"No,"* I mouthed.

Father too wore a mask, and though his eyes could be seen clearly, it covered the rest of his face. I wondered why he was trying to conceal his identity.

The woman's blindfold fell to the ground, and we set eyes on the most beautiful woman. Her pale, porcelain skin was dazzling.

Her deep turquoise eyes fixed on us.

I took a deep breath, unable to remember taking my last.

She struggled, but with hands bound tightly behind her back and with the unwavering grip of the four men, she failed to get loose. Within a moment, and with much panic, the men replaced the blindfold, covering the woman's face again. She was carried off into the dark.

As they disappeared from view, the woman cried out again. "Orpheus!" The name echoed into the silence.

Alex was on his feet and running toward the dungeons. I reached out to stop him, but failed. I scampered after him and soon caught up. We gazed down the long corridor. The men, Lord Artimas, and the woman were gone.

We explored the dungeons, looking for any sign of them. On finding nothing, we looked at each other in disbelief. I was shaken but selfishly reassured that Alex had shared witness. I told him of my plan to meet with Catherine, and we both headed away from the cells, back toward his bedroom. Alex changed clothes and shoved his soiled trousers under his bed. I was grateful they were not under mine. We scurried toward the south terrace.

"You're sure it was Father?" Alex asked.

"Yes."

"Do you think the woman was a witch?"

"She must have been, otherwise why would he—"

"Do you think she put a spell on us when she saw us?" he asked.

"No."

"You don't look too sure."

"Witches need potions," I said.

Alex was persuaded. Now all I had to do was convince myself. We reached the water's edge.

"You both look like you've seen a ghost!" Catherine said.

With a subtle glance, I instructed Alex to be quiet.

At the age of nine, Catherine was like a small doll, with beautiful refined features, a petite frame, and thick blond hair. Familiar golden locks cascaded down her back.

"You are both so late!" she obviously said for Alex's sake, having expected only me. "Still, you are here now. Ready for our forbidden nightly swim?"

I forced a smile. "You go on, Catherine, and we'll join you." I drew close to Alex. "We mustn't tell her anything, not until we have discovered what it's all about."

Alex grasped my arm. "We must speak with Father in the morning."

My reply was interrupted by a loud splash. Catherine had jumped into the cold water. Alex quickly undressed, then pushed past me and joined Catherine. Together, they swam out, away from the rocky shoreline. Unsettled, I glanced back at the castle walls, the many rooms and prominent turrets, and wondered if the recent events of the evening were a dark portent.

On hearing both Catherine and Alex call to me, I too undressed before wading into the chilly waves and pushing off from the rocks toward them. When I caught up, we all tread in the water while looking back at the castle's looming silhouette. I sighed, much relieved that things seemed to be slowly returning to normal. Our nightly swim had become somewhat of a routine in the summer. We had been strictly banned from such behavior, but had defied our parents. It had been I who taught Catherine to swim. I watched her with pride, she seemingly unaware of my attention.

Catherine laughed, pulling at my arms, and then pushing me away playfully.

Her expression turned to terror. "Where's Alex?"

I searched the surface. *"No!"*

We'd swum out too far, near the undercurrents.

"Alex?" Her voice was high-pitched, panicked.

I recalled where we had last seen him, swam in that direction, and dove down, frantically scrambling with outstretched hands. Lungs bursting, I returned to the surface empty-handed, gasping for air, only to dive again into the deep. My heart pounding, I grappled in the blackness. As if by a miracle, I felt Alex's hand lashing out and grabbed hold.

Swimming with all my might, I thrashed with my legs to speed our ascent, out from the wrenching current. My lungs were bursting.

I ignored the strain, determined to rise with Alex or not at all. With all my strength I yanked him up, his head now out of the water. Gasping for air, we both coughed and spluttered. Alex clung to me as I guided him to the water's edge. Catherine, a slower swimmer, followed behind. I pushed Alex, shaken and weak, up onto the bank. For a moment, he lay quite still, reeling with fear, staring blankly. I pulled him toward me and embraced him.

I caught my breath and turned awkwardly to help Catherine out of the water.

I shrieked.

Catherine had disappeared.

"Stay here," I ordered Alex and plunged back into the water, my arms reaching out, feeling blindingly in panic. After minutes of tirelessly searching, I caught sight of her. Catherine had been dragged down by a strong current and held there. She had been swept along the water's edge and onto the rocks, where she clutched at the jagged granite. Recovering her balance, Catherine pulled herself up onto the rocky bank, safe again on dry land. We ran toward her, helping her away from the water's edge. We collapsed by the wall of the castle, shivering in shock. I took Catherine in my arms, cradling her. She flung her arms around me and held me close. Alex covered her with her own dress before continuing to dress himself.

"I saw her!" she panted.

I glanced at Alex. "Saw who?"

"She came to me. St. Catherine of Alexandria!"

I dressed her, slipping the garment over her head, then pulled on my own clothes.

I had no idea what she was talking about and hoped she would not mention it again. I lifted Catherine into my arms and carried her up the stone stairwell and through the castle, closely followed by Alex.

"Take me to her—to the painting of her," Catherine pleaded.

"Tomorrow night," I said.

Catherine sobbed.

I carried her through the main hallway and into my father's drawing room. We all left a trail of dripping water in our wake, and I hoped it would dry by morning. Not wanting to cause either Alex or Catherine further distress, I remained calm, though I didn't feel it and wondered when my heart would stop racing.

Catherine settled in front of the painting by Raphael.

The portrait had been presented to my father as a gift of gratitude from a wealthy Italian merchant for the assistance he had received following the sinking of one of his vessels. The fine painting now hung in the drawing room of the castle, positioned left of the fireplace, large in its frame and spectacular in color. Catherine peered up in awe at the painting of St. Catherine of Alexandria, mesmerized.

Appearing so immaculate in her sainthood, St. Catherine gazed dreamily at the sky. Her vibrant blue dress extenuated her full and womanly frame, her hand placed over her right breast toward her heart in a feminine, humble pose.

Alex, as instructed, retrieved blankets to warm us. The huge log fireplace, lit earlier that evening, continued to blaze brightly, providing much needed warmth.

When Alex returned, he found Catherine resting her head on my shoulder, and he wrapped the blankets around us and the third around himself. He too looked up in wonder at the painting. He rested his head on my lap and we all sat quietly, gazing up.

"Tell me the story of St. Catherine again," Catherine said.

I hesitated.

Tears welled in Catherine's eyes. I scratched my head. Catherine again began to sob.

I nodded. "She was born into a noble family in Alexandria. Following a vision, she became a Christian, at a time when it was very dangerous to be one. A horrible leader by the name of Maxentius requested that she stand in front of his philosophers and present her faith, expecting that she would be converted away from her belief."

"She convinced the philosophers," Catherine said.

"She converted them to Christianity." I was happy to see her calmer. "Maxentius ordered their—"

"Death." Catherine nodded for me to continue.

I followed her gaze toward the saint's portrait. "Catherine also converted the wife of Maxentius and two hundred of his soldiers. He had them slaughtered as well. Catherine was very beautiful, and inevitably Maxentius fell in love with her and offered her a royal marriage—if she would but deny her faith. When she refused, Maxentius had her thrown into prison where she had yet another vision—one in which she wed Jesus of Nazareth."

"Becoming the Bride of Christ." She sighed.

Alex yawned.

I threw him a wary glance. "Eventually, in a blind fury, Maxentius condemned her to death and designed a tortuous device, like a spiked wheel, on which he intended her to die a painful and slow death. Catherine was tied to the wheel, and when it began to turn, it broke into hundreds of pieces, as if symbolizing God's wrath. Maxentius, still not convinced of Catherine's faith, had her beheaded, and her body was then carried away by angels to be buried upon Mount Sinai."

"Jadeon," Catherine said. "St. Catherine appeared to me and she said that I had to give you a very important message."

With sympathy, I peered at her, aware that she had experienced a terrible ordeal. A vision of Joan of Arc, whom St. Catherine of Alexandria had also appeared to, came to mind. "We swam out too far. It was my fault," I reassured her. "I should have been more cautious."

"No," Catherine said. "You will one day do something very important."

Alex discreetly gestured that Catherine was crazy.

I ignored him. "Catherine, did you hit your head? I can't see any cuts or anything."

"Jadeon, I am fine." She pushed my hand away. "There was a magnificent white light and everything. Honestly, I know how this must sound."

"Thank you for my message," I said.

She was not convinced.

"I'm pleased my life will have purpose, like Father's." It struck me that I had no idea what my father actually did.

At Catherine's insistence, we remained in the room with her, staring at the painting until dawn. Alex soon fell asleep, but I kept Catherine company, watching her for any signs she was still upset. Our parents had taught us swimming was the work of the Devil, and now we believed it. More disturbingly, I wondered if the woman in the dungeons had cursed us. Alex never brought it up, so neither did I. I wanted to find normalcy again. The way the woman had been treated went against everything my parents had taught us. I felt ashamed of such a family secret, and wondered how we could approach Father, certain that there would be some reasonable explanation.

* * * *

The year 1797 brought with it the bitterest of winters.

At age eighteen, I was fast becoming a man, and grew restless with having to remain in the castle to avoid the harsh elements. As usual, Father was engrossed in his business affairs and rarely had time for us. And Mother, who was pregnant, had become preoccupied with preparing both the staff and nursery. Thus I spent many hours alone, reading in the library or whiling away the hours studying the violin or piano—though Alex was the musically gifted one and always outshone me with his natural talent. Occasionally, he persuaded me to join him in a hunt, but as neither of us had a head for killing, we rarely brought home a trophy.

The year was sorely bitter in many other ways. My friendship with Catherine took an unexpected turn. Catherine's mother had insisted an escort be present whenever we spent time together. Having observed Catherine alone with Alex and me, she felt conflicted with her daughter's impending womanhood. Such an invasion of our privacy made it impossible for us to continue our friendship as we had done before. We stole moments when we could, hiding from her escorts, only to fear being discovered and the worst being thought of us. We could never relax and so our shared moments were always a strain.

My feelings for Catherine were so consuming that by Christmas I had eventually found the courage to ask my father's permission to marry her. Lord Artimas was not surprised by my choice of a bride, and was reassured the girl came from a good family. And despite her status being lower than ours, he conceded and gave permission for me to marry. Lord Artimas had lectured me accordingly. I, being the good son, had listened intently, though secretly I hoped he would soon shut up, so I could go to Catherine.

Dressed in my finest suit, I immediately visited her parent's home and uncharacteristically hugged her father. Her parents instructed me to await their dispatch when an appointment to meet with their eldest daughter would be arranged. Soon after, I received a letter from Catherine, agreeing to meet me in her father's church in Marazion.

Unable to recall ever feeling quite this happy, I galloped over the snow-covered hills leading to the chapel. My horse actually lost a shoe. Turning back was not an option.

The cold did not affect me.

Catherine knelt in prayer in front of the altar. I respectfully walked through into the empty chapel. The heavy perfume of incense lingered.

I paced.

Catherine genuflected before the large cross on which a crucified Christ hung at the front of the church. On hearing me, she approached briskly, meeting me halfway up the aisle.

"Jadeon, I think you know why I have asked you here. You know me better than anyone."

I held her hand to my chest and looked down at my perfect Catherine, my heart pounding.

"Well," she continued, "I have made a decision and wanted you to be the first person I told. I know you will give me your blessing."

I studied her expression, attempting to interpret her words. The ringing in my ears was distracting.

"Jadeon, I am going to take the veil."

My jaw dropped.

Silence.

The cold caught up and I could not feel my fingers.

"Well?" she asked.

"A nun—that's wonderful, truly!"

She smiled.

"For God's sake, why?" My voice strained, my decorum lost. "Catherine, are you sure? This is so serious—you can never marry. You have to shave off your hair, for goodness sake. And if you end up in The Order of Mary, that local convent, it would mean—" My lip quivered.

"It would mean that we would no longer be able to see one another, yes."

I slumped down in the front pew.

She sat down beside me. "It's what I want, more than anything."

I would not lose her to God.

I glared up at the cross and wondered what could be done. I studied her face. "I was hoping that you and I—"

Catherine offered a sympathetic smile.

I winced.

Catherine spoke, something about her vision of Saint Catherine of Alexandria, but her words faded. She believed this to be her destiny, and the good news was she had her father's blessing.

But she did not have mine.

Though I have no recollection of leaving the church, I do remember throwing up behind it. I spent the rest of the afternoon by the half-frozen river behind the chapel. The pain was so intense, it felt permanent.

I had reasoned with God, begging him to change her mind. On my eventual return to the castle, I could not help but think Catherine's background, with her family so entrenched in the Church, would have also influenced her decision. Just as my horse made it to the path leading up to St. Michael's Mount, Catherine's father, Father De Mercy, rode past me on horseback, coming away from the castle. Neither of us spoke. We just looked at one another. Pity was in the priest's eyes. I hated him for not warning me.

Alex greeted me. He had been waiting for my return, and I noticed he too had been crying, old tears staining his cheeks, his eyes red.

"She is gone!" I dismounted my horse and handed the reins over to one of the grooms. My head down, I walked past my brother and into the castle.

Alex ran after me. "I sent the servants for you, but they could not find you," he said.

"What?"

Alex, fretful, continued, "The midwives and physicians were called when she went into labor this morning, but everything went terribly wrong. They could do nothing for her. We would have had a sister. She passed, just after three. Thank God you have returned."

It dawned on me. Alex referred to our mother.

I went numb.

I I

⊕RPHEUS
Present Day

YOUR DAYS ARE NUMBERED. That is where you and I differ.

I am Lord Daumia Velde, a.k.a. Orpheus. The question is, "Who is the hunter and who is the hunted?" I would have no part in allowing Jadeon to write another word if I were not allowed to offer my part. Such is an indication of my character, as it is for Jadeon's, who permits me this luxury. Therefore, we will leapfrog our way through, each vying for your attention.

In May 1805, the night fog was all-engulfing as a large merchant ship swayed upon the turbulent waters of the North Atlantic. The vessel sailed along under the mastery of its experienced crew, now but a few hours off our destination, the Cornish harbor of Falmouth. One of the few passengers, I was hungry and stifled within my cabin, and decided to go out onto the bridge of the ship. I leant against the balustrade, looking out into the night and up at the numerous stars, soon to be covered again by the thick fog. How easily their beauty equaled that of the full moon, though these romantic ruminations were rare for one so seldom sentimental.

It was midnight, and several crewmembers struggled frantically to reel in the large, flapping sails in order to ballast the rocking ship. The crewmen were so engrossed in their work that I, their grand passenger, who was unaffected by either the blustering weather or its effect upon the sturdy vessel, went unnoticed. My tall and proud stature was an obvious indication of my noble birth, and my attire of dark, fine silks and luxurious velvets were a distinct intimation of my great wealth. What my presence did not indicate, however, was who I really was.

During the long journey from Spain, I attempted to subdue my appetite, but this had been a challenge. I was reluctant to finish the crew off, as I would have done easily upon land. This would have been quite absurd, as the safe arrival of this vessel was dependant upon them. I may be wicked, but I am not insane.

With my energy in decline, I would have to drink soon, and my dark olive skin was paling. That decision made, the next one was who would best suit my taste. I observed the crewmembers, considering who would be missed least. I smiled, such supremacy was empowering.

My grin faded as I recalled the reason for my journey. Sunaria . . . I saw her face—a vivid, bright memory of unusual turquoise eyes, perfect complexion, soft raven hair. She was of such beauty that she had often left me speechless. To watch her seduce her victims had been a sensuous delight. She had been entirely mine for over three hundred years, my bride, partner, and lover. We had been virtually inseparable, two perfect immortal beings, delighting in our dark ways as nightwalkers and reveling in our powers.

However, England had been her downfall. She insisted on traveling here to find her family's descendants and observe how they had progressed over the years.

"Complete folly," I had warned her.

Nevertheless, she would not relent, in her own stubborn way. Her foolishness proved my argument. She was discovered and trapped by those who called themselves the Keepers of the Stones. We had known of this ancient order, but such an alliance had always seemed of no real consequence.

Her trip changed everything. The league took her to some dark and depraved room, cut her wrists to drain her of her very life source, her sacred blood. Then, while she was still alive but weak, they dragged her off into the night, to the place of death they call Stonehenge. The Keepers of the Stones had then carried out an excruciating ritual. Her death was to be slow and painful. She was tied to the stones, then left for the cruel, harsh sun to do its worst. Her life was extinguished. My bright flame was snuffed out. In that moment, part of me died with her.

It was torture to go on without her. For sixteen agonizing years, I lived in the shadows, hiding from all and everything, sleeping most of the time, waking to feed when desperate hunger took a hold, only to return to my slumber. Rather than face my grief, I chose to sleep through it. Gradually, I regained my strength and the will to live, driven on by the overwhelming urge to seek revenge.

My last vision of her—as bonded vampires such as ourselves can share each other's visions—was terrifying. Sunaria had been blindfolded in order to protect the very men who held her captive, as her own waking nightmare would easily be conveyed to another vampire. Their fear was realized. Through her mind, I had witnessed her last excruciating days by way of her thoughts, joining her within the dark room where she was drained of her blood during that dark ceremony. I listened to the ritualistic chanting and felt the very cuts in her wrists as if they had been my own. Nevertheless, there was some hope of vindication.

When the blindfold had fallen off, she had a clear glimpse of two boys, their similarity discernable. They had looked on in frightful wonder, and she imprinted their faces upon her mind so clearly, I completely shared their image. Though I could do nothing for her, I promised her I would find them. Although with the passing of time the brothers would grow into men, I knew I would recognize them again and they would be the ones to lead me to her murderers.

My hunger intensified. I decided my next victim would be the captain of the ship, who spent most of his time in a drunken stupor in his cabin, and therefore would not be missed. His lieutenant, his second-in-command, would take charge of the helm and navigate the ship into the Cornish harbor.

Now all I had to fathom was how to get into the captain's room without anyone noticing. As I pondered on this, the eleven-year-old cabin boy came into view.

I signaled to the child and pointed to my cabin, indicating for him to meet me there. The boy had been the one to bring me my meals, though unbeknownst to him the rations had never been consumed, but thrown overboard.

Sitting in the darkest corner of my cabin, I hoped my sallow complexion would not startle the boy, and gestured for him to approach.

"What is your name?" I leaned forward.

"Samuel, sir."

"Samuel, there is something I would like you to do for me." My Spanish accent effortlessly lulled the boy. I studied him carefully.

"Yes, sir?" Samuel frowned.

"I want you to keep this a secret. Tell no one, and you will be well rewarded. I will give you a gold coin now, and one when the work is done. Come closer." I placed a coin in the palm of the boy's hand, and then closed his small fingers over the large doubloon.

The boy's eyes grew large.

To my horror, he began to remove his shirt. Startled, I jumped to my feet. I staggered backwards, knocking over my chair.

I gestured. "Stop. Replace your shirt. I did not mean—"

Samuel stared at me. He buttoned his shirt.

"All I would ask of you," I stuttered, "is such a small thing. I wish to visit the captain, and I know that at night his door is locked. I ask quite simply that you unlock it at three in the morning."

At this time, there would only be a handful of crewmembers working, minimizing the risk of anyone observing me entering the captain's cabin.

"Samuel, I will wake him and discuss important business of which he must be informed. There, that is all I ask of you. Please remember not to wake him. It is business of State, do you understand? Three hours from now, unlock his door, and when I take my leave from him, I will present you with your other gold coin."

"Sir, I think the captain would be very angry if I . . . I mean, he is very fussy about his room and who goes in and—"

"I understand. Has anything I have done, even in these last moments, made you doubt my word or my honor?"

"Sir, you promise to explain everything to him?"

"Of course."

He stared down at the coin before tucking it safely into his shirt pocket.

I felt sorry for him. His behavior had been a clear indication of his abuse.

The appointed hour arrived. I hovered before the entrance to the captain's quarters and turned the handle and opened the door, reassured that Samuel had done his bit. With caution, I stepped into the dark, sparse room. There upon the small bunk in the corner lay the ship's captain, a large man still fully dressed and snoring loudly upon his back. Hunger drove me on. I sat on the side of the bed, leaned over the oversized man, and then turned his head, exposing his pulsating jugular.

Instinctively, I nuzzled in, mouth against skin. The salty, sweaty taste stung. Enraptured, I shuddered when my fangs punctured his fleshy neck. An immediate rush of blood ran from vein to mouth— drinking, satiating, and glutting. The blood that flowed through his veins now flowed through mine. Eyes closed, I welcomed a flurry of emotions, though not the foreign wave of dizziness . . .

I was drunk.

By the foot of the bed lay an empty bottle of Cornish rum, consumed by my victim. The contents of the bottle now surged through me. In my rush to feed, I had missed this detail and now saw the ludicrous side of my predicament.

The ship rocked, causing me to lose my balance, and I fell. I tried to regain my poise, roaring with laughter, swaying from one side of the room to the other, determined not to jeopardize disposing the body. The captain would soon be dead. The telltale fang marks could threaten my safe position upon the ship. I had to regain composure and think as clearly as my intoxicated head would allow.

Carrying the portly man upon my shoulders was reasonably easy, but the careening ship proved challenging. I proceeded along the side of the deck, hiding in the shadows of the lifeboats before staggering to the balustrades. I rested the stocky officer up against the rail, lumbering with the rocking vessel.

Feeling a tap on my shoulder I turned, surprised to see the ship's navigator. His concerned expression equaled my own.

I drew toward him, heady with the rum, and laid the captain's body on the wet planks of the boat.

"Thank God you found him," the navigator said. "One day our captain will be so drunk, he'll fall overboard!"

"I caught him retching over the side. He's completely out."

"Come, I'll help you carry him," the navigator said.

I feigned that carrying the captain back to his berth was arduous and silently chastised my carelessness. On arrival, I discreetly pulled up his shirt collar as I settled him back onto his bunk.

On the following evening when the sun had set, I withdrew from my quarters and made my way toward the starboard. The crew unraveled the huge white sails that had been reeled in during the storm. A gust of wind caught the flapping canvas, propelling the vessel rapidly over the now-calm ocean.

I approached the navigator.

"Our Captain died last night," he said. "Men are all rattled. It's a bad omen."

The navigator informed me how the captain's burial had been a traditional ceremony—his body wrapped and cast overboard.

It was over. All evidence was now weighed down and resting soundly on the bottom of the ocean.

III

JADEON

LUCKY FOR US, Alex and I had inherited our parents' good looks. I adored spending time with him. His cheerful nature was often a pleasant contrast to mine. At age twenty-three, Alex was a striking man. He was popular with the local girls and I quietly envied his blond curls and blue eyes, which reflected his ebullience. Although not quite as tall as me, his exquisitely chiseled features made the girls dizzy. He seemed not to care. Although I'd ceased teasing him long ago about pirates, I replaced that joke by ribbing him about his many admirers. Very often, I pushed him so far he ended up in a rage, which entertained me to no end. But he would soon come around and see the humorous side.

This day, Alex had searched my usual haunts, eager to pry me off the castle grounds. He found me sitting at the water's edge, engrossed in the pages of a well-worn novel. Alex hovered over me now, glancing occasionally at the sunset, attempting to assess my mood.

"Jadeon, change your mind. You haven't been out for the longest time with me."

"I'll come with you another time. Next week, perhaps." I stared at the horizon.

"You said that last time and the time before."

Looking up at Alex, I envied his sense of freedom. Unable to shake the feeling that I should be somewhere else, I felt uneasy. "Take my horse and saddle if you like," I said. "I couldn't stand being around drunken men right now."

"What if I just stay here until you change your mind?"
"Then you'll be very bored." I sighed to exaggerate my point.
"I'll keep you company."
Nearby, two squawking seagulls pecked at a half-eaten crab.
"Jadeon?"
"I just need some time. That's all. Go and enjoy yourself."

With a pat on my shoulder, Alex reluctantly left me and headed for the stables. He was not the only one who tried and failed at getting me out. My father had given me a horse, an expensive well-bred stallion, in an attempt to console and encourage me to be more social. He had wasted his money. What I really craved was my father's approval, but he was too overwhelmed with his own grief and preoccupied with his own affairs to really give us any thought. Alex never seemed to mind, but I always felt whatever I did was never enough. Father's volatile character pushed me away. At the time I believed he had forgotten us. However, it was not only the death of my mother that pained me, but the void I felt from the loss of Catherine's company.

If it had been possible to avoid myself, I would have done so. After a while, even the servants would scurry away when they saw me coming, nervous of the broody lad who paced the castle walls with the weight of the world on his shoulders, but no real responsibility to show for it.

As usual, Alex left me sitting at the water's edge, gazing out to sea, deep in thought. He saddled my spirited black stallion. And as an experienced rider, Alex quickly mastered him. He rode out over the gravel pathway toward the mainland town of Marazion, estimating his arrival at the warm tavern to be within the hour. Alex had arranged to meet with his friends at the Master's Arms, a popular watering hole located in the center of town, well known for its fine ale and guaranteed lively company. As he rode up the hill passing the small cottages, he considered that on such a fine evening, and riding such a stately horse, he would even consider a visit to the neighboring town of Penzance.

IV

⊕RPHEUS

I HAD NOT FORGOTTEN my promise of another coin for Samuel. I remained on the deck for the remainder of my journey, hoping to catch sight of the small cabin boy. The ship navigated through the busy Falmouth harbor, making good time, skillfully avoiding the other fishing and merchant vessels. I offered condolences for the captain's death and inquired into Samuel's whereabouts.

"We have not seen him for some time," the navigator explained, "but he will be fine. In time, he'll resurface."

Upon disembarking, I considered it curious that Samuel had not approached me for his second doubloon, but the hustle and bustle of the busy port soon distracted me. I arranged for my few belongings to be delivered to the local tavern. However, I would not sleep there. I headed to the town of Penzance, the town where Sunaria had last resided.

I soon settled into a new way of life. I often left the province in order to feed and satisfy my insatiable appetite, preying on those who lived reclusive lives so as not to arouse suspicion. Occasionally, I would find myself in a dark alley or down a dusty road, threatened by a drunken sailor or a roving vagabond. Audaciously, I snapped their mortal coil.

One evening, as on so many, I perused the taverns and inns of Penzance in an attempt to gain information. Dressed in the guise of a rich merchant, I wandered into The Old Galleon Inn, the largest and loudest of all the taverns. I sat in the darkest corner, my hands wrapped around a cup of warm ale that would never touch my lips.

Six rowdy men burst through the doors of the tavern, obviously drunk. Raucously they ordered drinks from the cheerful innkeeper, shouting and laughing. Annoyed with their behavior, I stood to go but slowly sat again.

There was something strikingly familiar with one of the six men. Older, yes . . . his face now full, height taller, shoulders broader, his stature that of a man. But it was he. My heart pounded. It was indeed one of the boys who had witnessed Sunaria's torture.

I scrutinized the young mortal. The man conversed with his exuberant friends, unaware of my stare. His distinctive aristocratic accent and affluent attire gave away his position. He was the son of a lord. I judged from their fresh order of drinks I had a few minutes before they would leave. I withdrew from the tavern.

There are places about Cornwall where one is advised not to venture, dangerous and dark territory where men of crime and evil roam. It was to one of these places that I now headed. I soon saw what I had come searching for, and by reading one of the two highwaymen's minds, was ensured of the criminal's weakness.

The two men walked side by side, apparently scheming in the shadows. They were alone, and at such an hour there was no one else about. I moved quickly, approaching the men. With shocking speed, I easily broke the neck of the weakest, smallest man and then threw him to the ground. The other man froze with fear. I drew toward him with equal speed and grabbed him by his throat.

"Silence," I threatened. "Make a noise and I'll crush your neck, just like your friend here." I smiled, making sure the man saw my elongated, razor-sharp teeth.

The highwayman stared in terror and nodded.

"I know all about you, everything, but I am willing to forget all that I have seen. I want you to do something for me. If you decline or think you can run later in an attempt to evade me, you are quite wrong. Listen carefully and carry out my demands exactly as they are given to you. Waver from them and I will kill you. Comply and you will be well paid."

I explained his assignment, tightening my grasp around his throat.

Again, he nodded.

I returned to the tavern. Discreetly, I studied the young man and violated his thoughts. He staggered out into the night, leaving his friends to continue with their revelry.

I followed him.

He had obviously enjoyed another evening out and was rather inebriated. His judgment lacking, he trusted his horse more than himself to find its way back along the path through the woods to the castle. It was eerily quiet.

So distracted was he that he did not immediately notice my highwayman galloping toward him. His pistol pointed, he fired a shot. The bullet raced through the air, missing the young man by a hair. His stallion bucked and reared up, front legs flaying out, treading the air. Unable to control the careening animal the young man fell off, hitting the hard ground winded and shaken. His stallion bolted, leaving behind his master still sitting dazed on the ground.

The highwayman dismounted. Aiming his gun again, he stomped to the fallen rider. The young man cowered. Both looked in my direction as I cantered toward them, taking the aggressor by surprise. I aimed my pistol at the thief, shooting a fatal bullet directly into the highwayman's chest. Blood gushed from the wound and he fell to the ground, dead.

The young man staggered to his feet.

I dismounted and strolled toward him.

"Are you all right, sir?" I offered him my hand to assist him.

"I think so." He backed away and leaned upon a large tree, attempting to regain his poise. He looked down at the dead man who had almost killed him. "You just saved my life."

"So I did."

"I am Alexander Artimas."

"Alex, it looks as though your horse has no head for adventure. Lord Daumia Velde."

"Lord Velde, I am honored. My father is Lord Artimas. We live not far from here. The castle, you know of it?"

"Yes, it's familiar," I said.

"How will I ever repay you?"

"Oh, I will think of something."

Alex blushed. "Please allow me to repay you in some way for your kindness. Come back to the castle, and I will—"

"I have another engagement that I must attend to. Perhaps if you like, we could meet another time?"

"Perhaps tomorrow night?"

I mounted my horse. "I am a guest of the Brandenburgs while they are out of town. They have kindly allowed me to stay in their spacious home. Do you know of them?"

"Yes, I think I do. Do they live at Woodrow Mansion?"

"Come for dinner, tomorrow at eight." I kicked my horse and galloped off through the woods.

V

JADEON

FINDING AMUSEMENT WHERE I could, I leaned on the doorframe of my brother's room, arms folded, affectionately smiling as I watched Alex trying one suit on and then another, casting down the last with frustration.

"So, are you sure it wasn't a woman who saved your life, Alex? You can tell me." I howled with laughter at my brother's reaction. "For a start, you didn't invite him here for Father and me to thank him for saving your—"

"I did invite him, but his business keeps him from this part of town for now. I will invite him here again. Oh! These ridiculous dress shirts. Here, help me, will you? Instead of hindering."

"You look like a fine gentleman." I fiddled with Alex's necktie. "Extend to Lord Velde our thanks, and be sure to offer an invitation from Father to him so he may dine with us soon. We both look forward to meeting your new acquaintance."

"Yes, of course. Are you sure the white does not make me look too pale? I cannot make up my mind."

"Well, you'd better hurry. It is past seven-thirty now. Was your appointment not at—"

"Oh my goodness, he was very specific about the time." Alex realized I was mocking him, and he hit me.

"Knowing you, you'll probably be unfashionably early." I lingered at the top of the stairs and watched Alex walk briskly toward the castle entrance. "Be safe," I called out to him.

With evening came the familiar silence that befell the castle. Taking my usual path, I headed toward my father's private reading room where I often whiled away the hours lost in a good book or studying an old journal. Facing the fireplace, I took advantage of one of the warmer rooms. This room was rarely visited due to its extensive body of scholarly works, featuring a huge collection of foreign books and numerous philosophical doctrines.

Father had provided me with a key and gave strict instructions not to allow anyone in here owing to the Church's attitude toward non-Christian text. Of course, the moment he mentioned to me that such material was frowned upon he sparked an interest, and I soon became an avid student of both Eastern and Western philosophy, devouring the complete works of Aristotle in a summer.

I once tried to discuss the subject with Father De Mercy, but after he threw holy water on me several times, I learned to keep my thoughts to myself.

Engrossed in the ancient text of Homer, it took me a moment to realize someone had entered. Due to my positioning the chair obscured me from sight, but with a slight turn of my head I had a good view the room. My father had not noticed me. He hovered before the main bookcase and reached up for a book. However, he just tilted it back, revealing a small brass handle. I remained silent and watched.

The bookcase swung open.

I jumped with a start.

Lord Artimas disappeared into the blackness.

I sprang up out of the chair and sprinted through the door before it closed behind me, throwing me into complete darkness. Exhilarated to be shaken out of my gloom and ready for action, I reached out, fumbling along, treading carefully. The ground beneath me disappeared. I was at the top of a flight of stairs. Taking my time I descended, using my father's footsteps ahead of me as my guide. The spiraling stairway continued down until the drop in temperature revealed I was close to sea level. Flickering light guided my exit through a camouflaged door, leading into the dungeons that appeared as part of the wall itself. Puffs of air left my lungs and I hoped this would not give me away.

Large torches lit up the passageway. Having passed this very spot on so many occasions, I had never noticed anything out of the ordinary. Several men headed toward me and I ducked back behind the carved stone door and held my breath.

When they had passed, I inhaled gulps of cold air and peered out. I watched the men disappear into one of the largest rooms that lined the dungeons. Listening at the door I couldn't help remembering what I had witnessed as a child, though Alex and I had made a pact never to speak of it. As time passed I considered it merely a nightmare, but now, as I lingered before the wooden doorway, I knew it was very real. Scuffling and voices echoed from within.

Annoyance rose. I was angry with my father for still keeping secrets from me. I reasoned I was now a man and would behave as such, thus deserving to be a member of his alliance, ready to shoulder what he had hidden from me all this time. I rallied myself and clutched the doorknob.

I sprang into the room.

Empty.

To my astonishment, no one was there. Round and round I turned, surrounded by four stone walls. I ran to each side of the chamber and explored the solid rock, fingering the cold granite, convinced that somewhere a secret exit was present. Frustrated, I found none.

"I'm ready!" I shouted, my words echoing back to me.

Silence.

I hoped I could muster such confidence again. A small glinting object lying on the floor in the corner drew my attention. I reached down and picked it up. It was a pendant engraved with the name *Jacob*.

I turned it over and over again, studying the solid silver and admiring the delicate filigree of the chain. On closer inspection I noticed a smear of dried blood on several of the fine links.

My focus turned once more upon the chamber, looking for any other clues that might lead to the owner of this necklace.

Unwilling to contemplate the fate of the wearer, I tucked it into my pocket. Unable to recall a servant with that name, I headed out of the dungeons.

I would ask around.

VI

⊕RPHEUS

WITHIN THE CELLAR lay five dead bodies pushed up against the far wall. As an uninvited guest I had resided here in the manor for two days, feeding on the unsuspecting residents upon my arrival. I winced with disgust at the scene, irritated by the familiar stench that emanated. This part of the kill was tedious. Mr. and Mrs. Brandenburg and their three servants had been taken by surprise. I now considered if there was time to dispose of their bodies, though sensing Alex's arrival, the answer was no.

Swiftly I took the steps three at a time out of the basement toward the entranceway. Distracted by thoughts of the decaying flesh, I forgot to wait for the knock on the door before I opened it. I quietly chastised myself for such thoughtlessness.

Alex inhaled, taken off guard. He admired my attire. I was dressed in the finest black linen, a style that was purely European.

"Good evening, Alex." I stepped out, walking past him with a smile. I approached Alex's horse and untied the beast, which initially seemed a little uncomfortable with me. I led the stallion into the stables situated at the side of the property. Alex followed and watched me position the horse in front of a drinking trough. It leaned its long neck toward the water and drank while I patted its neck. "Such a fine creature."

"Thank you." Alex studied me. "And thank you for yesterday." He seemed a little nervous. "You risked your life, and for that I am deeply grateful."

"It was a good thing I was there." I stared at him intently.

"Yes," he said.

I turned back to his horse. "You're lucky. He's of good stock, very well bred."

Alex appeared uneasy. "He's my brother's horse. Jadeon lets me ride him occasionally. Well all the time, actually. Our father gave the stallion to him as a gift."

"I see. And what was your gift from Lord Artimas?"

"Well, um . . . He did give me a new sword."

"A new sword? How curious, to give your brother this fine horse, and you . . . a sword." I tilted my head.

"I—I never thought of it like that." Alex frowned. "But he might as well be mine. I ride him all the time."

"But he's not yours."

"No, he's not."

"Fascinating," I said.

"It's not what you think."

"And what is it that I think, Alex?"

"That my father favors Jadeon over me."

I approached him and straightened his necktie. "The oldest is very often favored by the father and the youngest by the mother," I said. "I expect your mother adores you."

"I—"

"After all, Alex, you are possessed of a handsomeness not easily equaled. Women swoon at your feet and men . . . covet you."

He was speechless.

"You have not yet realized your true potential. Perhaps that is where I come in?" I said.

"I'm not sure I understand your meaning."

"Now that I have saved your life, I feel somewhat responsible for you."

"I would never—"

"Expect it, I know," I said. "Come, you must be thirsty after your journey. You can freshen up before dinner."

"Thank you, sir."

"Call me Daumia." I led him back toward the house and we entered the manor's foyer. I stood close behind Alex and removed his cloak.

He took a moment to recompose himself.

In the lavishly decorated lounge I uncorked a bottle of red wine and commented that the servants had not arrived to prepare dinner that evening, informing Alex that if they did not arrive soon we would be forced to dine out. Alex gratefully accepted the full glass. He took a large gulp of the wine and then another.

Alex's gaze perused the elegant room—the fine furniture, the expensive beeswax candles, and the huge fireplace burning fiercely.

"So the Brandenburgs are out of town for the summer, you say?" Alex said. "When are they due to return?"

"Soon I hope." I stood in front of the fireplace, momentarily transfixed by the flames. "I enjoy the company of such remarkable people. It is unfortunate that they are detained. Come warm yourself by the fire."

"The wine is warming me, thank you. My father extends to you his invitation and would be delighted to have you as his honored guest."

"Thank your father for me, and as soon as my business arrangements are complete, I would very much like to dine with your family."

"My father—"

"The Brandenburgs have a wonderful painting by Joseph Turner," I interrupted his thoughts. "He's such a gifted artist. I'm sure you know of him."

"Yes, we have one of his paintings too. My father has a superior collection of art. I would be honored to show it to you if your time permits such a visit."

"Let us view the family's collection. Although small, it is rather fine." I led Alex into the drawing room.

Silently, we both admired Turner's painting.

"See how he uses the finest brush," I commented. "The way he accentuates form and color."

Alex stared at me. Not returning his gaze, I allowed him to continue as my eyes wandered over the painting, and Alex's wandered over me. For a moment I was taken aback with the frisson. Alex captivated me with his boyish charm. He emanated an innocence that was unexpectedly hypnotic.

I snapped myself out of my trance. "His use of light is really quite wonderful, would you not agree? I think we take such things for granted."

It was easy to read his mind. I was pleased to sense Alex was as equally fascinated with me. "So, you are hungry? I know a quiet tavern. We will take dinner there. These servants, they are so unreliable."

We headed out on horseback. On our arrival at the tavern I guided Alex toward the darkest corner where we talked uninterrupted. As the evening progressed, Alex opened up. I ensured that the compliments flowed, as did the wine. Alex was fast becoming enamored.

Alex stared at my right hand. "That's an interesting ring you're wearing," he said.

"It was a gift from someone who was taken well before her time." I again lifted the goblet to my lips and feigned a sip.

"I'm sorry to hear that," Alex said. "You were fond of her?"

I nodded and rubbed the ring in remembrance of Sunaria, who had given it to me. "Alex, tell me about your family. Let's start with your brother, Jadeon."

Within the gloomy tavern, Alex relayed the story of how both he and Jadeon had grieved for their mother that awful winter. It had been she who had brightened the castle with her vivacious temperament. Since her death, they had only entertained at the Mount in order for their father to find suitable brides for his sons. Their immense castle was not the comfortable and pleasing home it had once been. It had become as lonely and empty as the very souls that continued to live within its walls.

"Now Jadeon just mopes around in a melancholy mood. He rarely goes out," Alex said. "He spends his time reading, studying music, and generally daydreaming."

"Catherine. She remains in the convent?" I inquired.

"Yes, Jadeon sometimes goes down to the grounds outside the convent and sits, hoping to catch a glimpse of her. It's so sad."

"Grief can incapacitate the soul."

"You're referring to your friend?" Alex said.

"Yes."

"I am sorry to hear that. Would you like to talk about her?"

"No. And your father, tell me of him," I said.

* * * *

Alex and I enjoyed many an evening together. Alex believed that by day I attended to my business dealings, having no idea that in truth this was when I slept. It was a divine pleasure to manipulate him, as only a demon can, and soon Alex had grown distant from his family. Alex's feelings of affection toward me were inevitable. He was swept away with emotion, infatuated with the most exceptional man he had ever encountered, and the very fact I chose to spend my evenings with him truly flattered him. His company was refreshing.

Alex was well educated and therefore a superb conversationalist. He was bestowed with a delightful humor and a kind nature. I also took great delight in teasing him. I gradually became aware that I had begun to feel passionately for Alex, but knew my plans would not and could not be hindered in any way. Despite this, I found myself obsessed with him. In many ways Alex filled the void Sunaria's death had left. Alex soothed my grief, so much so that he consumed my thoughts.

Alex's visits to the Brandenburgs' home became a frequent occurrence. Although suspicions would predictably rise due to their strange disappearance, it was difficult to extract myself from such a luxurious residence. Alex never mentioned the Brandenburgs. He was all too happy with the circumstances of us having a place where we could enjoy our undisturbed privacy.

As on so many evenings, he arrived at the manor. As I had instructed him, he rode his own mare and arrived as pre-arranged—later than usual. He led his horse into the stable. When he knocked at the door of the manor house, he was surprised there was no answer and for a moment he wondered if he had been mistaken to the time or place of our meeting. Then, with an eerie feeling of being watched, he turned and jumped with fright.

I was standing right behind him.

"Where the hell did you come from?" Alex gasped.

"What kind of greeting is that for your old friend? Really, I must teach you some manners. Now where should I begin?"

Alex's cheeks blushed brightly.

"You are forgiven, for now." I walked toward him.

Alex noticed I held something in my hand.

"What is that?" he asked.

"It's a blindfold."

"For what purpose?"

"For you."

"No, no, really I—"

"I have a surprise for you." I turned Alex around firmly, ignoring his attempts at resistance. I pushed up against him and placed the thick strip of black silk material around his eyes. "Do you not trust me?"

"Of course I do. I trust you with my life."

"Good answer." I escorted Alex by his arm, our bodies locked together. I guided him to the large gardens situated behind the manor house.

"Really, is this quite necessary?"

"I like it when you resist me. It's quite charming. Alex, I have a gift for you."

After walking along the grassy bank for several minutes, we

stopped. I pulled Alex's hands up and placed them upon the large dappled mare, pulling the blindfold off him. Alex gawped at the beautiful beast, its mane long and flowing, its fine leather saddle carved out by Spanish artisans.

"Now you have a horse as fine as your brother's," I said.

He was speechless. He patted the horse, then looked back at me. "Why? How can I accept such a gift? Daumia—"

"Then you insult me. Accept as a gentleman accepts such a gift from a friend. And besides, this animal will not bolt at the firing of a gun. She is brave and well trained, unlike that donkey of your brother's."

Alex admired the exquisite animal, running his hands over the fine horse. He laughed excitedly. He turned and gazed up at me, confounded with my generosity. Our eyes locked. Alex drew closer to me. I tilted my head and smiled.

"I . . . I owe you so much," he said.

I stared at his full lips.

Alex's mouth loomed close to mine. I placed my hand upon his chest, stopping him from moving any further.

"I am so sorry." Alex drew back.

"No," I reassured. "Someone comes." I stroked his cheek.

Alex looked around the garden. He blushed. "I don't see anyone."

"Someone approaches."

Again Alex glanced around the garden. As he did so, his eye caught sight of a woman. She had just turned the corner of the manor house and headed toward us. Alex was completely astonished that I had detected her.

"I have good hearing." I backed away and strolled toward the woman. With a quick turn I said, "No, do not be concerned. We will have plenty of time to explore your desires." I threw him a captivating smile, then turned on my heels and walked toward the now fast approaching female.

Alex watched the stranger and I talk. The woman, easily in her fifties, was dressed in long full skirts, her expression one of concern. Alex assumed she was a servant of the house.

I bowed respectfully, then guided the woman away from Alex in order that he not hear our conversation.

"Come, madam, what is it that I can do for you?" I asked.

"Sir," she began, attempting to pull away from my grasp. "I have come to see the Brandenburgs. My daughter is Mrs. Brandenburg's housemaid. She comes home every few weeks, on the third Sunday of the month, her day off. I came by the house two days ago and several days before that. No one was home. But for her to go away for so long, she has never done that before. Do you happen to know where she is?"

"Yes, of course. First, please allow me to introduce myself. I am Lord Velde, a guest of the Brandenburgs. They have traveled to Europe for important business. Now, your daughter—"

"Mrs. Lafity," she followed breathlessly. We turned the corner of the manor and walked to the front of the estate. We soon arrived at the entranceway and headed on in.

"Is there a Mr. Lafity at home?" I asked.

"No, I am a widow. I just do not think she would leave on such a big trip without sending—"

"Really, I am so sorry to hear that, but at least the other children keep you company?"

"No, Emily is my only child. I live alone."

"Well, let me give you something for your troubles. Won't you come this way, as I am sure Emily has left a note in the drawing room for you. Not to tell you that she was traveling abroad with the Brandenburgs is so unlike her."

"Indeed, sir. I should not want to trouble you in any way."

"Really? Well then, come quickly," I said. "And perhaps a little drink is in order to calm your nerves."

"Are you sure it's not a bother for you?"

"Not at all. In fact, it's rather a lovely surprise."

She followed eagerly, taking in the luxurious décor, enjoying her first real look at her daughter's place of employment.

"Now, I think this is the note." I picked up a piece of paper from the oak writing bureau and handed it over to her. She read, slowly and with difficulty. I glanced through the window, confirming Alex remained outside, and moved quietly behind her, wrapping my left arm around her waist and my right hand over her mouth suppressing any screams. After a tilt of her head, my fangs bit into her neck. Delighting in the moment my eyes closed as the sweet taste flowed.

Alex, curious who the woman was and why she had come uninvited, decided to follow me after several minutes. On entering the hallway, Alex heard us in the drawing room. He proceeded in that direction.

She struggled frantically, as they sometimes did. As the blood loss affected her she weakened, drifting off into a faint, and I placed her down upon the floor, into death.

With a leap from the room I headed Alex off, greeting him before he entered and caught a glimpse of my delicious tussle.

"Oh, there you are," I said.

"What did the woman want?"

"She came to apologize for not providing us with a meal the other night. She's more than made up for it."

"Really. How?"

"Alex, I am sorry. I have urgent business which has just arisen that I must attend to. It will not take me long. Go to Mousehole where there is an Inn called Le Vive. Await me there. I should not be long. Perhaps an hour or so."

"Can I not come with you?"

"You know better than to question me."

Alex was taken aback.

"Le Vive, go . . . now," I said.

Alex turned and headed for the door. Before exiting, he gave me a final glance.

I smiled to soften the moment. "I expect you to run her hard."

"Excuse me?"

"Your new horse."

"Oh, right. Of course."

Alex withdrew. He headed to the rear gardens again, this time with a bounce in his step.

I returned to the drawing room and stared down at the muted-grey corpse. "Come on." I hauled her over my shoulder. "I'll show you where your daughter is."

On arriving at the small town of Mousehole, Alex enjoyed the view and was invigorated by the salty fresh air. He surveyed St. Michael's Mount, admiring the grand castle in the distance. Entering the inn he ordered some wine, and taking a corner table positioned himself with his back against the wall. He looked about him, noticing only two other men sitting at another table not far from his, engrossed in conversation. Alex fretted over how his father would respond when he presented his new horse. He hoped he would not be angry, but he knew that his father would be suspicious of what his son had done to deserve such a fine gift. Alex was even concerned that his father might not allow him to keep her.

The innkeeper's wife approached him, shaking him from his thoughts.

"Your room is ready for you, sir," she said.

"I am sorry. You are mistaken. I did not request a—"

"It was booked by Lord Velde, room ten. Here is the key."

"How do you know it is for me?"

"Well sir, those two men are locals, and you are the only other man in here."

"I see. Well, thank you . . . um, my horse?"

"Taken to the stable. My husband is having a stable boy feed and groom her, as Lord Velde instructed."

"Thank you. How many rooms?"

"Just the one, sir. He said you would have returned from a long journey and would be in need of a good night's sleep before you continued on."

Alex peered out of the window and caught sight of the towering castle silhouetted in the distance.

"Here you are then. It's through that door behind the bar and up those stairs."

Alex took the key from her and headed up.

Alex opened the door to the small room, his eyes adjusting to the dim lighting. He could just make out a large bed, a side table, a washing basin, and a drawing table with a large bottle of rum placed upon it. Intrigued, he entered the room, walked over to the dressing table, and found a candle next to the opened bottle of rum and two silver goblets. He lit the candlewick with one of the matches placed beside it then turned to get a better view of the room. He jumped with fright, almost dropping the candle, when he realized he was not alone.

"Daumia! How could you have traveled here so quickly? I did not see you enter the tavern."

"Oh, Alex, questions, questions. You really are a frightful bore sometimes. I left shortly after you and came in through the back," I said.

"I see."

I walked passed him, moving toward the dressing table. I poured rum into the two goblets, filling them to the top and picking up one, handed it to Alex.

"I have just had some wine." He accepted the silver cup. "I do not need anything more to drink."

"Really? Well, for what I have planned for you, I would recommend at least a sip. No?" I took the vessel from him, placing it down on the side table. I turned toward him and commenced unbuttoning his shirt, silently.

Alex stood, chest bare, though apparently relieved that his breeches and boots remained. He watched me place his shirt on the back of a chair. I returned the cup of rum to him. He gulped down the liquor. The thick rum burnt his throat and as I walked away from him toward the dressing table, Alex's expression reflected the discomfort of the rum.

"How is your drink?" I smiled before facing him again, just in time for my young friend to recompose himself.

"Wonderful," he rasped, his throat burning.

"Good."

A knock at the door startled him. Alex reached for his shirt.

I pulled it from his hands, placing it back behind the chair. "Come in," I said.

The door opened.

Alex was surprised to see a young woman appear. She closed the door behind her. Alex withdrew toward the window self-consciously, looking at the young female. Her age was similar to his own. She wore the dress of a servant girl, her mousey hair flowing around her face, tied at the nape of her neck in a bun. Her waist was small, her breasts large. Alex glanced at me as I leant against the wall by the door. With a nod, I permitted the girl to proceed. She followed my direction and approached Alex, who by now understood the scenario.

She knelt down at his feet and pulled at one of his boots. Alex lifted his foot in order to help her. Calmly, she tugged at his other boot. I approached him and topped up his cup. Alex gulped the rum. I backed up and leant against the wall, again fixing my gaze on Alex.

Alex begged me with his eyes to stop her. "Daumia, this—"

The girl, unabashed, undressed him. She pulled his arm and pushed him onto the bed. She glanced up at me for permission to continue. With a nod from me, she too undressed.

The great castle was visible from the window. Deciphering the information that Alex had provided, it was evident that his father Lord Artimas was indeed the Stone Master. I was so close now I could almost taste the Grand Master's blood.

My eyes wandered back to Alex and his harlot. Strolling over to them I topped up Alex's goblet, which stood empty on the side table next to the bed. Peering down at the girl I reached over to pull out her hair tie, freeing her curls to cascade over her face and shoulders. Perspiration shimmered over her body.

Face flushed, Alex glanced at the cup of rum on the side table again, not reaching for it but wishing he could.

I leaned toward him, running my fingers through his hair, ruffling it playfully. I backed off and sat down in the corner chair, watching on as the two mortals thundered toward ecstasy. Admiring the image, I savored the sensuous ambience and brought my cup to my lips, breathing in the full exotic aroma of the thick, warm rum.

When it was over and Alex was sated I ordered the girl to leave. She curtsied, accepting several silver coins from me before exiting.

Alex lay naked upon the bed, breathless and entirely vulnerable. He was besotted with me. His seduction was complete.

I handed Alex his shirt and sat beside him, buttoning it up for him in silence. When he was ready, we headed out of the room and down into the dark tavern.

"Wait here for me," I instructed him. "I'll be back in an hour."

I headed out into the night, hungry and intending on feeding quickly before returning to my protégé.

Alex sat in the darkest corner of the tavern. With nothing other than his thoughts to keep him company, his musing would soon turn to me. With my hunger satisfied, I returned to find him sulking, bothered that he had been left alone for so long.

"Why could I not come with you?" Alex asked.

I sat opposite him, my cheeks apparently flushed from my feed. "Must you spend every moment with me?" I asked.

Alex frowned.

Someone was staring at me. I turned, surprised to see the young cabin boy Samuel staring back. On recognizing the child, he reminded me of my journey from Spain.

"Daumia?" Alex vied for my attention.

I had only been able to extract and interpret a few mental fragments from the boy's thoughts, realizing that he knew what I was, but unable to ascertain how.

"Daumia?"

"What?" I said.

"You seem distracted."

"I was considering your father's invitation. Inform him I'd be delighted to attend St. Michael's Ball."

Alex beamed.

I wanted to run after the young child, though realized how such an imprudent act would appear. I had to let him go.

"I will send my servant with an official reply." I turned my attention to Alex again.

"I'm looking forward to introducing you to Jadeon," Alex said.

"I'm also looking forward to meeting the young Lord Artimas. I'm sure we have much to discuss."

"And the art collection. I promised to show you that."

"Just to spend an evening in your company gives me the greatest pleasure, but if you wish to flatter me with such introductions and a tour of the castle, I am honored."

"It is my pleasure." Alex smiled.

"Talking of pleasure, tell me what it was about tonight that you

found most pleasing."
    Alex blushed.
    I ordered more rum.

VII

JADEON

HUNGOVER AND DIZZY with pleasure, Alex saddled his horse in the stables and rode home. He admired his new mare with her ease of stride, still in awe of such a generous bestowal. He knew she was as fine a horse as mine. He was well aware that it was wise to inform Father immediately of the new equine boarded in the castle's stables. Lord Artimas had taught his sons etiquette if nothing else, and Alex intended to request an urgent appointment with him first thing in the morning to inform him of the circumstances of his gift.

On arriving home Alex was informed by Arthur, our father's private secretary, that approximately ten o'clock that morning would be convenient to receive an audience. Alex then ran to my room. On not finding me, he searched the castle in the usual places and eventually found me in the vast reading room, our father's main library. It was here the servants were encouraged to take reading lessons, though few took my father up on his offer.

I sat at the large mahogany table surrounded by various books. The athenaeum had one of the most comprehensive collections in the county, shelved in their hundreds along the lofty four walls of the room. This was another of my favorite places. I often sat in here alone exploring the extensive collection that could never be read in one lifetime.

"Good morning," Alex greeted me.

"Excuse me sir, this is a private reading room," I jested.

"Jadeon, don't be so—"

"Oh, it's my younger brother. I did not recognize you."

"I know we have not seen much of each other lately, but you have been your usual self-absorbed self and I have been my usual social, have-a-wonderful-time-and-live-life-to-the-fullest self."

"Ouch." I held my hand to my chest as if wounded.

"Sorry, but you know how you are." Alex took the chair next to mine and looked down at the many books strewn upon the table. "I have to see Father. Lord Daumia gave me—"

"A new horse, yes. I heard the rumor. He must be fond of you."

"I just hope Father lets me keep her."

"Of course he will."

"What are you doing then?" Alex said.

"Well, Father was even more serious than usual the other night at dinner and said he had something very important to tell me, something about some kind of ceremonial tradition. He has made me come in here for the last six nights to read these."

I had in fact ignored my father's instructions and had soon found other stuff to read. I fully intended on glancing at the material but thought that I would wait until the last minute and hoped to get away with it.

Alex picked up and opened the heavy leather-bound books one by one. "Am I also to carry on the tradition?"

I lowered my voice. "Look, I'm not even meant to be telling you any of this, so keep it very quiet. You know how Father gets. Apparently it's something to do with being the eldest. He told me that I will be informed of the honor and initiated by ceremony, as tradition dictates, on my twenty-sixth birthday in two weeks."

"Of course, your birthday."

I hated birthdays. I loathed getting gifts and opening them up only to have the giver stare wide-eyed, hoping I liked it, and having to do my best to convey that I did. "I haven't celebrated a birthday in the last two years, and now—"

"Father has lost it," Alex said. "Look at this subject matter—witchcraft—and, oh my goodness, what is this *Nightwalker Lore* penned by Fabian Snowstrom? What kind of name is Snowstrom? On the other hand, is it you who is delusional? What is a nightwalker anyway? Can I come to the ceremony? I am surprised there isn't something amongst all these about Frenchmen. You know how Father is about foreigners."

We laughed hysterically.

Arthur interrupted us. The old well-dressed man appeared agitated when he glimpsed the titles on the table. Obviously they were for my eyes only. Arthur glared at me with disapproval.

I glared back until I had forced his disgruntled gaze toward Alex.

"Your father can see you now, sir. He cancelled an appointment for you. Go immediately to his office and present yourself," he said.

Alex looked at me for support and I gave him an encouraging wink. He leapt to his feet and obediently headed for his appointment, closely followed by Arthur.

I opened up the book titled *Nightwalker Lore* and a card fell out from between its pages. I read the faded note aloud. "Jadeon, consider the coincidences that you do not see." Fabian Snowstrom had signed it. I flicked through the book and read a few lines.

So boring.

I threw down the book. *Well, Father, if you're trying to confuse me, you've succeeded.* I headed toward the kitchen, hoping to persuade the cook to prepare me a mid-morning snack.

Alex knocked at Lord Artimas's door and waited. On hearing Father's gruff voice, he entered. Before him Lord Artimas sat at his desk reading intently. For a long while he seemed not to notice Alex. After several minutes Father peered up, his expression stern.

"Pray tell me, Alexander, why was there a new mare in my stables this morning that neither I nor my veterinary surgeons have permitted to board?"

"Father, that is why I requested to speak with—"

"What if the animal has a disease and infects my stock?"

"The horse was a gift from Lord—"

"And what did you do to deserve such an animal?"

Alex tried again. "Lord Velde saved my life, Father."

"I am quite aware of that. So why is it not you giving him a horse? Why does he bestow such a gift upon you?"

"I do not . . . I cannot say. We have just—"

"In what manner have you become acquainted?"

Alex blushed.

"Well? Is it business? What kind of arrangements have you made with him?" Lord Artimas placed his hand against his chest. He was silent for a moment, as if trying to regain some composure.

"I apologize if I have offended you, sir," Alex said.

"Alexander, you must understand, I have enemies that would destroy this family. We must be more guarded. You must be more guarded."

"Surely those were the old ways?"

Lord Artimas glared at Alex.

"Father, Lord Velde is of noble birth. A gentleman of Spanish

Royal decent. And he is a good man and of the highest order."

"I have heard of his family. He is indeed of noble birth, but I would like to meet him for myself. Two weeks from today I have instructed for a grand function to be arranged. This ball will celebrate your brother's birthday. Perhaps we can marry him off after all. And be forewarned, you will be next. You will extend an invitation to Lord Velde, and he will accept. If he does not, you will break this liaison off immediately. Do you understand?"

"Yes, Father. I have already extended your invitation to Lord Velde and—"

"Check with the stables. If they destroyed your horse, it was for the best."

Alex struggled for air.

"Alex," Lord Artimas said. "If I seem harsh, it is because I have your interests in mind."

Alex lingered, hoping for some sign of affection or approval.

"You may go," Lord Artimas said.

Alex searched for words.

"You are still here?" Father inquired.

Alex withdrew.

I found Alex down by the water's edge and stood behind him, holding a bottle of rum and two goblets. "All is well. Turns out you now own the most expensive and well bred horse in the stables, and mine has been demoted to mule!"

"And she can stay?"

"She can stay. I warned the stable workers that no one was to harm your horse. No one."

Alex sighed. "I'll take that drink now."

"And talk?" I sat down beside him.

"And talk," he said.

I poured two large cups of rum and handed one to him.

Alex relayed his experiences with Lord Velde, leaving out any information that would indicate they had ever shared an intimate moment. We sat and talked into the early hours of the night in an attempt to catch up on all the time we had lost over the last few months. I reassured him I would do everything in my power to encourage our father to be welcoming to Alex's new acquaintance, expressing my delight that I would soon be meeting with the man that my brother had spoken of so highly.

VIII

⊕RPHEUS

AFTER ENJOYING AN extended sojourn within the luxurious residence, I left the Brandenburg's home, having overstayed my welcome. No trace of the family or their staff would be found, and I had kept such a low profile that my stay would go undetected. It was during my search for a new residence that I came across a witch's coven. At first I had considered finding refuge there, but with the discovery of Athena, a female vampire who had ensconced herself within the clan, I considered it would be prudent to avoid them. Fascinated with the occult, I took a few moments to peer through an open window, closing my mind to Athena.

I perceived she had sensed my arrival in Cornwall and had considered coming in search of me. Though concerned I might covet her den, she had reconsidered. She selfishly obsessed over her darling witches. It was easy to probe their thoughts and spy on their ceremony.

With the witching hour approaching, the ceremony was in full swing. The eleven witches stood at the feet of their mistress, their goddess, and offered her their exotic ritual. The coven had been in existence for over thirty years, the very affirmation of their faith in the arrival of their deity, whom they worshiped with fervent sacrifice and idolization.

The coven had embarked with just three women, all midwives. They had developed medicines and magical spells to assist the other villagers with every conceivable ailment as well as ease the suffering of labor pains for those with child. These were the women with whom everyone sought counsel when in need of medicinal sustenance.

But the tide turned now with frightening rumors that other sister cults had disbanded, their members burnt at the stake or even drowned as Christianity swept the nation. Before long the coven had grown in number as witches sought solace within this small house deep in the countryside in the county of Redruth, Cornwall.

If an affirmation was needed for these sisters of witchery, then Athena was it. Though unknown to them, her real name was Grace. She had arrived during a ceremony when they performed an incantation summoning up the goddess of wisdom, Athena, their magic so powerful that it succeeded with unexpected triumph. She descended from the air, as one would expect a goddess to, and invited the worship of the sisterhood. They soon discovered her powers, and if any doubt entered their minds she would soon dispel such thoughts with proof of her birthright, using feats of magic and mind reading.

For those who pleased her most, which all of them strove to do, she would reward their loyal devotion by allowing them to drink her sacred blood from the ceremonial chalice, permitting them to experience her sensuous elixir. Soon the witches of the sect were in awe of this powerful being, and with her promise of great rewards were soon lovingly enslaved.

For Grace—now Athena—the arrangement worked out wonderfully. She would sleep during the day, completely safe from the sunlight and protected by the women who watched over her, bestowing the adoration she believed she so richly deserved. As far as she was concerned, as an immortal she was a goddess. After all, she would never die. Was this not a gift of the gods? She had been born two hundred years earlier into the life of a servant girl, her parents both dead before she was nine years old. She had lived an uncompromising life.

Made a vampire at the age of twenty-one, she discovered that mortals were vulnerable and easily manipulated, especially with her gift of reading minds—as easy, she had thought, as reading the lines in a book for those of noble birth. She would go out into the night to feed after she had been luxuriously bathed and dressed by her loving consorts.

At nineteen, Sarah had hardly been in the cult for a year. With apprehension Sarah approached the goddess, frightened to make eye contact but excited to drink and feel as she had when first initiated. In a moment of bravery, she glanced up at Athena who sat proudly upon her royal throne, appearing so exquisitely regal.

Sarah sighed as she took in the image of the goddess before her:

her long brown hair tied, her skin pale, and her fine features flawless in the candlelit room. Athena returned her gaze with brown illuminant irises, attempting to hypnotize Sarah. Fully aware that Athena could read her mind, Sarah ensured her thoughts were those of servitude.

Although Athena had drunk the blood of a mortal far from this place previously that evening, she still looked down with hungry eyes at the beautiful girl and attempted to quell her desire.

"Step forward." Athena offered the silver goblet to the girl.

Sarah peered up in awe.

Athena lifted Sarah's chin in order that she would watch as Athena dramatically cut her left wrist, aiming the red blood into the goblet. The cut on Athena's wrist miraculously healed. Sarah's gaze fell downward to the full silver chalice, now held close to her mouth.

With a nod of permission from the goddess she drank tentatively, at first savoring and then gulping the blood that overflowed and trickled onto her chest. Sarah stared blankly as the empty goblet was taken from her. The witches guided her to the table at the center of the room and she lay down upon it. They observed in wonder.

Then it began. Sarah writhed, her eyes rolling back as the sensations pleasured her. For a moment, Athena was concerned that she had given too much to the young girl. Sarah shuddered as wave after wave of ecstasy passed over her.

Athena enjoyed the sensuous display. Unable to quell her need, she drew closer toward Sarah. Athena commanded the witches to turn their heads, and they reluctantly complied. Athena tilted Sarah's head, exposing her neck, and nuzzled in to suckle. Sarah flinched, then softened beneath Athena, who lapped at her paling skin. Resisting drinking further, Athena pulled away, stemming the bleeding with a gentle finger.

Before the end of the ceremony, I had to withdraw from the witches' orgy as I could no longer bear being so aroused. I flew through the woods and headed for the nearest brothel, paying several coins to the innkeeper before being guided to a back room by the prettiest young redhead. With the vision of what I had just witnessed still fresh in my mind, I doubly enjoyed the girl's affections. I eventually left her lying fatigued upon the bed, resisting the urge to drink from her, willing myself out of the room. Her death would have been a topic of conversation within the village, and I was trying to keep a low profile.

Within an old chapel I descended into the lower chambers, delighted to discover a new coffin that had been constructed for some poor soul who had not yet died. I took advantage of the tenant's absence and pulled the heavy lid down, sealing myself in, grateful for the rest.

Oblivion.

I was awoken by the harshest scream.

My head banged against the coffin lid. I leapt out. My heart pounded. Then I realized that the startling shriek had not come from anywhere near the chapel but had been transmitted to me from Athena. She was calling to me. I flew out of the dark room only to stagger back, stopped in my tracks by sunrays that flooded in from the top of the stairs. It was impossible for me to take another step, impossible to save her.

The waking nightmare unfolded.

I withdrew into the darkest corner, crouching low and hugging my knees, recalling when Sunaria had called to me and I had been powerless. Here, now, another vampire begged me to save her.

Athena had been so engrossed that she had not sensed the five masked men until they had burst in. All dressed in black, the assailants worked quickly with their torches of fire, setting aflame the witches who ran screaming. Athena was noticed immediately, her pale telltale beauty revealing that infamous fashion of a vampire. She rose into the air but the men were upon her, grabbing at her ankles. Athena struggled fiercely, her inhuman strength throwing some of them off balance. But there were too many of them. Swiftly, they tied her hands behind her and bound her feet. Then, securing the blindfold, they pulled her from the burning house and dragged her into their darkened carriage.

I mouthed their name, "Stone Masters," and threw up.

IX

JADEON

I AWOKE WITH A START.

"Wake up. It is time," Lord Artimas said as he loomed over me.

Rubbing my eyes still bleary from sleep, I squinted at his ominous silhouette. My head throbbed, a painful reminder of the previous evening when Alex and I had consumed an entire bottle of rum. I was scared Father would get a whiff of my breath and poke me with his stick again.

"Wear something dark," he instructed. "Meet me downstairs in the study."

He withdrew.

"Yes!" I leapt out of bed and promptly fell over. I checked the door to make sure he had gone. I dressed quickly, eager to discover what all the fuss was about. My boredom was slipping away. For some reason my trouser leg seemed to elude me, and I hopped round like a crazy person. My head throbbed and I cursed my brother for making me drink so much rum. Or was it the other way around?

Fully aware that if I was not to anger Lord Artimas it would be wise to be within his presence immediately, I descended the stairs two at a time.

On entering my father's study, five of his acquaintances addressed me. This looked serious. I was taken aback by the assembled entourage. Immediately I recognized the garments of the assembled men, all clothed similarly to my father in black attire with masks around their necks.

Catherine's father Edward De Mercy was present, dressed in his priest's garb. He nodded in greeting. I still blamed him for Catherine's decision but per etiquette, politely nodded and acknowledged two of the other men as Lord Hawke and Lord Theron, whom my parents entertained frequently. Still, it was difficult to subdue my enthusiasm which was hardly in keeping with the mood.

The men provided me with a dark robe and handed over a mask. I hoped they did not notice that my hands shook. They all fussed about me, checking the mask's fit. This accomplished, they pulled my mask around my neck, like theirs, revealing my confused expression. I wondered what Alex would make of all this.

"Listen carefully," my father began, "for on this night and those following, you will be initiated into the oldest order. I am the Master of the Stones, and you will one day take my place. This honor, bestowed upon you by your ancestors, carries with it much secrecy and it will be up to you to continue with the occupation that has gone on for thousands of years. You will maintain its concealment at all times. That even means keeping this secret from your brother. Alex can never know of who or what you are. Do you understand?"

I nodded. *What the hell was this?*

Lord Artimas continued. "We are an Order that has existed since the year 2900 before the birth of Christ our Lord. Our ancestors were chosen to maintain peace and safety within the land from those who would fulfill the will of the evildoers.

"We continue these duties today. Witches, demons, walkers of the night who suck the very life from humans by drinking their blood, these and many other such beings exist. And it is our duty, as it will be your duty from this day forward, to destroy any and all such creatures that exist.

"There are many of us. That you will learn. We send out men to find and study the evil ones, the Devil's own. And upon finding them we decide their fate and the manner in which they should die. The responsibility is far-reaching, and I do not expect you to comprehend it immediately. But before this night is out and before you reach your twenty-sixth year, you will become our loyal apprentice in all things. Are you ready?"

Everything that I had witnessed over the years finally fell into place—my father's distant disposition, his constant immersion in matters of state such as these, his indifference to his sons. I remembered the young girl who was dragged from the room near the dungeons. Irrevocably, I was being drawn into something scary and I wanted to resist the pull, but it was too late. I checked the serious expressions of the other men and wondered if I could decline the offer.

"Well, speak, boy," my father said.

"Lord Artimas, I am honored, but I—"

"You have much to learn. Soon you will gather the true magnitude of who and what you will become, and the responsibility therein."

Lord Artimas, escorted by the five men, led the way down into the castle vaults and I followed behind. All this time I had been eager to be in on the old boys' club, and now all I wanted to do was withdraw. I wondered how much of my time would be taken up with wearing this outfit and hanging out with the oldies. We came to a stop before the room that I had been banned from. The men secured their masks and I followed suit. The mask stifled my breathing and I couldn't wait to take it off.

As though reading my mind, Lord Hawke instructed me, "Until we say otherwise. Understand?"

I nodded.

On taking a large key from his pocket, my father turned the lock and stepped inside then gestured for me to follow. My eyes adjusted to the dim candlelit room.

I flinched, quickly composing myself so as not to annoy my father.

A woman lay splayed out upon the sizable oak table at the room's center, tied down with shackled limbs to the floor. My flashback to the beautiful woman of sixteen years ago came with waves of dizziness that unsettled me. I walked around to see her more clearly, noticing she too was as beautiful as the first. Brass chains secured her.

Her eyes fixed on me. "Jadeon, please help me," she begged.

My tongue cleaved to the roof of my mouth.

"Silence!" my father said. "See how they manipulate, Jadeon. They use their evil to read your thoughts. Guard your mind."

"Who is she?" I asked.

"She calls herself Athena. Do not let the appearance of the body of a young girl fool you. She is unimaginably old."

My once-innocent life dissolved as I viewed the seemingly harmless girl. I considered rescuing her, but when she spat at my father and revealed her fangs, I changed my mind, glancing at her shackles and hoping they would hold.

Her cries faded with my light-headedness. I resisted gravity's pull toward the stone floor and leaned against the wall to support myself.

"Let's begin," my father said.

I was wary. There was more to it.

Father's men guided me to stand at the feet of the girl. Father

Edward De Mercy stood in the corner of the room, holding holy water in a golden cup, occasionally splashing it upon the terrified girl. The other men positioned themselves on either side of the table—two men on one side, two on the other—as my father, lord of ceremony, took his place at the head of the table.

Could it get any worse? My question was soon answered.

The men chanted an eerie noise—at first a muffled echo that increased to a distinctive vibrant echo. My father picked up a baroque knife from the altar behind him. One of his assistants held the silver chalice below the woman's outstretched hand. She squealed as my father cut into her wrist.

Rum rose in my throat.

Her blood trickled into the cup.

To my amazement the wound healed immediately, only to be incised again.

"We drain their blood," my father said, "not so that they will die. It is impossible to kill them this way. But it weakens them." He cut into her wrist again. "See how the wound heals quickly. We must not allow her to regain her strength. Come, son, take this knife and do as I have done."

Beads of perspiration spotted my forehead. I stared at my father. His displeasure forced me to approach the girl. Shaking, I took the knife and studied it, hoping this would cause his impatience to grab it off me.

He glared at me with an insistence that was impossible to ignore.

I offered the knife back. "Perhaps next time?"

My father's gaze bored into mine. "Now," he ordered.

Her cold arm pulled away from my grasp. I glared down at her veins. "Is this really necessary?"

The girl's shrill screams pierced the room.

"Gag her!" my father shouted.

"What has she done?" I asked.

"Murder."

"Still," I reasoned.

Again he glared.

"I can't," I said.

"You are my son." He glanced at the others.

His words ran deep. Biting my lip, I made a light incision with a shaking hand, mesmerized with the speed that it healed.

"Deeper," Father instructed.

I cringed.

"I know the first time is the worst." He pointed to her wrist.

Clenching my jaw, I hacked through her flesh.

More screams.

I felt monstrous.

Blood poured into the ornate cup. Father emptied the overflowing chalice into a large rococo bowl set on the altar behind us.

She struggled. Her wound healed with preternatural speed. This was an abomination.

"Take me with you," the girl begged. She read my mind again.

"Silence," my father said.

Please, she begged, sending her thoughts through mine this time, ensuring others would not hear. *Your father keeps you prisoner within these castle walls. Your brother Alex, too. Let me go, release me, and I will help you escape.*

I shuddered. "She is in my head. I hear her!"

"So is the way of the Devil," my father said.

As the ceremony progressed, I observed the girl weakening. She fell in and out of consciousness only to regain some strength and plead. I lingered by the door until Lord Hawke grabbed me and directed me to watch from a better vantage point.

I quietly cursed him.

Her chains were removed and they rebound her hands and feet with coarse rope. Forcefully, they pulled her upright and placed a blindfold. Once it was securely fastened, they dragged her out of the room.

Thank God it was over.

Having had enough of the barbaric, I reluctantly followed them toward the corridor that led to the dungeons, wondering where we headed.

My father led us to the furthest of a long line of cells, and upon entering pulled one of the stones that jutted out innocently from the wall, camouflaged by its surrounding stones. With such a movement, the wall shook and a stone doorway swung open.

We continued along a passageway that led beneath the castle. This was where these men had disappeared all those years ago when I had followed them round the corner only to lose them. We trekked on for what seemed an eternity. Eventually a glimmer of light hinted that our exit neared.

Perhaps I could slip away.

My father was a fit man, and now I realized why. The men roughly hauled their staggering victim out into the night and through the locked doorway, completely hidden by trees, where I recognized the shadowy woods of mainland Marazion. Cautiously, with our prisoner in tow, we descended the steep slope toward the three horse-drawn carriages stationed below.

My father reassured me that when we arrived at our destination, I would have a greater understanding of our purpose.

It did little to comfort me.

* * * *

We traveled over several nights, keeping our captive secret, staying in accommodations along the way, specially pre-selected inns and fine homes owned by other associates. Torn, I craved the naiveté of my old life and yet was eager to unravel my family's secrets.

Weary from our journey, I was grateful when informed we had arrived in Salisbury. Limbs aching, I climbed out of the carriage and paused on the grassy bank, gazing up in awe at the overbearing structure before me. I caught my breath as my eyes absorbed the magnificent view.

"Stonehenge," my father said.

The megalithic circle of stones towered like grand rocky gods reaching inexorably toward the stars. I stared in wonder, struck by the outer circle with its continuous lintels and estimated their height to be over sixteen feet. Within the outer ring appeared a horseshoe of bluestones towering over the central sacrificial altar stone. To the northeast, beyond the outer ditch of earthwork, stood the bulky heel stone as if guarding the stones as one of my father's sentinels stood upon it. I rallied myself and placed my mask over my face before proceeding toward the central stone where my father now stood. The sunrise was imminent.

The girl, who remained bound, blindfolded, and gagged, was shoved to the center, closely followed by Father De Mercy, who chanted ancient incantations and sprinkled holy water. Typical. When some of it landed on me I wiped it off, annoyed. The night chill was bitter. I regretted not wearing warmer clothes.

Lord Artimas guided me to the outer rim of the stones and in hushed tones explained, "Construction began in 2950 B.C. The first pillars, transported by sea, established the most profound statement of human supremacy. The stones were dragged from the Preseli Mountains in West Wales. Later, Sarsen stones were brought in to intensify the dramatic effect of the first, designed initially so that during the midsummer morning, the sun rises between the central stone, on which a vampire is placed, and the heel stone."

His words fell behind as I tried to keep up.

"Therefore," he tapped my shoulder to get my attention back on him, "when the sun comes up and is at its most potent, it directs concentrated rays upon the nightwalker, who chained steadfastly to the central stone, is killed instantly, unable to escape the powerful rays that incinerate it to ashes.

"In time we discovered that the ceremony can be performed all year long. However, it is not enough to scatter their ashes to the wind, as with certainty they could reform. We must separate and pour them into the naturally formed fissures carved into the top of the inner circle of stones—thus ensuring that the ashes never reconstruct. For if they did, they would easily revert to their former selves. The stones are so substantial they can never be breeched or shattered. They are indestructible. This ceremony has taken place since man first realized that such creatures exist, and we eventually fathomed how we could destroy them in order to protect man's very survival. We fought back."

It was all very convincing and for the first time since this nightmare had begun my guilt subsided. I hoped I had what it took to make my father proud. It was good being so close to him, even under these conditions.

Athena was positioned face up on the central altar, her long brown hair falling over her face and down the sides on the oblong stone. Chains were placed around both her hands and feet and then pulled downwards as the other end of the metal restraint was fastened with spikes and nailed firmly into the ground. Her mask and gag were removed, and her gown, now dirty and torn, was pulled down roughly. Her dress was purposefully ripped open to expose the flesh above her heart.

The men worked fast, placing large flamed torches in between each stone so that the monument shone with a mystical light, revealing its true magnificence. From a distance, it would appear to be an intimidating Druid monument. The wooden altar, taken from Cornwall, was now positioned close to the central stone behind us and the silver goblets and knives were placed upon it in an organized fashion. When it appeared that all was in order, Lord Artimas took his place again at the head of the stone and picked up one of the knives.

I hoped my nerves were ready for the unimaginable.

"How do you plead?" Lord Artimas asked Athena as she sobbed.

"Do you admit to the murder of the innocent?" he continued, not waiting for her response. "Do you admit to serving Satan? It is with truth and honor that I command your spirit into the afterworld, where you will be judged accordingly."

My eyes were transfixed on Lord Hawke, who accepted the knife from Lord Artimas and drew toward the altar. He proceeded to cut deeply into Athena's wrist. My father lifted the silver chalice and placed it under her hand. Holding it steady, he caught her blood as it poured into the cup, filling it to the brim.

Not wanting to see anymore, I let my gaze wander.

Despite the spaces between the stones, they seemed to close in on us. Having read about this place, I was not prepared for actually being here. As I ran my hand over one of the cold pillars, fascinated with its hugeness, it was easy to become intrigued not only with how it got here, but also how deep it went.

So many questions.

"Jadeon!" My father redirected my attention to the girl again. He ordered me to stand with him and instructed me how to proceed. With grand authority, the hypnotic chanting began.

Athena had lost so much blood my mind could not fathom how she still breathed.

"It is with thanks that I, Master of the Stones, take nourishment from this evildoer, in order that her transgressions be absolved and taken into me."

To my horror, my father lifted the cup to his lips and drank the very blood he had just drained from Athena. He then appeared to enter a blissful trance-like state, dazed and in obvious pleasure. Studying the faces of the other men, I saw that their eyes fixed on my father, as if hoping they too would get a taste. Lord Theron took a knife from the table and proceeded to cut off the woman's hair, quickly retrieving it from the ground and placing it at her feet. Lord Artimas recovered.

Shifting my feet, my gait felt unsteady.

"Take your rightful place here at the center of the stones and drink," my father commanded again. "Now, son, accept your birthright and partake of your first drink, for on this night and with this act you are one with the stones, such an honor only bestowed upon the Master and his apprentice."

Lord Hawke cut deep into her flesh again. I obediently held the cup under her and turned my head away, only to feel my father's hand at the back of my head, redirecting me toward the blood pouring into the cup and overflowing onto my hands.

I peered down at the silver chalice and wondered if I had staggered into a nightmare. The men watched in reverence. Lips pursed, my head arched back, subtly avoiding the ridge of the cup.

This was diabolical.

My father placed one hand on my shoulder while his other forced the base of the cup to my lips. I gulped it down, hoping such speed would prevent me from tasting, but both aroma and flavor were surprisingly pleasant. Astonished by the sudden warm flush which was similar to the epicurean effect of wine, I swooned, swept away by the delirious sensations. My head fell back and someone assisted me onto the ground. Spellbound, I struggled with the loss of control. Wave after wave of a strange carnal rapture enveloped me, transporting me to a time before, when I was Master of Ceremony myself.

This was madness. Having entered it, my mind sought a way out. The stones now spoke to me, a clear and familiar language. Panic-stricken, I was painfully self-conscious and so embarrassed but this drunkenness was impossible to shake off.

A blinding white, the connection my father had spoken of. My mind continued to play tricks and I felt myself ascend. Looking down I clearly viewed this gathering of ancient rocks, designed and set in perfect fashion. Despite the ecstasy, I struggled against the desire, descending with speed now, falling rapidly toward the earth. I lay again upon the floor, enraptured by the stones' power, sensing a merging. I became the stones.

It was the laughter and cheering in celebration that roused me from my trance. My father's voice instructed me to stand and complete the work. Lord Hawke pulled me to my feet and I opened my eyes, staggering toward the girl. My cheeks were red, my pulse racing. I was utterly humiliated. The admiring stares of the men and my father's proud smile softened the moment. Dizzy and still reeling with pleasure, I wished this entire spectacle was over. Lord Artimas handed the knife over to me, instructing me to pierce Athena's heart.

My stare pleaded with him.

"Take the knife and stab her heart. Forgive her for her trespasses. Remember, it is within your power to do so," my father instructed. "Make it slow, so that she feels the full force of her punishment."

I hovered over Athena and stared down at her.

"Do it!" my father ordered.

I raised the knife high up above her, unsettled to see that her eyes were focused upon mine.

"He knows who you are, Jadeon," she said, "and he promises revenge." Athena turned her gaze toward my father. "Lord Artimas, Orpheus is coming for you."

I wanted to hear more. "Who is—"

"Jadeon," my father said. "Finish it."

I clutched the blade's handle and lifted it high into the air. I paused. My father wrapped his fingers around mine and with full force he brought the knife down into her chest, piercing her heart.

Athena's scream was deafening. My father pried my fingers off the knife, leaving it in place. I staggered back nauseous, fixated by the blood that poured from the wound. A death rattle rose from the girl and she became quiet. A bright prism of light descended, seemingly emanating from the very stones. Dawn arose, flooded the area, and danced around us.

I shielded my eyes, taking small glimpses at the blinding rays that magnified and reflected. A beam of light focused directly upon where Athena lay, and with her screams came the melting of her flesh. The light burned through her and within her. Aflame, she burnt from the inside out. The knife that had penetrated her heart fell with a clang.

My blurred eyes blinked at the central stone covered in Athena's remains.

One of my father's men gathered up the ashes. He worked quickly, dividing the residue out into cups, scraping it off the sacrificial altar.

We headed back to the stagecoach which had been stationed at the perimeter of the monument. Out of its window was a clear view of my father's loyal servant positioning a small ladder at the base of each inner stone, then climbing to the top rung. He poured a few ashes into the cracks just below the lintels.

Lord Artimas peered intently at me. "Lord Theron and I have agreed that Alex and his daughter are to be married. Do we have your word that such a union will go unhindered?"

The lightheadedness made it difficult to focus.

"Well, boy?"

"Father, I—"

"I take that as a yes."

Our carriage lumbered forward with a jolt as the horses responded obediently to the stagehand's crack of the whip. For Alex's sake, I had to see a way out of this for him. My eyes closed and I rested my head on the leather headrest. Immediately my father chastised me, saying that it was imperative I remain awake. He warned that if I were to sleep too soon after the ritual I would suffer later from memory loss. The thought sounded appealing, but the heel of his shoe convinced me otherwise.

Athena, the goddess of wisdom, would reign no more in her small kingdom of witches. All that was left of her, other than her ashes, was her taste in my mouth. I sucked my bottom lip with utter surprise at my own reaction and wondered when I would be able to drink like this again.

X

⊕RPHEUS

ATHENA WAS DEAD.

The Stone Masters had blindfolded her, fully aware that in doing so other vampires would be unable to track her. Strategically, they had arrived at Stonehenge minutes before sunrise ensuring no vampire could interfere with their ritual for fear of becoming victims themselves. Their tactics were wearing thin. I was prepared to go into the very heart of the secret society if that was what it took.

To mark Jadeon's initiation into the Stone Masters, Lord Artimas had arranged a grand ball under the pretense of his son's birthday celebration. The Artimas function was now a few hours away. I held the official invitation, animated at the thought of being welcomed in.

I stood naked, gazing at the exit of the chapel. The heady aroma of incense hung thick in the air and filled my nostrils. A small disguise was required. If my plan was to succeed then the next action was crucial. My paling features were a telltale sign to those in the know. To penetrate the castle undetected and without raising alarm, I had to darken the color of my skin.

The sunset pulled with it the last remnants of shimmering light.

Taking a deep breath I approached the doorway. Perfect timing was imperative. I would have to move swiftly. With my hand on the cast iron handle of the finely engraved wooden door I turned it and darted back into the shadows, avoiding the sunlight that flooded in. Standing tall, I stepped out of the chapel and into the light, raising my arms out, turning around several times, allowing the rays to caress my body. My skin smarted. I leapt back inside, closing the door on the way, relieved that the tingling soon wore off. The color of my skin was a light golden brown.

Delighted with my success, I returned to where my clothes lay and began to dress, wary of the sun's fading rays that weakly flickered through the doorway. My ability to tolerate the light was a sign of my increasing immunity and strength. Such is the benefit of senescence. Lost in thoughts of Sunaria, who named after the sun had cruelly died by it, I could not help but ponder on the irony.

A voice startled me. It was a woman's...no, two...a conversation. People headed in my direction and I currently stood naked from the waist down. Two angelic nuns entered through the doorway. The ethereally dressed women were oblivious to my presence. They revealed their names. The younger of the two sisters was Martha, and the older Catherine.

I smiled.

XI

JADEON

THIS WAS NOT what I had expected. A barrage of business meetings now almost sounded appealing. To think I had been in a hurry to get invited into the old man's club. Now all I wanted was to avoid them.

I turned to the books once again only this time actually reading them, devouring the pages to unravel the confusion. I was stunned at what I learned, my eyes opened to horrors that sounded more like the ravings of madmen. It seemed that pagan rituals were rampant and were going on too close to home for comfort. An uneasy feeling came with the realization that the rest of my life was to be dedicated to slaughtering the damned.

But there was no way out.

The fact that I could not tell Alex was unbearable. We had always shared in everything and in that way helped each other see through whatever concerns we had, problems that now seemed insignificant, petty preludes to this. The drag in my stomach worsened with thoughts of Alex's impending marriage. This pressing matter weighed heavily.

For a week I had tried to discuss with Father the wisdom of such a match, and each day he bore me down with his terrible gaze and put me in my place.

To add insult to injury, Father had then given me the dubious honor of informing his youngest. Fearing such a conversation would place an irreversible rift with Alex I paced the corridors of St. Michael's Mount looking for a solution.

Anxiously I made my way to Alex's room. Within the castle final preparations for the grand ball were underway, and I dodged the servants who scurried around, getting things just right for when our home would be invaded by hundreds of guests. I was counting the hours until they would be gone.

On my arrival in Alex's bedroom, the tailor fussed around Alex engrossed in his work. Alex admired his reflection before the mirror. Arthur had been trying to arrange my brother's fitting for days, though Alex's sporadic appearances had proven challenging.

I had carefully rehearsed and re-rehearsed my speech. Father had told me all arrangements were set and all that was left was for the groom to be informed. This was unbearably cruel, but Father was determined.

Swallowing hard, hoping the lump in my throat would not give me away, I spoke. "Lady Emily Theron will be attending the ball tonight, Alex."

"So?"

"It will be nice for you to see her again. It has been such a while since we saw her last."

Alex glanced at me and smiled. "You're kidding, right?"

I cringed.

"Jadeon, what's on your mind? Birthdays are not all that bad."

"This one is."

"Is Father giving you a hard time?" he asked.

"Father has requested that you escort Lady Theron tonight."

"But I'm hosting Lord Velde."

"It would be wise if you humored Father," I tried.

"You should escort her. She's fond of you, I'm sure."

"It is you she likes."

"What makes you think that?"

"Inside knowledge."

"I don't do boring."

I addressed the tailor and gesticulated toward the doorway. "Please," I said.

The tailor quickly withdrew.

"He hasn't finished," Alex said.

"We need privacy. There is something I have to tell you," I said, picking up objects within the room, looking at them nervously, and then placing them down again.

"What?" Alex said.

"Oh God, Alex, I am so sorry—"

"I'm sure it isn't as bad as—"

"I need you to remain calm," I said.

"My horse?"

"No."

"What then? Tell me?"

"You are to marry Lady Theron."

Alex laughed. "That would be absolutely—" He caught my expression in the mirror and spun round. "This is a joke?"

"I'm sorry." I shook my head.

"You're serious?"

"I am."

"This is not a cruel prank?"

"Please, it's for your own good. Father and I have decided—"

"Father and you? Since when has it been Father and you? I will not marry her. Call it off immediately. I do not even know her."

"I cannot. It is done and set."

"Excuse me?"

I had to be strong for us both, to behave in a manner that set an example of authority. As the eldest it was my duty to shoulder this.

"Jadeon, say something."

"Emily comes from a noble family."

"That's not what I meant. This doesn't sound like you." He wasn't wrong.

"This is not about me, and it is not up for debate."

"You know this is madness."

"I should have chosen better words . . ."

"You marry her."

"These things are not to be tampered with. In time, you will understand."

"There is no understanding your betrayal," he said.

"Please, Alex, I—"

He turned his back on me and faced the mirror. Even with his back turned away, his panic was palpable. I deserved it. Full of guilt, I headed out.

"Wait," Alex called after me.

"Yes?"

"Perhaps if you reasoned with Father."

"I don't know if—" I read the desperation in his face. "I will do what I can."

"Hey, isn't it your initiation into the old boys' club soon?"

"That's already happened, I—"

"Again, I'm the last to hear," Alex said. "You may have your secrets, but I too have mine."

"And what is that supposed to mean?"

Alex faced the mirror again.
His silence forced my withdrawal.

XII

⊕RPHEUS

CROUCHING LOW IN the shadows I hid behind the pews, awaiting my chance to either bolt away into the night or down into the basement of the chapel. I observed the two nuns carrying out their work in earnest, both dressed in their long white linen habits. They silently tended to the small church, thus allowing me to listen to their thoughts. I ascertained that sixteen year old Martha had recently arrived at the convent. However, it was Catherine who interested me—the woman of Jadeon's affections.

Easily absorbed with Catherine's thoughts, I detected she continued to feel a great deal of fondness for Jadeon, thinking about him frequently. Switching my concentration to the youngest nun, I was surprised at how mundane her thoughts were and decided that I would have to leave soon before I collapsed from sheer boredom. Much to my pleasure, a rat scuttled close to Martha and her screams disrupted the silence as she leapt onto one of the pews. My boredom subsided.

Catherine did what she could to calm Martha, who though shaken, attempted to recompose herself. Fear struck again as out of the corner of her eye Martha caught sight of me and screamed, pointing in my direction. Catherine turned to see what had distressed the girl.

I stood up.

Catherine gasped.

I stared defiantly, aware that I was still naked from the waist down.

For the young Martha, this was all too much. Jumping down from the pew and almost ripping her sash, she ran from the church, the noise of her wails resonating. Catherine's glare equaled my own.

"This is a house of God!" Catherine exclaimed, and before she could stop herself her gaze fell directly upon my nakedness. "Sir, I beg you, please cover up. You can see I am a nun."

I took great pleasure in staring back at her and proceeded to pull the rest of my clothes on, my eyes frequently glancing up at the captivating nun who bravely stood her ground.

"Sir, if you are in need of help, some medicine or food, we can provide such things for you."

I approached her. She caught her breath. Catherine stepped backwards, moving away from me.

I followed.

Catherine banged into the font and froze.

I leaned forward, pressing against her and placed my hand inside the chapel's font and wet my forefinger. She struggled, but with my weight pressed against her she was powerless. I placed my finger on her full lips and into her mouth and stroked her moist tongue.

Instinctively Catherine suckled.

I stared down at the beautiful innocent creature, enraptured, and now understood how Jadeon had become so obsessed with her. Removing my finger from her mouth I took hold of her hand, guiding her forefinger into mine.

Catherine's eyes rolled back, teetering. Her legs gave way.

I caught her, preventing her fall.

Thwack!

A sharp pain struck the back of my head. I let go of Catherine and spun round to see Martha holding a large silver candlestick.

I laughed and dodged another strike from the candle. "So I take it a *ménage a trois* is out of the question?"

Martha was startled that her attack had no effect on me. I lunged toward her and she screamed and leapt back. I howled with laughter.

Martha grabbed Catherine's hand, pulling her toward the doorway. On reaching the chapel exit, Catherine turned and stared at me.

I smiled at her.

"He is the Devil!" Martha shrieked.

I leant against the chapel door and watched the two nuns running into the night. "You flatter me, Martha," I called out.

Catherine's subtle perfume carried in the air. I breathed her in, then shook myself from my reverie. I had a ball to attend.

* * * *

Within an hour, I stood on the shoreline of St. Michaels's Mount. Other guests were arriving and I strolled with them toward the castle steps. This was indeed a stately event. All had dressed in their finest attire. At the entrance of the castle I saw Alex, Jadeon, and the man whom I assumed was their father, Lord Artimas. He was exactly as Alex had described. All three were busy greeting their guests. I paused for a moment and rallied myself. I was about to come face-to-face with a Stone Master. I had to convince Lord Artimas, who had an eye for vampires, that I was human.

Lost in the crowd, I took a moment to study the other guests and familiarize myself with the castle. Looking back again at the grand entrance steps, I was surprised to see Jadeon Artimas staring at me. He whispered into Alex's ear. Alex's face lit up.

I approached them, all the time scanning Lord Artimas's mind for any indication of his suspicions of me. I bowed deeply, greeted them and threw a quick glance at their father, ready to retreat if needed.

Lord Artimas turned to me. "Sir, it is with great pleasure that I invite you to St. Michael's Mount. I am forever in your debt."

"Lord Artimas, I am honored to have finally met. Your son has spoken such inspiring words about you," I said, almost cringing at the niceties.

"Lord Velde," Jadeon said, "we are honored that you could join us. Perhaps later I will have the opportunity to become more acquainted?"

"I would like that very much, sir." I studied Lord Artimas, reassured that I was in.

I followed directions into the lobby and left my hosts greeting their other guests. I looked about the finely decorated castle vestibule, observing the men and women mingling with one another. Taking a moment to read their minds I couldn't help but laugh at how warmly they greeted each other, while their thoughts certainly did not reflect such sentiments.

I strolled into the main ballroom and immediately recognized the music played by the orchestra, recalling that Ludwig Van Beethoven had been one of Sunaria's favorite composers. I avoided the regally-dressed servants who offered guests a rich assortment of fruits, meats, and sweet delicacies, and instead admired the rich burgundy and purple velvet drapes strewn upon the walls of the ballroom, providing an elaborate backdrop to the baroque décor. The grand chandeliers hung low from the ornate ceiling, reflecting the candlelight exquisitely off their finely cut crystal.

Over three hundred guests had been invited, and I wondered how many were staying within the castle walls following the festivities. The dancing couples were dressed in their finest apparel. Light from the chandeliers shone upon them. I sauntered about the room lingering close to the walls, aware of the glances and even some stares from admiring mortals. I reminded myself I was not here for entertainment.

Alex soon joined me and together we stood in the corner of the sumptuous ballroom, talking discreetly to one another, occasionally looking toward the center of the room where some of the guests mingled loudly and others danced. The playful mortals waltzed around and around, their perfectly timed gliding steps all in unison moving flawlessly to the orchestra.

"My, you have caught the sun," Alex said.

"I was outside quite a bit, selecting horses to send back to Spain," I lied.

"But I thought Spain had the best horses?"

"Ah, I did say that, didn't I?"

"Well, I know first hand of your excellent choice in livery."

"How is the mare?"

"She's settled in well. I ride her every day."

"I am glad to hear it," I said.

Jadeon appeared and we welcomed him into the conversation.

"Your party is a success," I said.

"Yes, it appears to be going well," Jadeon said. "Alex tells me you live in Spain. How long will we have the pleasure of your company?"

"I return to Spain in a few weeks," I replied, but I was secretly planning to visit Italy. To judge by Alex's expression, he had not considered that I might leave Cornwall. "But you are both invited to visit me in Spain," I said.

Jadeon smiled. "Perhaps next summer?"

Alex looked vexed.

Jadeon reflected concern. "Alex has a lot on his mind right now."

"I have been condemned to a slow death," Alex said.

"How so?"

"Father has arranged—"

"For him to marry," Jadeon said.

I feigned ignorance, though I had extracted the facts before they were spoken.

"Perhaps you could request to be hung, drawn, and quartered instead?" I said.

Jadeon's expression was priceless.

Alex laughed. "At least the suffering would not last quite as long."

"Well, I for one adore weddings." I winked at Alex.

Alex sighed. "Daumia, you're not helping."

"Perhaps I could meet her?" I said.

"You and me both."

"You approve of your brother's union?" I asked Jadeon.

"It's complicated. But I have promised Alex that I will talk with Father about—"

"I want to meet her, get the girl," I insisted.

Jadeon was a little taken aback. "Well I . . . very well."

Alex and I accepted the goblets of wine offered up by a waiter. I returned my gaze to Alex. I hated the fact he was in an unwanted engagement.

"May I present the honorable Lady Emily Theron," Jadeon announced.

I turned toward Jadeon and looked at the two women he escorted, obviously both friends.

Jadeon gestured. "Lady Theron, Lady Raynor, may I introduce Lord Velde."

"You most certainly can." Emily glanced up at me.

I read her mind and smiled. "Madam." I bowed, taking her hand and kissing it. "I am honored to make your acquaintance."

"And I yours, Lord Velde." Emily was breathless.

"Alex tells me how delighted he is that you are soon to be wed," I said.

"Yes, thank you, sir." Emily blushed.

"Have you known each other long?" I inquired.

"Quite long."

"How long?" I pressed.

"Well, I—"

"How much time have you spent in each other's company?"

Emily grew silent.

"I see," I said.

Tension hung thick in the air.

"Perhaps a dance." Jadeon motioned to Lady Theron.

"One moment please, Jadeon." I leaned toward Emily and whispered into her ear. "I know your secret."

Emily gasped.

"How awkward," I smiled, enjoying taunting her.

"But how do you—"

"Your mother told us," I misled her.
"My mother told you I am preg—"
Alex spat out his wine.
Emily looked at Alex, her face reddening.
"Really?" I said.
Jadeon cringed. "Oh, God."
"And it looks as though Alex is not the father," I said.
Emily was perplexed.
"Well, we are off to tour the castle," I said. "Alex has promised to show me the family art collection. I hear they have a Rembrandt. And coincidentally, I too own a painting by the same artist—*Belshazzar's Feast*. Why, if ever you are in Spain I would take such delight in showing it to you, but with a new baby on the way you won't be doing much traveling."

Emily's friend led her away.

"That'll put a strain on the mother-daughter relationship," I said.

"I am not quite sure what just happened there," Jadeon said.

"It was perfectly clear to me. Your father sacrificed his son's happiness for a friend whose daughter is with child."

Jadeon was stunned. "How did you know she was—"

"Well, Jadeon, if you have to ask," I said.

Jadeon flinched. He excused himself.

"Looks like your brother is off to tell Papa that the cat's out of the bag," I said.

"You just saved my life for a second time." Alex took a large gulp of wine.

"So I did," I said.

XIII

JADEON

I HAD TO FIND FATHER, warn him of Emily's condition and break off the impending marriage. Father would never condone such a union. Although devastated for her, such a turn of events was great news for my brother, who was probably celebrating with Lord Velde somewhere. With the formalities over I hoped to join them again.

It seemed that I had been searching for my father in the many rooms of the castle for half the night. The festivities of the ball continued and in one embarrassing moment I came across Lady Theron and her daughter in the anteroom, ensconced in an argument. Offering my apologies for interrupting I leapt out of the room.

Eventually I bumped into one of the male servants, who had apparently been searching for me with a message. The young man breathlessly informed me that Lord Artimas was holding a meeting in his study and had urgently requested my presence. It made me wonder if the news of Lady Emily Theron's predicament had reached him. There was no doubt that it would be zealously deliberated. With a jump in my step I headed to Father's offices.

On my arrival, Lord Artimas was completely enraged. Father De Mercy attempted but miserably failed to calm him. My father's colleagues stood by, watching on.

A small boy cowered in the corner, dressed in the clothes of a ship's cabin boy.

"Jadeon! Where have you been?" my father asked.

"Looking for you," I said.

"I requested your presence half an hour ago. Urgent business—"

"That's why I am here."

My father frowned.

I guided him to the back of the room. I lowered my voice. "I feared the news would have gotten to you before—"

"You knew about Velde?" he asked.

"What? No. This is about Emily?"

"Not now," he snapped.

I stood my ground. "Alex's intended is pregnant."

Lord Artimas looked tense. "I know."

"And you blessed this marriage?"

"Lord Theron—"

"I don't care. Alex is your son and you have forgotten that. This life has hardened your heart. I will not allow you to marry him off in this way."

"Jadeon," my father replied softy, "if you do not find your brother within the hour, your defense of him may well prove fruitless. Lord Velde may have already killed him. Alex was used, and now that Velde is in—"

I reeled. "What are you talking about?"

"Lord Velde is not the Spanish lord he appears to be," he said. "Your brother Alex has befriended a—" Lord Artimas glanced at the boy. His gaze fell upon me again. "Alex ensured this man's entry into our home," Lord Artimas said. "This cabin boy has informed us that when he sailed aboard the ship *The Blue Rose* on its journey from Spain he met Lord Velde, a passenger aboard this vessel. He commissioned the boy to unlock the captain's door with the payment of a gold coin. Lord Velde murdered the ship's captain. The boy witnessed the murder."

I wanted to bolt, to go and find Alex, but Father clutched at my sleeve.

The cabin boy was directed to stand in the center of the room.

Fearfully he said his name was Samuel and recounted his story before the imposing gathering. The boy stated he had hidden from view within the captain's cabin on many nights in order to have a warm, dry place to sleep. On that fateful night he had witnessed the gentleman actually bite the neck of his master, and then like an animal drink his blood.

Although the cabin boy had attempted to warn the navigator and other crewmembers, they had not believed his story. Adding insult to injury, they had taken the coin the man had given him. Samuel continued to explain that while on land leave his ship had docked in the harbor. He had recognized Lord Velde with a stranger in the old Marazion Inn, and had soon discovered the name of the other gentleman to be Alexander Artimas.

I pulled away and headed for the door.

"Wait," my father snapped at me. With a pointed finger at Samuel, he said, "Continue."

On recognizing the man, Samuel had informed his uncle the innkeeper. His uncle immediately informed Father Edward De Mercy. This time the boy's story was believed and he was brought to the castle in order for Lord Artimas to question him further. Samuel was reassured that these men found his account credible. He was thanked for his bravery but sternly warned that he should never speak of it again. Samuel's uncle escorted him toward the door.

I almost tripped on the boy on the way out.

"Be warned," my father called after me. "If you see Velde, do not approach him but send word. Guard your thoughts. He will kill you if he realizes that you know his identity."

As I withdrew, Father ordered his men out and directed their search.

I recalled Athena's words at my initiation ceremony.

He is coming for you, she had threatened.

I should have listened.

XIV

⊕RPHEUS

ALEX AND I STROLLED along the sprawling candlelit corridors and perused his father's fine paintings. I recognized the cabin boy, escorted by an older man, heading fast toward us, and nudged Alex into a deep shadowy alcove, leading to one of many rooms.

"Alex," I said, "there is something I have been meaning to ask you."

"I'm intrigued."

I pushed Alex against the wall and remained still, hoping they would not detect movement as they passed by the alcove. Samuel's mind confirmed my suspicions. The boy had witnessed everything that had occurred on the ship and Samuel had just shared his experience with Lord Artimas.

"That was close," Alex said.

I stepped back. "Too close."

"Well, you have something to ask me?" Alex said.

I sighed. "Would you consider coming with me?"

"Back to Spain?"

"Not exactly."

"Then—"

"Would you . . . like to be more than you are?"

"I don't get you," he said.

"Are you ready to live the life you always dreamt of?"

"Free of my father?"

"Free of everything."

"How?"
I was thoughtful.
"What do I need to do?" he asked.
"Are you prepared to come to the end of the world with me?"
"Where do you have in mind?"
"I want to give you a gift."
Alex stared at me.
"There will be no turning back," I said.
"Sounds serious." Alex smiled.
"For now, perhaps just a taste?"
"How much time do I have?"
"None." I lunged, pushing him against the wall. Turning his neck to the side, I bit.

He shuddered.

We shared the frisson. Alex tried to push me away. I held him fast. Our two bodies were locked together by the strength of one. I opened my mouth wide to receive the sudden gush and savored the wave of pleasure.

Through clenched teeth, he moaned.

Leaning against him, it was a thrill. Our emotions intermingled.

I broke away.

Alex fell, dazed. He stared off, blinking.

I applied pressure to quell the trickling blood. "Alex, do you trust me?"

A tear fell from his eye.

With a bite into my wrist I'd drawn blood. "Drink."

He turned his head away.

I thrust my wrist against his lips and pulled his head back, bestowing only enough blood to cause memory loss. I closed Alex's eyes and wooed him to sleep.

I dragged his body into the darkest shadows of the alcove.

XV

JADEON

FRANTIC, I ENTERED the ballroom where I had last seen Alex with Lord Velde. An overwhelming guilt caught in my throat. Had I been less self-absorbed and more attentive to him, he would not have sought friendship elsewhere. Pushing through the crowd, almost tripping on the long generous dresses of the female guests, I was caught up in a frenzied dizziness by the twirling dancers. Beads of perspiration spotted my brow when there was no sign of Alex.

Taking three steps at a time, I ascended the central stairway and headed toward the candlelit corridors. Alex had mentioned showing off Father's art, and as the majority of it was presented here it was a good place to start. The passageways were empty. I bolted outside toward the secluded rear of the castle near the waters edge, aware that this was a favorite place for both of us. I searched along the castle walls. The cool sea air stung my nostrils. A storm approached. I turned to head back toward the castle steps.

I flinched. Lord Velde stood before me.

Must close my thoughts.

"Did he tell you that was possible?" Lord Velde asked.

He drew toward me.

Stunned; a barrage of thoughts.

"Please call me Orpheus."

I recalled where I had first heard his name, called out by the terrified female held captive here.

"Her name was Sunaria."

"Where is Alex?" I asked.

My hands shook and I held them behind my back, hoping he would not notice. I had to keep calm.

"He's taking a nap," he said.

"Will you take me to him?"

"Why wake him?"

"I need to see him."

"Do you now?" He smiled.

Silence. His stare was shocking.

The quiet threw me. "What is it that you want?" I asked.

"I want her back."

"I'm afraid that—"

"Impossible, I know. Your father—"

"The girl we saw, she was Sunaria."

"She was the woman I loved. She was no threat. She lived in the shadows, harmless and innocent."

"As innocent as a vampire can be," I replied, wishing I had not.

"You judge her? And yet you never met her."

"She murdered—"

"Your brother is in love with me."

I shook my head. *"No."*

"You know this to be true. He is infatuated with me."

"What is it that you want?" I considered my chances of escape.

"What I want . . . and do not attempt to run, for I will stop you. What I want is merely revenge. A life for a life. Your brother, Alex, is to be that life."

"There must be another way."

"No."

"Perhaps a duel?"

He shook his head. "It's not enough."

"My father's men are on their way as we speak."

Orpheus glanced at the castle. "This very night . . ." He knelt down and picked up a small rock, standing again. He crushed it effortlessly, exaggerating his point as the rock dissolved into dust. "I will extinguish your brother's life." He pulverized the stone.

"Stay back!" I said.

"Or you will do what? Have you any idea what it is to love a woman with your entire being as I did? Oh, but you do! Her name . . . yes, I hear it now—Catherine!"

Trying to fathom how he knew about her, a wave of panic hit me. "Do not say her name!"

"Beautiful long blond hair, full lips, fuller breasts."

"I said do not—"

"Your mind is as transparent as your brother's," Orpheus said.

"We will duel and that will decide this."

He vanished.

I searched the area. "Orpheus?" I called out.

The air was chilling. Crashing waves hit the rocks and sprayed foam. Cursing my ineptitude I headed toward the castle.

Halfway up, Orpheus reappeared before me as though out of nothing.

Relieved I had a second chance, I began, "You have been wronged. For that I am sorry, but Alex is—"

Orpheus held a necktie. "I'm going back to him. Only this time, instead of helping Alex with his tie, I'll strangle him with it."

I recognized the material. It was Alex's.

"Yes. Pity really, because he's so vibrant, so—Alex."

"You dare touch him!"

"Consider this place without him." Orpheus turned.

I flew at him.

Orpheus leapt out of the way and I hurtled to the ground. Easily, he flipped me onto my back and his fist struck my chest. Air left my lungs. Struggling to catch my breath I clutched at his jacket, fearing he would disappear again.

"You were saying?" he said.

"Don't harm him."

"Are you begging?"

"Take my life instead. Take me in his place."

"How honorable. But you see, you have no idea what you are offering. I am taking your brother to Stonehenge to perform the very same ritual that was performed upon Sunaria, before I strangle him. That is how it must be for me to feel any kind of peace again."

Orpheus helped me to my feet.

Everything was wrong.

"Take me," I said.

Orpheus appeared to think upon this for a moment.

"This is nonnegotiable," I said.

"Very well. There is a boat waiting by the water's edge. Once upon the mainland you will see my carriage. Its horses are white. This will take you directly to Stonehenge. If you deter from this route at any time or delay it, I will kill Alex. Do you understand?"

"How can I leave you here with my family, all these people?"

"Our agreement is over, then?" Orpheus pulled on the necktie, testing its strength.

"Wait!" I said. "If I do this thing, you must assure me, promise."

"I am a gentleman who seeks nothing other than some kind of retribution for the death of a loved one. Such a thing is a nobleman's right."

I could see no other way through this. Father was here. He could take care of the guests. I would take care of Alex. "How will I know that you will not kill him anyway?" I asked.

"So long as I can take the life of an Artimas, I will be satisfied. A life for a life. Yours instead of your brother's."

"Very well." Although reluctant, I walked past Orpheus and headed toward the boat docked in the bay. "Orpheus, if you harm my family, if you break your word, I shall personally pour your ashes into the stones."

"Spoken like a true Stone Master." He handed me the tie.

I stared at it. Not wanting to give my thoughts away, I quick-footed it down to the boat. Although this man had strength and speed, I hoped my adroit mind could outwit him.

XVI

⊕RPHEUS

ALEX EVENTUALLY PICKED himself off the floor. Realizing his favorite necktie, a gift from his brother, was gone, he did a quick search. Miserable not to find it, he headed down the corridors back to his room. He was uncertain what had just occurred. With his memory foggy he tried to fill the gaps. Had he offended me? He believed he must have done something to displease me.

He recalled an altercation but could not fit the pieces together. He considered that perhaps his engagement to Lady Theron, though now probably broken off, might have roused my jealousy although he reasoned I had dealt with the situation calmly at the time.

He rubbed the area where I had bitten him, soothing its sting. On looking down at his hand, he was dismayed to see some residual blood.

Some kiss, he thought.

Alex needed to be alone for a while, away from the meandering crowds partying within the castle walls below. On nearing his own room he was surprised to see his father leaving it, approaching him with worrying speed. Alex reasoned that news of the conversation with Emily had reached his father and he steadied himself. He pulled his collar up.

"Father, please let me explain," Alex said.

Lord Artimas was accompanied by four other men, whom Alex recognized as lords from other nearby estates. His parents had hosted them on many occasions. One of them, Lord Hawke, had presented him with his first fencing sword.

"Where is he?" Lord Artimas appeared distracted, impatiently glaring at his son.

"Who, Father? Good evening, sirs. Lord Hawke, it is wonderful to see you again." Alex politely greeted his father's associates.

"Lord Velde. Tell me where he is," Lord Artimas said.

"He is gone, Father."

"Gone where?"

"I know what this is about. I can explain." Alex lowered his voice in fear of offending Lord Theron. "You see, Lady Emily Theron is pregnant!"

"And how do you think Lord Velde knew?"

"Did you know?"

Lord Artimas ignored his son's question. "You believe that, do you? That you can tell from looking at a girl who does not have a belly that she is pregnant? If you believe that, then you are . . . For God's sake, he read her mind. Your Lord Velde is none other than a vampire!"

Alex placed his hand upon his neck again. He backed away from Lord Artimas, staring at him and attempting to fathom his words. Lord Artimas flicked back Alex's shirt collar and viewed the two fang marks.

"No!" Lord Artimas steadied himself against the stone wall. "How could you have allowed him?"

"Father." Alex stepped backwards. "It is not what it seems."

"Do you see?" Lord Artimas said to his men.

With a nod from Lord Artimas, they lunged toward Alex and overpowered him.

"Father, please."

"My son." Lord Artimas caught his sobs.

Lord Artimas followed closely behind the entourage. Struggling frantically, Alex was dragged into the dungeons. They shackled him to the central table, securing his arms, tying his wrists upward and binding his feet together.

"Blindfold him, for God's sake!" Lord Artimas commanded.

The room was prepared, the altar set, the knives sharpened, and the silver chalices placed. Lord Artimas shook, stifling his tears while preparing the instruments. The preparations complete, Lord Artimas's men offered their words of consolation. The ceremony began, the ritualistic chanting resonating. Lord Artimas took the knife from the altar and with a shaking hand placed it close to Alex's wrist, doing what he could to ignore his son's pleas. Lord Artimas cut deeply into his son's flesh, surprised as the blood flowed easily into the cup below. Despite Alex's deafening screams, Lord Artimas persisted.

The door flew open. My menacing silhouette appeared at the entrance.

Lord Artimas glared at me.

The shadows danced over me. "He is not a vampire," I said. "I merely bit into his neck."

Alex cried out. "Oh, thank God, Daumia! Please hurry, the pain! I cannot bear it!"

"Why him?" Lord Artimas asked.

"To gather up all the lords of the Stones and to ensure that they, and you, would be in the same room at the same time. Artimas, see how his wounds do not heal as those of a vampire would? You are a stupid man."

"I do not believe you! The marks on his neck . . ."

"You mean you would actually murder your son with such little evidence? How little you think of him."

"You manipulate everything."

I snapped. "Someone put pressure on that boy's wrist before he bleeds to death."

Lord Artimas raised his hand, an indication his men were not to move.

"He is no longer your son. You do not deserve him," I said. "Alex is mine. You have taken my Sunaria from me. Now I take your son from you."

"There are five of us and one of you," Lord Artimas pointed out.

"Any last words?" I said.

Four of his men approached me. Before they could close in I descended upon one of them, lifting him high into the air. I flew toward the ceiling, dragging the startled man with such force that his neck was broken on impact. I dropped him to the floor with a thud. Lord Hawke threatened me with his knife until he too found himself flying through the air. I caught him and forced the man against the ceiling.

Lord Hawke flinched in terror as I removed the knife from his grasp and turned it toward his throat, hacking through his fleshy neck from one ear to the other. The blood poured from the gaping wound, gushing down onto the other two men watching helplessly below.

"Do you now comprehend who I am?" I shouted and fell upon the two remaining men now covered in their friend's blood, fracturing their necks easily. I again settled before Lord Artimas.

"Alex, lay still, do not be afraid," I reassured him. "I shall not let you die."

Alex roused. He struggled to see over his blindfold.

"Looks like the party is over." I glanced at the corpses around us. With flashing speed I tore away some of the material thrown over the altar, binding it tightly around Alex's wrist, stemming the bleeding.

Taking the knife he had used to cut the wrist of his son, Lord Artimas attacked me. I thrust him backwards and he staggered back upon the altar, causing everything placed upon it to come crashing down. I pushed him up and onto it. Lord Artimas lay dazed. The knife fell from his grasp. I sat astride his body, holding his arms down. I turned his head and exposed his neck, biting down hard.

I drank.

Lord Artimas fell in and out of consciousness.

With a Stone Master's blood running through mine, I freed Alex from the shackles. I kept his blindfold on despite him begging me to remove it. He was bewildered and weak, and could hardly stand. I pulled him to his feet and picked him up, carrying him back up to the private rooms of the castle, careful to avoid any guests who had strayed from the party below.

I carried Alex to his own bedchamber, placing him upon the bed, adjusting his limbs to ensure his comfort. I removed his blindfold, pulled the blankets up over him and sat for a moment by his side, gazing down at the wound on his wrist. It was not fatal, but it was nevertheless deep, increasing my concern that it would become infected. Alex was in shock.

I ran my fingers affectionately through his hair, wiping the tears from the boy's face, watching him drift off to sleep. Standing, I lit a nearby candle, providing some light for the room and ensuring Alex would not wake in total darkness. When I was satisfied that Alex was safe, I made my way back down to the dungeons.

Lord Artimas had staggered toward the doorway. I dragged him back into the chamber and pushed him up toward the altar, allowing him to fall to the cold stone ground before sitting him upright with his back leaning against the table.

"Your heartbeat is slowing. You are near death." I took the knife that had fallen to the floor and placed one of the cups under it. I cut deep into my left wrist and allowed my blood to pour into the silver goblet. I placed the cup against Lord Artimas's lips. He turned his head away.

"I go now to turn Alex, then on to kill Jadeon," I taunted.

Lord Artimas labored to breathe.

I again rested the cup against his mouth. "Drink or die tonight." I

forced the red fluid into his mouth.
Lord Artimas swallowed.
"Stone Master, you now reserve the weakness of a man and the vulnerability of a vampire. And the sun awaits your presence, my lord."

XVII

JADEON

I WAS READY FOR HIM.

I waited in the fractured stillness within the pillars of Stonehenge, exhausted from my journey but determined to stop this madness. The night chill helped me to focus. After three and a half days of travel in Orpheus's carriage, my confidence had risen and my strength was surprisingly good, despite eating and drinking little.

Leaning against one of the central bluestones I scanned the horizon, wondering from which direction he would appear. A noise startled me. But it was just an animal or a bird. Again I steadied myself. The dark hour of the morning offered little light other than that from the few stars. Large towering trilithons glistened. My mind played tricks upon me. In the distance the figure of a man fast approaching came into view.

My wait was over.

Orpheus lingered at the furthest edge of the sarsen circle. His eyes gleamed in the darkness, staring. "During part of the ceremony," he said, "they cut off her hair, her long and beautiful hair. You should have seen her. She was exquisite. Her ashes now lie in the stones behind you."

I followed his gaze.

"You are to become the next Stone Master. You are destined to continue these rituals."

"And you are destined to continue to murder the innocent," I said.

"No one is innocent. No one, not even your Catherine."

"She is of no consequence. I am here now. Our arrangement is made."

"I shall put you out of your misery." Orpheus drew near, grabbing hold of my arm. He pulled me onto the central altar, forcing me down. The towering stones loomed.

Orpheus pushed strands of hair away from my face.

"You look so similar to your brother. You share the same bone structure, same eyes." He climbed upon the altar stone, sitting astride me.

I swung my hunting knife and buried it into Orpheus's stomach. Thrusting it deep, I pushed him away and scrambled off the stone.

A strong arm dragged me back. His blood covered both himself and me and the wetness of it made my hands slip against him.

Orpheus held me down.

He pulled out my knife and held it against my neck. The sting from the tip persuaded me to hold still. With his other hand he lifted up his shirt for me to see his injury heal. Orpheus smiled, amused.

All that I had read in my father's books came to mind and I cursed myself for not believing. What a fool to think I could take him on.

He threw the weapon to the ground and held me. "Impressive. I never knew you had it in you," he said.

With shocking speed he bit into my neck.

I will not die like this.

With the sharp sting I struck out, shocked by the assault, alarmed by my irregular heartbeat. He was locked against me.

I fought to stay awake.

Flashes of thoughts came and went.

"Jadeon, Jadeon!" Catherine called to me. I wanted to warn her, tell her she was not safe. Unable to speak, I willed her away.

Wait, where was I?

I had somehow escaped this thing. "Catherine?" I called to her from the door of the chapel. She appeared at the altar, an ethereal vision of loveliness.

I was calm.

"Rest a while," she said. "Here, you must drink, and then you can lay down and place your head upon my lap."

I felt the ridge of the cup. Its cold stung my lips. I gulped the thick, warm elixir.

I know this taste.

So tired, pulled down by exhaustion, I tried to recall how I came to be here. Sleep dragged at me until I surrendered.

When I awoke, horror struck me that I still lay on the stone. My eyes were open to a bleary vision of Orpheus peering down, in his hand a silver chalice.

I had drunk from that cup.

"You dreamt of her," he said, "as I dreamt of Sunaria when I was turned."

I sat bolt upright, aware that something was wrong. I looked down at my pale hands, startled by their lack of color, and turned my gaze to the imposing pillars, wary of the sharpness.

"Head south for Salisbury Cathedral," Orpheus said. "Hide deep within its chambers. If the sun touches your skin, it will kill you."

I leapt off the central stone and searched the ground for my knife. It was gone. My surroundings were foreign. Something had drastically altered.

"Best hurry. The sun knows your name," Orpheus said.

I was relieved to still be alive. "But I thought you—"

"I am not a gentleman. I, like you, am a vampire, and therefore I do not keep my promises!"

Orpheus was gone.

"Alex!" I screamed.

I sprinted toward the center of Salisbury.

On eventually reaching the cathedral, I recalled visiting it as a young boy, and from memory—and indeed necessity—found my first new hiding place. The doors to the cathedral were open allowing me to swiftly enter the large tenement.

Overwhelmed, tears rolled down my cheeks and onto the floor. I staggered down into the basement and pushed open the door leading to a burial chamber where I crouched low. My world dissolved. Praying with what strength I had left, my mind was full of thoughts for Alex, Catherine, and my father. On returning to the castle, I would be a dead man. My father would be furious.

"You found it, then?" Orpheus' voice startled me.

"What have you done to me?" I yelled.

Tears streamed down Orpheus's face. "You see, it's like this," he sobbed. "I miss Sunaria, I cannot go on without her. I have done what I came here to do and now it is over."

"What are you talking about?" I asked. "Alex? Is he safe?"

"I am here, am I not?"

"Then we are even?" I said and rose, readying for my attack.

"Jadeon, at first darkness, go back to Stonehenge. There you will find my remains upon the altar stone. Separate and pour my ashes into the stones. If I cannot be with Sunaria in this world, then—"

He was gone.

The room was dark. I had been so intent on finding shelter that I had not realized this before. I looked around for the lit candles and was shocked to find none. I could see in the dark. My vision clear, I glanced around the room again, taking in my surroundings.

I cringed at the sight of the coffin, the lid half off, exposing its red velvet lining. I studied my pale hands, wary of their luminescence, bit my lip nervously and flinched with the jolt of pain. I examined my teeth, running my fingers along my incisors, alarmed to feel they had become sharp. Impossible.

An unfamiliar hunger came over me, and with a refined sensory acuity, I scanned the cathedral for the presence of others.

Horrified I cried out. "What have you done to me?"

Dizziness made me stagger. I craved the dark. Daylight outside irritated me. I would not sleep in that box, but I had to sleep, hide, disappear. Crawling, now sobbing toward the coffin I climbed inside and pulled the lid over me, entombing myself. Within the blackness came immediate relief. Drifting off, grateful for sleep's insistence, my circadian rhythm adjusted and my senses enabled the ability to gage the passing of time. Unconsciously, I waited for the day to be over.

Crazy dreams.

I awoke with a jolt, alarmed to feel the sides of the coffin.

Irrational thoughts.

I bolted up and banged my head. With panic, I pushed frantically at the coffin lid and jumped out, refusing to look back.

I stole out into the night and returned to Stonehenge.

Approaching with caution I stared down at the central altar and beheld the pile of ashes strewn over it. Orpheus had gone through with it.

Some relief.

I scooped up a handful and allowed them to fall between my fingers. The breeze caught a few. Eager to get it over with I separated them and poured the remaining ashes a few at a time into the fissures at the top of each of the inner stones.

Marveling at my ability to climb the stones, I reassured myself it was done then wiped my hands on the grass.

I was desperate to return to Cornwall as soon as possible but aware that I would never make the journey if I did not restore some strength.

Impatient and overcome with hunger, I huddled in the corner of the Salisbury tavern, awaiting my order of fresh soup and bread. I craved the warm liquid to quench my thirst. My jacket was securely buttoned. I was eager to hide my stained shirt, hoping that my unkempt appearance would not arouse suspicion.

The sparse dim room was virtually empty. A few regulars nursed their goblets. Their voices carried and yet their mouths did not move. A horrible insanity came over me as I perceived that it was possible to read their minds.

My skin was chilled yet my insides burned up. Staring down at my hands I became fearful of my pallor, but was jolted out of my quiet panic by the tavern server who first placed a cup of water before me then slopped the thick broth down. Its steam arose carrying with it a reeking odor. I dipped my spoon into the dirty soup and tasted it.

I gagged.

I checked the room to ensure my reflex had gone unnoticed. I stared at the cup of water and could not understand my repulsion. My experience had dulled my appetite. I yearned for something else. Something unspeakable. As the cravings dragged, I tried to understand them. Not only was I drawn to the other guests, but also felt a powerful pull toward the tavern wench.

I withdrew and headed toward the woods.

My death had been nothing more than a pause.

When the realization settled I fell to my knees and wailed, aware that what I once had been—human, mortal—was now lost. I grieved for my past. Then it came again, that terrible craving that held on fast. Fighting with my will and reasoning with it, I bit into my hand and drew blood. Like a child I suckled, experiencing a sense of relief for the first time. I had to eat. I could not eat. My urgency to return home was heavily outweighed by my desire to merely survive.

White eyes glared from the forest. The fox snarled at me then continued to gnaw through his hind leg which was ensnared in a manmade trap. When my stare had subdued the creature and his fear paralyzed him, I knelt beside the red-furred animal and nuzzled in. The fox's blood-soaked fur tasted foul. He sprang to life, a last-ditch effort to survive as claws scratched at my face, slicing through. Grappling with him, he was easily overpowered.

The fox was not enough. If there was a hell, then this was it.

My screams reached the blackness.

Lying on my back, the stars were familiar. Ursa Major, shaped like a plough, shone brightly. Catherine's favorite astrological alignment. I followed the two stars to the right of the constellation and found the North Star. This would guide me home. Mustering my strength, I crawled onto my feet and started running.

Hours from home a whiff of blood carried in the air and beckoned. I followed the fading lights to the lone cottage and peered through the window at the young man asleep in the rocking chair. He snored. An elderly couple lay where they were slain. The murderous robber had arrogantly fallen asleep in their favorite chair. I eased open the window and climbed in.

The odor was terrible. Old food still simmered on the hearth. Unable to resist, my eyes fell upon the buccaneer's neck, hypnotized by the blue that ran through it. My taste buds tingled, mixed with my bloody saliva. I fought with my desire and lost.

Unable to control myself, I nuzzled into his neck, amazed that he did not stir. How, I wondered while suckling, could such an attack not awaken him. I lapped at his blood, grateful for the bestowal, taken regardless.

At last, it was a wonderful sensation, a rise in my mood and a sense of wellness. With my familiar against me I luxuriated in the feed. Then they came—powerful images, portraits of memories and lingering thoughts.

Something inside me died.

* * * *

Within hours of burying the ashes, I arrived home but lingered on the shoreline, hesitant to discover what awaited me. As expected, the tide was in and water surrounded the castle. Reassured that no one watched me I flew high into the air, heading toward the chateau. The green-blue water shimmered beneath me.

When I reached land, I threw up blood.

Although this new ability to travel in this manner was exhilarating, there was something demonic about it which caused terrifying waves of fear. My father had spent a lifetime tracking and killing creatures of the night. My life was in his hands.

Quiet loomed in a once-busy castle, and taking my time my eyes wandered over the interior, hoping for some sign all was now well.

The quiet was eerie as I ascended the stairs.

A sigh of relief came when I set eyes on Alex, resting calmly within his bedroom.

Placing my hand on his forehead I gauged his temperature. His skin burned, the fever having taken hold of him. Studying him, I was reassured to find him still human. Taking a seat next to him, I gained some comfort from holding his hand. There was still hope that my disease was not permanent. More lies, only this time from myself. I refused to give up hope.

"Jadeon, is that you?" Alex opened his eyes.

"You have a fever, but we have the best doctors."

I noticed Alex's wrist had a bandage wrapped neatly around it.

"What happened?" I asked.

Alex struggled to push himself up. He rested back against the bed frame and clutched my arm.

"Where have you been, Jadeon?"

"It's a long story."

"You have been gone for . . . God, you are pale," he said.

"I am here now."

"He has gone mad."

"It's over."

"You spoke with Father?"

"Not yet. What do you think . . . happened?"

"Lord Velde saved my life. He stopped Father from . . . from killing me."

"Not Father."

"Yes, Father. Look!" Alex thrust up his wrist. "He did this to me."

Alex was shaken. When he was well again, he would be ready to face the truth.

"Where is Father now?" I asked.

"God knows. He has not come to visit me. Not that I want him to."

"I see." I tried to unravel his scrambled words.

"Daumia, he said that I had to give you something." Alex reached into the pocket of his shirt and pulled out a gold ring. He handed it to me.

I examined it carefully, recognizing the crest. A gradual fear came over me. The engraved scribe read, "Stone Master."

I heaved and struggled for words, "When did you last see . . . Velde?"

Alex, do not tell me the answer.

"He left a few moments ago, just before you arrived, Jadeon."

"No!"

"Yes. Why?"

"His ashes."

"What ashes?" Alex stared at me.

"Oh, my God! Father." I leapt up.

"Daumia mentioned he had a rendezvous with the Church."

I sprinted from the room.

I hurried to the convent in Marazion, riddled with guilt. My father's remains were now entombed with his enemies. And I had put them there.

There was no time to grieve. Only the blame was welcome.

On my arrival at the convent it was typically quiet, the air still, nothing out of place. I had to see Catherine. Aware that breaking down the door would cause the other nuns distress, I restrained myself and rang the doorbell, pacing the ground before the entrance. Peering into the courtyard through the wooden shutters I strained to glimpse any sign of danger.

A small frail nun soon arrived at the door.

I towered over her. "Catherine, where is she? Is she here?"

"Master Artimas, is that you?"

"Yes. Catherine?" I pushed for an answer.

"She . . . she is gone." The nun stepped out from the convent.

"What do you mean she is gone? Where did she go?"

"A gentleman came for her. She was reluctant at first, but he persuaded her. They were heading for St. Michael's Mount."

"How long ago did they leave?" I asked.

"Oh, a while back." She handed me a string of rosary beads. "Sister Catherine asked me to give you these."

I clutched the beads. "Thank you, sister. How did he persuade her?"

"Why, he told her you were distressed. I assumed it was because of Master Alexander's terrible accident. But now that I see you—"

"What accident?"

She appeared confused. "Why, Lord Velde informed us of the—"

"What accident?" I pressed.
"He said that your brother had been badly burned."
I staggered back.

XVIII

⊕RPHEUS

ALEX LINGERED UPON the castle steps, waiting for Jadeon's return. The night faded fast. He was well. No bandage upon his wrist now, and the fever had left him. I dreaded the moment but had to inform Alex that the time had come for me to leave. Alex pleaded with me not to go. I managed to subdue him with the promise I would only return for him if he calmed down.

Just minutes before I had rested on Alex's bed, staring down at the weakening mortal. Jadeon had left for the convent and I had taken great pleasure in watching him panic, knowing that Catherine was secretly locked up in the dungeons of his castle and he had not detected her.

I pushed some strands of Alex's sweat-soaked hair out of his eyes, reconsidering whether I could cope with leaving him behind. "Do you remember anything of our conversation the other night?" I asked him.

"For some reason things are still a little fuzzy. I don't really remember much about the night of the ball," Alex said.

"Taking a small amount of my blood can do that," I said.

"What?"

"That night, we shared a moment."

"I don't get you."

"I know, it's one of those things in life where an explanation inadequately explains the reality," I said.

"Reality of what?"

"Perhaps I could show you?"

He stared at me with his large blue eyes.
"Alex, it would be sacrilege for me to let you grow old."
"You're scaring me."
"The greatest bestowal of all is life itself."
Alex shuffled uncomfortably.
"It's time I gave you your gift," I said.

XIX

JADEON

A MAN POSSESSED, I flew toward St. Michael's, my skin tingling with the imminent sunrise. Alex lingered on the castle steps, waiting for me. I swooped down with dizzying speed and pulled him by his shirt collar, dragging him as fast as possible into the dungeons. We tumbled into the Stone Master's chamber and I slammed the door shut, shielding us from the light.

The items used in the sacrificial ritual were now scattered upon the floor. The dark room remained disheveled, a cruel reminder of what had transpired earlier that week. The four decaying bodies of the men remained strewn out in a hideous fashion. We both recoiled at the bloodbath. It was too late to escape the sickening stench.

Alex ran to the door and tried to open it.

"No," I shouted and pushed him away. "We cannot go out. The light, it will kill us."

"What are you talking about?" Alex panicked, his voice shrill. "How do you move like that?"

I stepped in front of him, blocking his path.

"Move out of the way," he said and headed again for the door. "I refuse to stay in here a moment longer. Open the damn door."

"You need to calm—"

"Let me out!"

"Please, let go of the door." I shoved him hard and he flew across the room, landing on the floor.

I had misjudged my strength. I locked the door and removed the key, grasping it, and knelt at Alex's side. "I'm sorry, I didn't mean to hurt you."

"Who did this to them?" Alex stared at the bodies.

"Alex..."

"Father?"

"Not Father, Lord Velde." I tucked the key into my coat pocket.

"No."

"Alex, we are in complete darkness and yet your vision is clear!"

"That's not possible."

"We are changed. We are..."

"What?"

I mouthed, *"Vampires."*

"You're talking madness. Did you have anything to do with this?" He pointed at the massacre.

"For God's sake, you must listen to me!"

He nodded.

I tried to calm my tone. "Do you remember when we witnessed Father and his men carry that woman from this room? Father held the title Master of the Stones. He led an ancient alliance. That woman whom they dragged into the dungeons was called Sunaria. She and Daumia had been lovers for centuries when Father killed her. "

"That was years ago. Daumia is our age."

"Daumia is a vampire, as was Sunaria."

Alex scurried backwards away from me. "You have lost it."

"I can prove it to you."

On the floor beside the altar I found Father's blood stained knife.

Alex cowered.

This was the only way of proving it to him, but more importantly, to myself. With shaking hands I rolled up my shirtsleeve and proceeded to cut into my left arm.

Alex's sobs grew louder.

Together, we watched my wound miraculously heal.

Time to face the truth. My mind reeled.

"That is not possible," he muttered.

"You're next."

"I believe you. I believe you."

I threw the knife down.

"But I hate the dark," Alex said.

"Now would be a good time to get over it."

"I don't understand."

"The name Sunaria called out was Orpheus. Daumia is Orpheus. He sought revenge for the death of his lover."

"And now you say we are . . ."

"He has transformed us both. I believe it is through the passing of his blood to us," I said.

"Not possible." Alex beheld my expression. "Oh, my God, what have I done? It was I who brought him."

"He would have found some way to get to us."

"No, Jadeon, I brought him here."

"There is something more pressing. I need you to remember everything Orpheus ever said to you. Places he has traveled to, homes he may own."

"No, I never want to see him again. I want nothing more to do with him."

"He has Catherine."

We stared in the direction of the dead men and cringed with the realization that we were trapped for the day with the decomposing bodies.

* * * *

The following night I attempted to impart some of the information to Alex that I had gathered. Alex coped better than I had thought he would, though looking back, he was still in denial.

Like I had been.

His disregard was only to be expected. To persuade Alex I dragged him to the library and sat him down, hoping the books would prove that I was not crazy.

He still thought I was.

With no time to pander to his moods I instructed him to stay home and guard the castle while I went in pursuit of Orpheus to bring back Catherine. Leaving Alex was unbearable, but I was pulled. Not finding Catherine was equally wrong. Her face haunted my every waking moment.

Hold on, I am coming for you.

Although my prayers were many, they included my hope Catherine would not be repulsed by me now. I hated the fact Orpheus had her. The thought of him touching her tortured me. I considered whether Catherine was strong enough to cope.

My rage was unbearable. On finding Orpheus, I would kill him. It was imperative I keep such feelings hidden from Alex. We lingered upon the steps of St. Michael's Mount and embraced. I reassured him we would soon be reunited. When certain he was ready for me to leave, I ascended high into the air.

With the faint detection of Catherine's presence, I sensed a glimmer of hope. I sent her a message out into the night. "I will not rest until you are home."

Impossible for her to hear.

Dismayed, I glanced down. Alex headed for the servant's quarters.

✕ ✕

⊕RPHEUS

OF WHAT DO VAMPIRES dream? Of times gone by, when they once walked as humans, when they ate, drank and made love as mortals do. During such times when enclosed within naiveté life was simplicity itself. Alex dreamed of Jadeon and Catherine as all three played within the castle walls, no cares other than that of avoiding their parents and stealing time together. The all-consuming nightmares came, too.

Alex had dismissed all the staff within the castle. Many of them had worked there for most of their lives. The task had not been easy, and despite not wanting to alarm them, he told them his father had died of an infectious disease. For their own safety they left.

Alone and bewildered, Alex walked the corridors. He longed for Jadeon, and despite all that I had done he still pined for my company. Wandering St. Michaels's he was lost within its vastness, trapped by what he had become. He dared not venture out, afraid of everything and nothing. He would wait. Jadeon would return soon. Then and only then would he explore the changing world that lay outside the castle.

Alex had made a room for himself after clearing the corpses and removing all evidence of the Stone Master massacre. Here he could sleep in safety, engulfed in total darkness during the daylight hours. His bed now lay in the corner of his dark domain. An ironic twist of fate that he had once been forbidden to even enter this room.

A noise startled him and he awoke from a troubled slumber. Three weeks had passed since Jadeon had left his side and for a moment he hoped it was his brother. Alex detected more than one person within the castle walls.

"Pirates!" Alex jumped up out of his makeshift bed. Unlocking the door he made his way toward where the men had now gathered.

He listened carefully to the voices within the large dining room, detecting several men, and was shocked to discover them busying themselves stealing the silver cutlery. He pushed the door ajar and watched the burglars place their finds into the hessian sacks they had brought with them. The men were large of frame, rugged in appearance, and dressed as sailors with dark breeches and dirty white shirts. Two of the sinister buccaneers wore bandannas. Alex's urgent need to feed partially distracted him from his fear. Their human odor intensified his hunger.

"Gentlemen," he announced, standing at the doorway. "You are trespassing. Leave immediately."

The men appeared startled to find anyone at all living within the castle.

The largest of the three, the apparent leader, neared him. "We had heard news that this place lay empty now."

"I live here, and those things which you are taking belong to me. Now leave." Alex entered.

"I very much doubt you can take all of us on." The pirate scowled.

"What makes you think I live here alone?" Alex asked.

"Lord Artimas is dead. You must be one of his sons. You live here alone, no servants, no guards. Even your dogs are all dead. We saw them lying upon the ground by the water's edge when we arrived."

"Care to join them?" Alex asked.

The imposing man sneered. "This is how it's going to be. You will allow us to proceed unhindered, and we will leave you alive. How does that sound?"

"Get out of my castle!" Alex yelled.

Alex staggered, stunned by the jab in his abdomen. He looked down, horrified to see the silver tip of the pirate's weapon protruding through his stomach, blood flowing readily. He fell.

The fourth man, initially undetected, now stood behind him and had run his sword through Alex's body. The sword was yanked out, causing his blood to spurt. Alex struggled to rise. Using all his strength, he staggered and pushed his attacker out of the way, shocked to view his blood on the pirate's sword. Alex fled.

He moved fast but they followed. The telltale trickle of blood that poured from his injury guided them to him. They followed him down the stairs, past his room and along the corridor where the many dark cells of the dungeon were lined on either side

They walked into each ready to finish off their victim. The trail of blood now ceasing they split up, each searching the cells for him separately.

One of the men continued along down the dark corridor and into the last cell. Finding nothing he turned to go, but on hearing a scratching sound stopped to investigate. The pirate was thrown back by the wall that swung out and knocked him to the ground.

Alex appeared from nowhere, pulling the man into the secret vault that led to the castle's clandestine underground pathway. He dragged him down through the dark passageway used before on so many occasions by Lord Artimas. The wall grated closed behind them and silence now replaced the man's screams. His colleagues ran into the cell, startled to find it empty.

With the struggling pirate cradled in his arms, Alex stood upon the dirt floor as he—the aggressor now—leaned into the man's neck. The full force of his victim's blood poured into his mouth and for the first time he felt fortunate. His eyes rolled. The man weakened, surrendering with the loss of blood. Alex could feel the mortal's heart beating, and though it slowed he continued to drink, quenching his thirst, savoring. He dropped his dead victim to the ground.

Alex gazed at his bloody shirt. He lifted the wet material to examine the fatal wound upon his abdomen, which to his relief healed before his eyes. He shoved open the stone doorway and sauntered toward the center of the line of dungeons. He used his new refined senses to locate the three remaining men. He could see the pirates standing at the end of the corridor and noisily entered one of the cells, glancing back to ensure he was followed.

Alex readied himself for them.

They soon trapped him at the entrance, their menacing expressions taking Alex off guard. They drew toward him, snaring him in the corner of the dark pungent cell. Alex rose up into the air and scampered along the dungeon's ceiling. Within a moment he stood on the outside of the cell, slamming the door with a clang and placing the rusty padlock in place, sealing the men inside.

"Wait!" The pirate's hands were wrapped tightly around the jail bars, his knuckles white.

Alex faced him.

"You must let us go, boy. We have a ship anchored just behind your castle. Set us free or others will come to look for us."

"Really?" Alex's eyes grew large. "I think that's probably the best news I've heard for weeks."

Alex was gone.

* * * *

The years advanced with an inevitable flow, proceeding with either speed or at a monotonous pace. Spending most of his nights reading in the large library, Alex made up for lost time. Although he had rarely ventured into the room on his own volition when a mortal, he found himself devouring the numerous collections of books and his knowledge of the world grew with each passing day. He took to studying music again, and as time was in abundance he eventually mastered both piano and violin, entertaining himself upon the lonely evenings.

The occasional uninvited visitor ensured he never needed to leave the castle and helped disrupt his boredom with the passing of such predictable seasons. Such visitors would come and go, and in doing so would often bring with them fascinating articles. Alex soon learned that to kill these victims before they used their machines of the new age was foolish. He would lie in wait for his captives, studying them while they demonstrated their contemporary appliances.

With the modern era came modern gadgets—electric shavers, music boxes, and even small talking contraptions which they called phones. He was able to master the workings of such devices, left behind unwillingly by those who provided his food source. He would drink their blood. Then taking their noise boxes, making them his own, he would listen and dance to the new way of creating music, distracted by the loud, deep base that played, only to sink into a depression when the thing would stop altogether, as if broken.

He soon discovered that some had a power source which could be removed and then swapped for new ones, replacing the round metal devices with the name *Duracell* or *long-life* written on their sides. To his utter joy, the music resonated magically once again from within the object's small structure. Gradually, he discovered more about the outside world from the radioed voices that came from within the music boxes when he turned the knobs this way or that. Despite his reluctance to venture out, he was able to get a taste of global events.

In this world outside his the population changed. The voices came and went, and yet he thought one generation easily reflected the next. The horrifying wars also occurred one after another as thousands upon thousands of people gave their lives for countries and places they had not even seen. Such dilemmas he found difficult to fathom, how mortals threw their lives away with such ease when their life span was already so short.

He was also struck by the changes in the way people spoke to one another. He had enjoyed the politeness in the way society conversed in his day, but this new way of speaking seemed aggressive and disrespectful.

He listened intently as individuals talked unashamedly about their intimate and even promiscuous sexual ventures, which in his day would never have been mentioned between siblings let alone to the world at large. Alex knew this modern way of life was not for him even if he had attempted to venture out. He was disturbed at how his mind would play tricks upon him.

Occasionally he would even experience hallucinations, thinking he could see Jadeon sitting with him or appearing in a doorway or the like. But these were but wishful visions. When two hundred years had passed, Alex gave up.

PART TWO

XXI

JADEON
Present Day

MY OLD LIFE HAD bled away.

I stood on the castle steps and scanned the interior, hoping to detect Alex inside and that he was okay. On entering it was a pleasant surprise to see that nothing had changed in all these years, though a musty aroma now hung in the air.

I craved being human. I wanted to walk in daylight, dine on an eight-course meal, and sip a fine wine out of a crystal glass.

These were stupid things. I yearned for Alex.

Hands in my pockets, I strolled into the entrance hall and lingered under the familiar crystal chandelier. Piano music played in the far corner of the great hall. The music paused for a moment, only to begin again. Alex had for a moment sensed me.

Closing my eyes, I dreaded seeing him, fearing having to face the boy I had left behind and scared of what I might find. Moonlight lit up the regal entranceway throwing dark shadows over the walls and stairway, the red worn carpet crushed underneath my feet. Painting after painting of ancestors glared down.

A knot in my stomach caught me and I reeled at the thought of reuniting. I was full of guilt. My anxiety welled. After chasing shadows for so long all that was left was numbness. And now, here within these walls, I was unraveling.

The music got louder.

He had not changed. I lingered at the doorway watching him,

taking in the image of my brother as he gracefully struck the keys. A sob caught in my throat. Alex must have assumed me dead. He may very well have wished it.

I scanned the great hall and cringed at the layer of dust on everything. The room was in a state of disarray. This reflected his spirit. Alex peered up at me but continued to play.

I deserved it. Tears rolled onto my cheeks.

Alex thought me to be an apparition, his wishful thinking gone mad.

I drew toward him. "Have the visions of me ever spoken to you?"

"Not until now." Alex ceased playing.

"How will you ever forgive me?"

He considered me, then leapt up and ran to me.

I enfolded him in my arms.

"I sent you messages," I said, "telepathic signals to tell you where I was."

"I am not too good with that," he whispered. "It's easier up close."

Were these his first words in years? Shaking, I studied him. Anguish tortured my breaths.

Alex's legs gave way. I caught him.

With my arm around him we walked to the anteroom, though the layers of dust were so thick. We only stayed a few minutes and eventually sat down on the main foyer steps.

I was home.

It was difficult to look at Alex.

Please do not hate me.

"I don't," Alex said. Wide-eyed he stared at me with that familiar fresh-faced innocence. He kept prodding me until I grabbed his pointed finger and with an affectionate smile shook it.

"Tell me then," he said. "He still has her?"

Finding the strength to talk, I relayed to Alex my attempts to track down Orpheus who had evaded me at every turn, cruelly teasing me, allowing me to get close enough to sense Catherine's presence but not see her. Time and time again I was left standing where she had once stood. The only clue that she had ever been there at all was her faint perfume. I had gone out of my mind obsessing over them.

With shame I faced up to the fact I had abandoned Alex. He seemed not to care, overjoyed to have me back.

He gave me another prod.

With a heavy heart I explained Orpheus had kept Catherine prisoner for several years until her hair, which had been shaven short while a nun, was allowed to grow long. He had waited patiently for her girlish figure to become fully matured. Finally, when Orpheus had found both her features and characteristics most pleasing, he had done the unthinkable. All this I had detected but had never seen. I had not given up, relentlessly following them around the world.

Eventually Orpheus's scent had grown cold.

Looking at Alex, the guilt weighed heavily. His clothes and skin were filthy and his hair disheveled. I had to take care of him, make it up to him.

But this was not enough.

Alex had lived a life of solitude for two hundred years. I wondered how he would ever forgive me, for I would never forgive myself.

First I endeavored to clean him up but soon realized there was no electricity within the castle. I guided Alex outside. Stripping both myself and Alex naked, I waded with him into the water until we stood waist-deep and then scrubbed him with ancient soap until he was clean again. I wrapped him in a towel and provided fresh clothes.

Lying upon our father's old four-poster bed, with Alex resting his head upon my lap as he used to do in years gone by, we enjoyed the closeness we had once shared as if nothing had ever changed.

We spoke tirelessly, sharing stories of our adventures, laughing at each other's exploits. As only Alex could, he awarded no blame to me for being away. Instead he melted against me, helping ease my interminable guilt. Alex questioned me relentlessly, seeing the modern world through my eyes. I was a little more familiar with the twenty-first century and had even learned the skill of driving.

"I have a Silver Jaguar," I said. "I can't wait to take you for a spin."

"So much has changed," Alex sighed.

"Why did you never leave St. Michael's?"

"For the longest time, I was nervous I'd miss you if you—"

I bit my lip.

"Then," Alex continued, "I kind of enjoyed my own company."

"I . . . let you down."

"When you left I had time to think about a lot of things. I should have seen through him. I should have sensed he was manipulating me."

"I should not have left the castle," I said. "It was my duty to fight at Father's side. Looking back, it felt right to guide Orpheus away, but he pulled the oldest trick in the book when he divided and separated us. That's why he—"

"He hasn't won. I just don't understand why he hated me."

"We do not think like him because we are so removed from his world. How could you have suspected? We were sheltered from all things of this nature. Father should have been clearer. Shoving a book at me didn't cut it."

"I tried to keep this place up but after a while I lost the will," Alex said.

"Who cares about the dust? Still, it might be a good idea to refurnish the place, modernize it perhaps."

"Does that mean men will come here?"

"I can deal with them."

"We will need money." Alex stretched.

"We can sell one of the paintings, perhaps two."

"Yes, let's start with the Joseph Turner. I never did like that one." Alex remembered how Orpheus had once admired the artist's work.

"So we must find an art dealer."

"Let's do it!" Alex sat up.

"Sounds good to me," I said, and from out of my jacket pocket I pulled out my mobile phone and dialed the operator, jotting down the phone numbers of several local art dealers. I dialed one of the numbers and waited for an answer.

"Hello, St. Clare's Art Gallery," the female voice said.

"Good evening. I have a painting I wish to sell. Do you buy paintings?"

"Yes, sir, we do. Is it by a local artist?"

"Yes, but he's dead now."

"Well, sir, then your painting may be quite valuable."

"Perfect. May I bring it in for you to view?"

"Would I know the artist, sir?"

"Yes, perhaps. Joseph Turner."

"*The* Joseph Turner?"

"Yes," I said.

"Oh, bugger off!"

I heard the click of the phone. She'd hung up.

"Well that seemed to go well." Alex had read my puzzled expression. "Turns out I am not the only person with a dislike of Turner."

"I think I know of the perfect place to sell the painting," I said. "Fancy a trip to London?"

* * * *

We were ready to travel to the city.

Alex's clothes were not exactly going to fit in but I reassured him that we would purchase a suit first thing.

"If anyone asks," I said, "you're going to a costume party."

I wore my usual attire, a stylish Savile Row suit.

"Going to a funeral?" Alex jested.

I threw him a wry smile. Crazy, I know, but I still cared about my appearance.

We made our way from the castle walls into the center of Penzance, flying through the air and landing in a dark alley just behind a spiritualist church. I carried the painting wrapped in an old sheet to protect it. We headed down through the old cobbled street toward my parked car. Alex stared in astonishment at the people who passed us by, amazed at the fashions that people wore, particularly the women's clothing.

Where they had once worn long full skirts, they were now dressed in short revealing garments. The colors seemed even more vibrant lit up by the street lighting. The majority of men wore loose-fitting clothing. The younger the youth, the looser the article worn.

To Alex, the noise of the outside world was deafening. Whereas there had once been horse-drawn carriages racing along the busy dirt roads, there were now huge speeding metal vehicles. Where marketplaces had once stood there were now glass-fronted stores selling their wares in the shiniest of packages.

Alex jumped backwards startled by two men who ran past us, their outfits identical. He pushed me out of the way, fearing for my safety. I smiled at Alex's response to the two joggers who passed by and attempted to explain, exploding into laugher at his expression. I wondered how long it would take before he felt comfortable.

Alex's gaze fell upon the silver Jaguar and he hopped in. With a turn of the ignition the engine started and we headed out.

As we drove along Alex often turned in his seat, catching glimpses at this thing or that. Wide open fields had been replaced by houses and other buildings, the vast Cornish landscape transformed into a flurry of human activity.

"Can I drive your car?" Alex asked.

I pulled the car over and Alex slid into the driver's seat. After the first few seconds of jerking forward, Alex quickly got the hang of the vehicle. We sped off. Alex drove the Jag hard.

A blue light flashed directly behind us, and though Alex found it distracting, he drove faster in order to avoid the irritating glare. Eventually, after screaming in his ear, I persuaded him to pull over. Alex slowed the vehicle and parked it alongside the paved road.

The police officer, who now stood at the Jaguar's driver's side, directed Alex to wind down his window, which I did for him.

"Good evening," the young officer greeted us. "Sir, do you have you any idea how fast you were going?"

"Extremely fast, I imagine." Alex smiled.

I cringed.

Alex smiled at the officer, studying his uniform.

"Sir, the speed limit is 35. You were traveling at 70. You just got yourself a ticket."

Alex turned to me. "He's obviously impressed."

The officer pointed his flashlight into the Jaguar. "Sir, may I see your driver's license please?"

"Driver's license?" Alex asked.

"Sir, have you been drinking?"

"I am beginning to feel—"

"Officer, I left my license at home," I interrupted. "I was giving my brother a driving lesson. Please just give us the ticket."

"Is this your vehicle, sir?"

My slow response caused the officer's suspicions to rise.

"Please step out of the vehicle," the police officer said.

I whispered to Alex. "Follow my lead." I grabbed hold of the painting and got out of the car.

The police officer froze, looking around for the two men who had but moments before stood directly in front of him. He could only stare at the abandoned vehicle.

* * * *

The Savoy, a hotel that I favored for its thick curtains and discreet staff, was perfect for our trip. We could safely sleep there with the 'Do Not Disturb' sign posted on the door. The hotel's luxurious furnishings were perfect and very homey. This was also a great place to purchase Alex's outfits from the hotel stores. The following evening, comfortably ensconced within our hotel room, Alex chose from the clothing selection brought to our room. He favored the blue denim jeans and white shirts despite my recommendation of smarter attire.

Carrying the Joseph Turner, now wrapped in a fresh towel from the room, we made our way down the Strand toward Trafalgar Square for our appointment at the National Gallery. We both admired the main façade of the magnificent architecture. Over the years successive extensions had been made, complementing the original grand design.

The vast museum ensured that the gallery's entire collection of about two thousand paintings, mostly by the old masters, were on display. You would never find a forgotten Monet or Degas concealed in an underground temperature-controlled vault. In 1897 those paintings deemed contemporary had been transferred to the Tate Gallery, but by the early 1990s many of the paintings were relocated to the Tate Modern.

I was in my element, stopping for a moment to admire Michelangelo Merisi Da Caravaggio's painting of the *Supper at Emmaus*, dated 1571-1610. The painting seemed more like a photograph with its realistic images and vibrant colors.

Alex pulled on my arm when I froze in front of another of the paintings. We had an appointment to keep and I was making us late. Mr. Teddington, a tall and wily man, warmly greeted us. We were escorted to his office within the large building. Mr. Teddington surveyed us suspiciously, and on viewing the towel wrapped painting, looked even more concerned.

"As I told you on the phone," he began, "I believe all Turners are accounted for."

"The painting has been in our family for years," I informed him, unwrapping the work of art carefully and placing it upon the table as instructed.

Mr. Teddington studied the antique portrait with an eyeglass. He peered at us in complete astonishment. Picking up the phone he requested a second opinion. Soon the room was filled with his colleagues, each taking a turn in viewing the painting with the eyeglass.

"Its worth, Mr. Teddington?" I asked.

"Difficult to say, though I do have a dear friend who works at Sotheby's. He should be able to arrange a quote and a buyer for you. Perhaps we would even be able to place the painting here for a while at the National, before selling it? This is quite a find. Are you sure you want to part with it?"

"Quite sure," Alex said.

"I also have in my possession *St. Catherine of Alexandria* by Raphael," I said. "Would you be interested in placing her amongst your collection? Only a loan, you understand. I do not wish to sell her, just present her within the gallery."

"Sir, we would be delighted," Mr. Teddington said. "Any other priceless pieces of art you have hidden away?"

I chose not to reveal that our collection would amaze the art community.

"I know what you're thinking," I said to Alex as we withdrew from the gallery.

"You love that painting. I just can't understand—"

"St. Catherine reminds me—"

"Of course," he said and rested his hand on my shoulder.

"Once we have Catherine back, I will be happy to have Raphael's portrait hanging in the castle again," I said.

On my initial return to St. Michael's I had stared at the painting, wallowing in the past and wanting to stay there. It was too much having this reminder of Catherine under our roof. My need for her never wavered. I was reassured Alex understood.

With the final transaction complete, the Joseph Turner painting sold, we returned to Cornwall. Alex and I busied ourselves with our plans to refurnish the castle interior, ensuring that its character was maintained complementing its unique style. Work began under the supervision of an interior designer. Alex stayed out of the way of the workers and I hovered over them, verifying our designs. Within a few months St. Michael's Mount was restored to its original unique beauty, though modernized. We now enjoyed electricity, running water, and luxurious furnishings throughout the castle.

I even took to painting again, making my way to the tallest tower and whiling away the hours until my brother dragged me down before sunrise. Alex was even able to persuade me to fence again and we rummaged around for our old dueling swords, pleased that time had not worn away either the epee's metal or our talent.

Our castle was fast becoming the ultimate bachelor pad. Knowing Alex as I did I was reluctant to introduce him to too much modern technology for fear he would become a man possessed. He needed to get out more, not stay in.

Alex caught my wandering thoughts. "What's an X-box?" he asked.

Burying my head in an old favorite book, I turned a page of St. Thomas Aquinas's *Summa Theologica* hoping Alex would become distracted and not ask me again.

Several weeks later I found myself alone in the castle. Though pleased Alex had ventured out on his own, after four hours I felt compelled to look for him. I found him in Café Art Tarot, located in the small town of Penzance not far from the castle. Despite the coffee shop being full, Alex went unnoticed at a corner table over which he had strewn magazines. Alex was engrossed, eagerly reading the pages of the glossy papers. Taking the seat opposite him I noticed a full teacup to his left, untouched.

"*Cosmopolitan!*" Alex beamed, referring to the magazine's title.

"I'm not so sure that's such a good introduction into the world of the modern woman," I said.

The waitress appeared and offered me a menu. "Or are you a vampire like your friend here?" she asked.

"Earl Grey tea will be just fine. Thank you," I answered her.

She returned behind the counter.

Alex threw me a mischievous smile. I blocked out the chattering thoughts of the other customers.

"I wish I could do that," Alex said.

"Close your thoughts?"

"Yes."

"I'll teach you," I said.

"Do you suppose he ever thinks about us?" Alex asked.

"Orpheus?"

"I still can't get used to that name."

"I often sensed that he regretted—"

"What?"

"Not taking you with him."

Alex sat back in his chair. "I wish things were different."

"I can't bear to think of Catherine frightened and trapped," I said.

"You are doing the right thing. Don't give up on her."

"I couldn't if I tried," I said.

"Perhaps she'll come to us?"

"That's just it, why the hell hasn't she sent a message? She must know."

"I'm sure there's a good explanation," he said.

"I just wished I knew what it was. How is the feeding going?" I asked.

"I think I've mastered it now," Alex said. "After drinking as little as possible, I persuade my—them—to drink from me. Then before I know it they've forgotten the whole thing ever happened."

Alex was like me, reluctant to say the word "victim." We had both naturally pursued those whom society considered evil and as such it had helped to quell the self-reproach. With a few sips of our blood our food source would have no recollection that we had even met.

I sighed. "Let's practice closing your thoughts down. Quiet your mind."

The waitress set a cup of Earl Grey tea down on the table. I thanked her.

Alex's gaze followed her back to the serving station. "What am I thinking?" he asked.

I read his mind. "Obviously I have my work cut out." I laughed.

Alex smiled and poured his full teacup into the plant pot on our table.

I cringed at his attempt to dispose of his tea. "Alex!" I whispered. "The plant's not real."

The tea seeped out from under the plastic pot, dripping on to the table. Leaving more than enough money to pay for our drinks, we withdrew from the café.

Alex laughed and I hugged him playfully.

Being with him again had changed my life. I savored every minute and sometimes just stared at my younger brother in gratitude for him. Although Alex had turned a little eccentric, it was actually quite charming.

We soon arrived at the castle. "Alex, someone's here." I defensively placed my hand against his chest.

We both sensed danger and quickly headed in.

Cautiously we entered the parlor. In front of the fireplace gazing up at the painting of our father stood a redheaded man. Rugged in appearance, of medium build, aged twenty-five in human years or so, he dressed in leather trousers and a black silk shirt.

He turned to face us. "I rather like what you've done with the place. I would have gone for a lot more black," he said.

I removed my jacket and placed it on the back of a chair. "Who are you?"

"Marcus. So we meet at last. I have heard so many things about you. Particularly you, Alex. I can see the appeal now."

It was easy to detect Marcus's vampiric traits. His movements gave him away.

"What do you want?" I rested my hand on Alex's shoulder.

"We've been keeping a close eye on you both. You've not been doing badly. Pity about the Jag. I'm rather partial to that car myself."

"Get out," I said.

"I am here on behalf of Orpheus. I have a message for you, Jadeon," he said.

"You know where Daumia is?" Alex stepped toward him.

Marcus smiled. "Daumia is fed up with this game of hide and seek. He wants it over with. He proposes that you leave him alone."

I neared him. "Or?"

"Or he will kill you," Marcus threatened.

"Where's Catherine?" I asked.

"Jadeon, Jadeon, you really are so predictable. You know, there are some women who like to be chased but Kate isn't one of them."

I thrust him up against the fireplace.

Marcus snarled. "Anything happens to me, and Catherine . . ."

he warned.

I let go of him. "I want evidence that she—"

"Sorry, no can do," Marcus said.

I stepped back. "I'm more than prepared to spend another two hundred years—"

"Perhaps Alex can go with you this time?" he said.

Alex looked pained.

"Get out before I kill you," I said.

"Have you any idea of what and who you are dealing with?" Marcus said.

I glared at him.

"Jadeon, have you ever played chess?"

"What?"

"Chess. You make a move, your opponent makes a move, etcetera. With Orpheus, you will never see him coming. He will derail your scheme."

"You are done. Now get out," I warned him.

"He will swipe you off your feet and he'll take both your queen and your king before you've even considered your strategy."

"Out, now!" I shouted.

"When Catherine complains about the way he dispenses with you, he can reassure her that he gave you every opportunity. So be it. Such is life. Or in your case, death!"

"Give this message to Orpheus," I said. "Tell him I am coming for him."

XXII

⊕RPHEUS

CAPTURED IN SLEEP, the dream holding her firmly, Ingrid Jansen struggled to awaken from her nightmare. She saw herself as a rookie police officer once again, standing next to a woman who was tied and gagged in a chair. Ingrid kept reassuring the woman that everything would be all right, though the woman was dead.

The emergency phone call had come through to the Salisbury police station at 2100 hours—a domestic disturbance on Rowland Street.

Ingrid was unarmed, her baton taken from her at knifepoint by the man and thrown out of the window, breaking it upon impact. Ingrid scanned the room for other objects that she could use to defend herself and checked for possible exits.

The putrid smell of rotting food hung in the air. Movement caught her attention, and for a frightful moment she glimpsed maggots crawling amongst the pile of unwashed dishes in the sink.

Unbeknownst to Ingrid, the police sharpshooter positioned just outside the kitchen was taking advantage of the broken window.

Her aggressor was becoming even more agitated. "You fucking bitch." He waved the knife at her.

Pandemonium, a noise shattering the tense atmosphere deafened her, stinging her ears as the gunshot hit just above its target exploding the man's head. Ingrid was splattered with brain matter. His blood covered her body and entered her mouth. She spat it out, resisting the urge to vomit.

I could bear her dark ruminations no more. It was time to wake her.

Ingrid stirred in response to the sensation of my fingers gently stroking her hair. She bolted up, heart pounding from both nightmare and the invasive tactile stimulation. She jumped out of bed wearing nothing but her underwear, and ran to the sitting room. Finding no one she continued to search each room, still dizzy from sleep. Finally she ran to the front door finding it was as she had left it—locked, bolt on.

She walked into the bathroom, splashing water onto her face then back into the sitting room, collapsing onto her couch. Pulling her golden chenille throw over her she sat staring into space.

Ingrid glanced at her watch. It was five in the morning. She was due to catch the train at 0700 at Salisbury train station. A Monday. And this week she was attending a police forensic psychologist's course at Scotland Yard.

* * * *

The course was scheduled for 0930.

Being her usual early self, Ingrid sat in the front of the hall in order to get the best view of the lecturers. She was delighted that her friend Dr. Elizabeth Miller was the senior speaker. Suddenly this all made perfect sense to her, for if not Elizabeth, who would have placed her name down on the course attendance list? Elizabeth had been with the police for eleven years, a senior forensic psychologist based at Scotland Yard. She had qualified with a Ph.D. at Oxford and had been recruited by the Metropolitan Police for her say-it-like-it-is attitude.

At thirty-five she was head of her game and well respected in the community. Elizabeth's African heritage gave her a slender height and combined with her dark features she was an attractive woman. She had married John, a police officer at a nearby station. Ingrid considered herself lucky to have a good friend in the force. She listened to her friend speak, in awe as Elizabeth conducted the lecture.

Ingrid thoroughly enjoyed her friend's articulate presentation and afterwards was delighted to accept Elizabeth's invitation to join her for a drink in Covent Garden.

In the secluded West End wine bar the two women nestled in the corner, sipping Chardonnay while exchanging news about friends and family.

"What a wonderful surprise, Ingrid," Elizabeth said. "When I saw your name on the list this morning, I couldn't wait to see you."

"Why surprise? Didn't you put my name on the list?"

"No, darling, but I'm so pleased you are here. We have so much catching up to do."

"If not you, then whom?"

"Your boss?" Elizabeth asked.

"No, he said he hadn't."

"A colleague, then?"

"No."

"Well, obviously someone has tried to get rid of you for a week from the station, and I am very happy that they did. I'm proud of you. You're really getting into this detective thing. Making enemies already, darling?"

Ingrid was thoughtful. "I know I can be a bit honest sometimes. Perhaps I've ruffled a few feathers?"

"So, my love, how are those nightmares of yours?" Elizabeth asked.

"Oh, God, I don't get one for months, then . . ." Ingrid trailed off.

"My course can be pretty intense. Some pre-course nerves?"

"No, I don't think so. And there was something else, too."

"Something else?"

"Don't go doing that psycho thing on me, Elizabeth."

"I'm sorry. Force of habit." Elizabeth winked. "Something else?"

"It's a bit spooky."

"You know how I love spooky."

"Well, I was having that same-old-same-old nightmares."

"Which one? In the apartment with that man without a head?"

"Thank you, yes that one, when—" Ingrid hesitated.

"When?"

"As I woke out of the dream I felt someone was touching me. You know, on my face and my hair."

"That's interesting."

"When I got up to look around the flat, no one was there. I checked everywhere—rooms, cupboards, under the bed. Nothing. I left my window open, but I'm three floors up so no one could have jumped up there."

"I love that quaint apartment of yours," Elizabeth mused.

"My dreams. Come on, what does it mean?"

"And I adore its high ceilings. Isn't it Victorian?"

Ingrid nodded. "The dream?"

"Well darling, do you want my honest opinion?"

"Yes, of course. You know I trust you," Ingrid said.

"When was the last time you dated?"

"What has that got to do with anything?"

"Oh, Ingrid, you're so busy being Miss Dynamic Police Detective, you're denying your natural—"

"Oh, God."

"Textbook, sweetie. Well, seriously, when did you last date? Six months, a year?"

"Two years."

"Oh my God, girl, you get yourself out there and . . ."

"Oh, I don't know. I hate all that . . . Well, you know, 'so-do-you-come-here-often' thing."

"Ingrid."

"All relationship roads lead to domestic drudgery," Ingrid said.

"Oh dear, you really are damaged aren't you?"

Ingrid poked around in her bag and pulled out a card.

"What have you got there?"

"It's a postcard. Someone left it at the front desk for me. It's of St. Catherine."

"Let me see." Elizabeth reached over and took the card from Ingrid. "She's beautiful."

"It's taken from a portrait that's showing at the National Gallery. The card's postmarked from here in London."

Elizabeth flipped the postcard over. "*Ingrid, eight o'clock*. That's all that's written on it? Looks like you have a secret admirer."

"I doubt that."

"Darling, trust me," Elizabeth said. "You are smart and beautiful, and that's why men don't approach you. Perfect skin, big brown eyes, full lips, tight arse. Why, if I wasn't married . . ."

"You're outrageous!"

"Now the National is the sort of place that you'll meet the best guys. You know, your type. Intellectuals always hang out at galleries, museums, etcetera. Go on and get down to the National!" Elizabeth winked. "Now I must dash, as hubby is cooking tonight and such an event is a bit like a solar eclipse. Blink and you will have to wait another hundred years for the stars to align. Now it is what—seven o'clock? Better get moving."

Ingrid peered down at the postcard again.

XXIII

JADEON

LONDON, THE CITY that no longer sleeps. It is here that I find some solitude, wandering among the crowds until my need for normality subsides. I love this vibrant town, more for its culture than anything. Sometimes Alex likes to come with me. Other times, like on this occasion, he wanted to hang out in the West End and take in a magic show.

Unable to stay away from Raphael's portrait for long, I returned to the National Gallery in need of my St. Catherine of Alexandria fix. I was so completely engrossed with the painting that my trancelike demeanor must have appeared eerie to the other guests who admired the artwork. It certainly drew the unwanted attention of one woman who neared me and studied my expression. She was fascinated that my focus never strayed.

I assumed she would eventually move on but for the moment, she like me, was predictably mesmerized by Raphael's portrait. Turning toward the pretty petite female, aged twenty-five or so, I stared directly at her, hoping it would make her uncomfortable and force her away.

She had a fragile beauty. She held my gaze.

I snapped my head back at the painting, unnerved.

She took a few steps back to survey the portrait more fully.

"Isn't she beautiful?" She drew closer.

Silence. I would try that.

"She's hypnotic," she said.

I shoved my hands in my pockets.

"You don't say much, do you?" The pretty girl smiled at me.

"Raphael does capture her essence beautifully," I said.

"Raphael. What an amazing painter."

Polite reply, politically correct social behavior. Now go away.

"This must be the best gallery in town," she said.

"You mean other than the Tate?" I asked. I had made her uncomfortable and felt shitty. "Do you know her story? The story of St. Catherine?" I asked her.

"Yes. I'm Catholic, so I was breastfed on saints."

I stared at her, amused that she blushed. Actually, the stranger was very beautiful.

"So was I, breastfed on saints, that is," I said to ease her discomfort.

"Perhaps that's why we are drawn to them now."

"Perhaps."

"Is this your first time to the gallery?" she asked.

"No, so many other paintings to see," and, I checked my watch, "the gallery closes in an hour so you'd better hurry."

She furrowed her brow.

I had hit a nerve with my rudeness. I sensed she was not used to men speaking with such disrespect. Interesting, not that I cared though. "Well it's been nice meeting with you but I have to go now, Ingrid." I strolled off, heading into the other room where more paintings awaited.

I was relieved to have extracted myself from the clingy girl. On the other hand, perhaps my fascination with her had thrown me. Abruptly I stopped. A dramatic portrait had caught my eye—Rembrandt's *Belshazzar's Feast*. I swallowed hard and looked around the room self-consciously. Orpheus once mentioned he owned the masterpiece. It astounded me to see it here.

The portrait was of a chilling scene of a regale in the kingdom of Babylon, a striking rendition on an old Biblical narrative. Several guests sat around a richly adorned banqueting table and drank from the sacred vessels stolen from the temple of Jerusalem. These princes, wives, and concubines of King Belshazzar appeared deeply troubled, startled by the sudden interruption of a blinding vision. At the center of the painting stood Belshazzar, equally alarmed by the mystical apparition.

Large in the frame, he was dressed in the lavish apparel of a king, his royal crown positioned high upon a generous turban. Defensively he held out his hand and glared wide-eyed in astonishment at the miraculous light that emanated from the hand of God who wrote upon the wall in Aramaic script.

Fascinated, I considered the gallery's interpretation of the painting. Belshazzar and his sages had studied the words written from right to left, perturbed that they were unable to interpret their coded meaning. The prophet Daniel was summoned by the king and deciphered the words for him—*Mene Mene Tekel Upharsin*—foretelling the fall of the kingdom of Babylon and the death of Belshazzar.

I mouthed the words, "*Mene Mene Tekel Upharsin.*" I shuddered in reaction to the precise Aramaic: *I will bring down the house of Belshazzar.*

I lingered before the painting and wondered yet again why after all these years Catherine had not approached me. She knew where we lived. She could easily have visited if only for a moment. She must have known I had pursued her relentlessly. Did Orpheus still keep her prisoner?

I was lost in thought.

"Excuse me?" That girl again. She had followed me.

Reluctant to engage I offered a polite smile and headed for the next room.

"How did you know my name? You called me Ingrid, and I never told you my name."

She was right. I chastised my carelessness. I studied her face, gauging my response. The twinkle of gold caught my eye.

Thank God for that.

"Ingrid, see." I pointed to her namesake necklace.

Ingrid blushed. "Boy, do I feel—"

"It's a beautiful name," I said.

"May I inquire on yours?"

"Jadeon."

"That's unusual." Ingrid followed my gaze toward a gentleman who was walking toward us.

I recognized Mr. Teddington.

"Lord Artimas," Mr. Teddington greeted me. "I was informed you were here tonight. How do you like the position of your painting?"

"Good evening, sir. Thank you for giving her such an excellent position."

"It is indeed our pleasure. Such a masterpiece deserves to be presented as such. Thank you for allowing the National Gallery to exhibit her."

"Ingrid, meet Mr. Teddington," I said. "He's the senior curator. Mr. Teddington, this is Ingrid."

Mr. Teddington and Ingrid shook hands.

"How long have you had *Belshazzar's Feast* within your

collection?" I asked him.

Mr. Teddington appeared to think on this for a moment. "I believe it arrived just after your Raphael was presented, certainly within a week."

My head spun. Orpheus, the bastard, was playing with me. "Do you happen to have the name of the gentleman who it belongs to?" I asked.

"Like yourself, he's a private dealer. He did mention to me that he owned a club in Belgravia. I believe he said that it was on Chesham Place. Does that help?"

"The name of the club?" I asked.

"It's named after the painting—Belshazzar's."

I hoped they'd missed my reaction and cleared my throat. "Please excuse us Mr. Teddington, we have a prior dinner engagement," I said and guided Ingrid out of the room and through the long corridors until we reached the gallery foyer.

"That man can talk for hours if you're not careful," I said, smiling though my heart pounded. Orpheus had positioned the painting in order to get my attention.

"It has been a delight." I shook Ingrid's hand. I headed for the gallery exit. "Enjoy the rest of your tour."

"So dinner's off, then?" she called after me.

I turned toward the fresh-faced woman.

Ingrid blushed. "You just escorted me to the door."

"I did, didn't I?"

"I would love to talk more about Raphael. I didn't mean to be forward," Ingrid said. "It's just that you seem so knowledgeable about art and it's such a refreshing change from my world."

She was certainly convincing. I tried not to stare but my gaze wandered over her figure.

Her eyes reflected that she had noticed. "Perhaps you're like me and don't get out much," she said.

I smiled. "I would very much like to take you out to dinner." I tried to shake off this sudden desire.

Ingrid beamed.

I hailed a taxi to the Strand's Savoy Hotel. On our arrival I escorted Ingrid to the hotel's restaurant, Simpson's in the Strand. The maitre d' informed us that her attire of black trousers and leather jacket were unsuitable to dine at The Grand Divan. I offered my apologies to Ingrid. I had no idea that such rules were enforced. It was unusual for me to frequent these places. With a firm hand I led Ingrid down the long corridor to the stores and small booths within the hotel lobby.

The fact that she was uncomfortable made me wonder what it was about overpowering her that gave me such a rush.

We entered the Versace store. Guessing her size I took a dress from the rack and held it against her. Replacing it I found another more suitable outfit.

"This one," I offered her.

Ingrid glanced at the price tag.

"Consider it a gift," I said.

"I can't possibly."

"Really, I insist."

"Perhaps there's another restaurant that's not so fussy about—"

I took Ingrid's hand and gently pushed her into the changing room. I instructed the store's female assistant to help find Ingrid the appropriate shoes, giving her instructions to charge the items to my room and provide anything else Ingrid may need.

Ingrid stepped out of the changing room.

Quickly, I closed my mouth.

She was striking in the small black halter dress. She twirled, seemingly unsure whether this was such a good idea. Whereas the clothes Ingrid had previously worn had hidden her curves, she now stood before me the very essence of a woman.

Ingrid suspected I had ulterior motives.

"Ingrid, I'm the consummate gentleman," I said.

"In other words, you're quite safe. You're not planning on having your wicked way with me?"

"Well . . ." I glanced at the shop assistant, surprised by Ingrid's statement.

Ingrid looked me up and down.

Reading her mind I said, "I'm not gay." I regretted my outburst immediately.

"I never said you were," Ingrid laughed.

No, but she had studied my tailored suit and dashing looks and wondered if it was too good to be true.

"But you did choose Versace," the shop girl pointed out.

"Now a man can't have good taste?" I said.

"Good point," said Ingrid. "Let's eat!"

I requested that Ingrid's clothes be sent up to my room for safekeeping. We headed back to the restaurant and after one of the staff recognized me, we were provided with the service that would ensure Ingrid a pleasant evening. Such was the benefit of having inherited a title.

To dull her senses I ordered champagne. It worked perfectly, quickly lulling her thoughts which raced along at a frightening pace. Even so, at times I had trouble keeping up with both her external and internal dialogue.

"So tell me about your career choice."

"I'm a policewoman." She watched my reaction.

I had already sensed as much and did my best to feign innocence, having avoided the law for all the obvious reasons. Although I never considered myself a criminal, being a nightwalker could easily be considered such.

Bugger it. I was going to enjoy myself.

"Do you enjoy your work?" I asked.

"I love it. Couldn't see myself doing anything else."

"Are you married?" I asked, already aware of the answer.

"I hope not. Here I am having dinner with a dashing . . ." Ingrid blushed.

"Go on. Dashing . . ."

Ingrid beamed. "Charming young man. Are *you* married?"

I smiled as Ingrid hung on my answer. "I hope not. Here I am having dinner with . . . an exquisite woman."

Her scent was alluring.

"You know Jadeon, there's something about you that is really old-school."

"I get that a lot." I smiled.

"Are you wearing contacts?"

I knew silence was the best answer.

"They're just an unusual brown, that's all. Your irises are luminous."

"Thank you, I think."

"This is such a perfect restaurant. Do you eat here often?"

"No, I . . ."

"You don't eat much do you?" Ingrid said. "Funny how you ordered desert, and yet . . ."

"You have a keen eye, Ingrid."

"Comes with the territory."

"How long have you been a policewoman?"

"Since I was eighteen." Ingrid laughed. "Are you doing the math on my age?"

"I am."

"And you're an art dealer. What a delightful time you must have spending your days in art galleries."

I smiled.

"So tell me what it is about your work you love the most," Ingrid said.

"I adore how an artist portrays daylight, the way a master captures an aurora, or the perfect sunset. And you?"

"I love it when I catch the perpetrator. I never give up and I never let go. I'm like a bulldog."

"More champagne," I offered.

With dinner over, I escorted Ingrid to the hotel's elevators. I turned her to face me when I realized that my mirrored reflection was absent.

Ingrid studied my worried expression.

"I don't like heights," I lied.

On entering the hotel room I guided Ingrid to the large sofa. Kneeling at her feet I removed her shoes before joining her on the couch. I ran my fingers through her hair, desperately wanting to linger but knowing that I should not.

"It's late, Ingrid. Why don't you stay?"

"But where?"

"I have to see a . . . gentleman about a painting," I said.

"Boy, you art dealers keep strange hours."

"You have no idea."

Ingrid scanned the room. "You have a suite?"

"Bed's in there." I pointed to the adjoining door.

"Very nice."

I opened the door for her and she entered.

I liked the feeling of being close to a female again. In fact, Ingrid rather reminded me of Catherine. Perhaps that is why I allowed myself this little indulgence.

I withdrew.

Instinctively Ingrid tiptoed around the room and explored, searching for any evidence that might reveal more about me. She would find nothing. Had it not been for the champagne dulling her senses, she might have found that suspicious. Walking into the bathroom her gaze fell upon the huge bathtub. Ingrid locked the bathroom door.

Without hesitating she removed all her clothes, carefully placing her new dress on a coat hanger on the door. Pouring the thick liquid soap into the bathtub she watched it froth under the running water, breathing in its opulent foaming scent. Climbing in she enjoyed the warmth, surrendering to the feeling of relaxation.

The following morning I arranged for room service to deliver a delicious selection of pancakes, fresh fruit, orange juice, and Earl Grey tea. Although it was a decadent move I thought it a nice gesture to provide Ingrid with her favorite breakfast.

XXIV

ORPHEUS

WITH MY MATCHMAKING skills a success, I awaited Jadeon's visit. He had enjoyed the few hours he had spent with Ingrid and was sorry to leave her company, but he knew as well as I that to pursue any kind of relationship with a mortal was futile. He was also eager to head toward Belgravia and check out my club, exhilarated to be so close.

Two hundred years and at last he stood outside my domain—Belshazzar's. The darkened windows made it impossible to view the interior and he was unable to judge what kind of place this was. A bouncer stood on guard at the doorway. Jadeon approached him.

"What is the code word, sir?" the guard asked.

Jadeon studied the muscular tattooed bouncer, a worthy opponent to any unwanted visitor. The guard unknowingly informed Jadeon of the password.

"Of Vampires and Angels," Jadeon answered.

Jadeon was welcomed in. Pausing for a moment he checked behind him, aware that this was his last opportunity to turn back. He stepped in and walked through the dark hallway.

Taking in his surroundings he made his way along the eerie passages, glancing up at the many chandeliers guiding his way. Continuing down the dark sinister corridor he approached the large double doorway, which opened for him, and entered the wine bar.

Tables were everywhere, the room full of both humans and vampires, though he detected the mortals had no idea whom they were socializing with. The gothic and renaissance décor provided an eclectic accent. The aroma of burning candles and incense bestowed a heady scent, and the music enhanced the atmosphere. Jadeon easily counted at least one hundred guests. Everyone was dressed well. The theme appeared to be that of black attire and leather, both men and women obviously of wealth. This was an exclusive club. *But what kind of club?* he wondered. *And for what purpose?* Walking toward the bar he was immediately greeted by the bartender.

"Bloody Mary it is, then." The man poured a thick red concoction into an iced glass.

Jadeon sniffed the familiar aroma.

Looking around the room again, he observed others drinking the same as he and he wondered how they got away with consuming such a concoction. Self-consciously Jadeon sipped from the glass, appreciating that it was indeed blood and he was thirsty. He glanced back at the man behind the bar, uneasy to see him staring back.

"Another?" the bartender asked. "It's on the house. You're a first-time guest, so anything you want is yours."

"Who owns this place?" Jadeon asked.

"I think you know," he said.

A tall woman approached Jadeon. "I haven't seen you in here before."

"This is my first visit." Jadeon took another sip from his drink.

"Well aren't you the lucky one? First-time visitors get special treatment, don't they, Lance?"

Lance slid an iced cocktail in her direction.

She ran the tip of her forefinger around the edge of the glass. "Can I interest you in anything?" She leaned forward on the bar, allowing Jadeon to see easily down her silk top.

He shook his head and attempted to keep his eyes focused on hers, aware that her satin blouse was completely transparent. She laughed in response to his shyness, drawing unwanted attention in his direction. She leaned toward Jadeon, close enough to kiss him.

Jadeon stepped back, taking her hand and gently pushing it away, conscious that others may be watching. She laughed again as a hand appeared on her shoulder and she was guided out of the way. A female nightwalker now stood before him. Jadeon was struck by the appearance of her red hair and blue eyes.

"Please excuse our guests. They get a little carried away. They just can't wait to get started if you know what I mean."

Jadeon stared at her.

Opening up her mind, she invited Jadeon to read it. In doing so he realized that this club was not just a place for social drinking and light entertainment. The female presented the clearest of visions of what occurred within this very building several floors below.

Powerful and clear images of the activity within the rooms were revealed, and the visions were of a sexual nature. This was a club in which an individual's fantasy could be realized. While he surveyed the many naked and partly dressed bodies intertwined it became clear to him the focus here was on obtaining both sadistic and masochistic pleasure.

Glancing around at the people within the room, Jadeon knew many of them would soon be joining those below. He wanted to flee, considering that he could perhaps return when he'd had some time to contemplate his next move. In reality, he knew it was too late. He might never get a chance to be this close to me again. He steadied himself, attempting to look a little less conspicuous. He knew that if I were here I would detect him. And he was right.

Jadeon felt a bump and turned to see a young male in black leather behind him.

"Just say when you want to come and play," he whispered close into his ear. "I'll heat the wax."

Jadeon stepped away. Gradually a sensation of dizziness disorientated him. He realized his drink had been spiked. He placed it down on the bar and scrutinized the bartender, attempting to gauge the poison. Jadeon took a seat at an empty table positioned in the corner. He sat with his back against the wall, hoping the dizziness would pass.

The feeling of warmth rapidly came over him and he relaxed a little. The music played with his mind and he enjoyed the rhythm. A corseted female sat next to him. He studied her, finding her dark features, curvaceous body, and tight leather outfit alluring. She sat for a moment looking at the chattering crowd. The ebullient mix of party guests conversed noisily, engrossed in their conversations, consuming their beverages.

Initially unsure whether it was the atmosphere or the blood that had given him such a heady sensation, Jadeon's symptoms now confirmed his suspicions. Whatever had been placed in his drink was seriously taking effect. He rubbed his eyes to clear his vision. Disconcerted, he realized the female stared at him. She pouted seductively, her mouth sensuously full, her lipstick blood red. He scanned her thoughts, amazed to see visions of angels which appeared to fly through the air or float dreamily in front of him.

Such visions reminded him of paintings by Raphael. He became lost in their beauty, his thoughts drifting off.

As the illusions continued he felt her discreetly place her hand on his thigh, but such a movement was obscured, shielded by the table from the view of others. Jadeon closed his eyes, lost in the images. He was aroused as the thick aroma of incense filled his lungs and the loud, thumping bass affected him. Opening his eyes Jadeon struggled to gain control, pushing her hand away.

With a wry smile and the huskiest voice she said, "Well, if you change your mind."

Standing up with a feline elegance she turned from him, walking toward the rear of the room. Jadeon watched her stand before a doorway. It slid open automatically and she stepped into an elevator. Holding out her hand to him with a coy expression, she gestured for him to join her. He found it difficult to concentrate. Her musky perfume lingered. The elevator door closed.

And then he saw me.

Jadeon's heart skipped a beat. I stood with my back to the bar, my elbows leaning on it casually, surrounded by several others. Jadeon recognized Marcus and was curious about the girl with us with the shocking purple streaks highlighting her hair. Dark circles under her eyes hardened her features.

We had walked in when Jadeon had been distracted. He now stared intently, though I ignored him. I was dressed in the fashions of the day, wearing black trousers of the finest leather and a white shirt. Jadeon attempted to read my mind but, unable to do so, continued to view those who surrounded me. We laughed loudly, joking with each other as all activity centered around me.

My eyes now fell directly on Jadeon's. My smile faded. My gaze returned to my friends and I continued to converse, having informed Jadeon with a glance that I knew he was here.

The young girl standing with us looked strangely out of place to Jadeon. Her clothes, denim pants and an inexpensive shirt, were dissimilar to what the other club members wore making her stand out. Upon reading her mind, the only one of the group Jadeon could penetrate, he sensed she wanted something from me and she was willing to do just about anything to get it. Fascinated, he scrutinized her.

I broke off his concentration. I was heading for him.

I loomed over Jadeon. "Looks like you've been stood up," I said.

"I'm here alone." Jadeon glared.

"No, you?" I signaled to the barman to bring drinks. "We fulfill most fantasies," I said. "However I dare say yours are a little unusual. Be reassured, I'm open-minded."

I sat down opposite Jadeon.

"Where's Catherine?" he asked.

"Who?"

"You know why I'm here."

"So what's Alex up to these days?" I asked.

"Over you," he said.

Two beverages were placed on our table.

"You use to be so eloquent when it came to social graces. What happened to Mr. Nice Guy?"

"You happened."

"A little gratitude would be nice."

"For what exactly?" Jadeon said.

"What year is it?"

"What?"

"What year is it?" I said.

"What has that—"

"You were born in the late 1700s, which makes you . . . old."

"Orpheus?"

"And yet you sit before me in the twenty-first century."

"You made me into . . . this?"

"I gave you eternal life."

"You massacred my family."

"Okay. Bored now."

"What was put in my drink?" he asked.

"Our blood donors are rather partial to chasing the dragon and such like. It gives it a kick."

"Bastard."

"I thought it might loosen you up a bit. God knows you need it," I laughed.

"I just need to speak with Catherine, hear that she is . . ."

"You always were an old romantic."

"Where is she?"

"She's here. Downstairs probably, drinking some innocent's life. No, wait. I think I see her giving some poor masochistic a run for his money!"

"You disgust me," Jadeon said.

"You flatter me."

"Let me see her. You and I are both tired of this charade. It's going nowhere fast."

"I can't deny that you are rather tiresome. It has been like trying to swat a bloody insect that refuses to die—buzz, buzz, and bloody buzz. Enough is enough. You're right. Let's ask Catherine to tell you herself." I rose. "Shall we?" I gestured to the elevator.

"I don't think so," Jadeon said.

"My club, my rules." I signaled to Marcus, who had remained standing at the bar, the girl now gone. He headed toward us.

I led Jadeon to the back of the room.

"Shall we?" I gestured to the open elevator.

He hesitated.

"Come now, so close. Below, she waits for you," I said.

Jadeon stepped into the small space. Before the doors closed several of my cliques joined us. I checked the time on my Rolex. We descended into Belshazzar's lower rooms.

XXV

JADEON

WITH ALL MY WILL I resisted the urge to place my hands around Orpheus's neck and strangle him. I had to keep my head for fear of what he would do to Catherine. Of course, he was well aware that he had the upper hand and I hated him even more for it. Orpheus led me down the long dark corridor running beneath the club.

Behind us walked four of his cohorts, including Marcus. Their sinister presence increased my uneasiness and unnerved me when they returned my gaze with a menacing stare. Hearing an occasional noise emanating from the rooms we passed, one after another, confirmed that the activities within them were of an erotic nature.

Orpheus stopped in front of one of the doors and placed his ear up against it, listening. Turning the handle, he gestured for us to be quiet. Opening the door, he allowed me to peer into the room. The scene astounded me. A blond woman was tied with leather straps to the rear wall, her head flung forward as if in a faint. She was completely naked and her fair hair fell over her face. Two women stood in revealing outfits, playing and taunting with the girl. The blonde raised her head and cried out for more. I was relieved to see none of the women in the room were Catherine and scowled at Orpheus.

They laughed at me.

From within the room, the two female vampires bowed respectively to Orpheus and his entourage. The door was closed shut.

"I think we'll have more luck in here." Orpheus led us into another of the rooms, similar to the first and obviously used as such judging by the décor of shackles on the walls and the leather accoutrements.

The purple-haired girl who had previously been standing at the bar with the others was now leaning in the corner. I studied Orpheus's motives for having her here.

Orpheus smirked at me.

I was done. I lunged at him.

In a fury, his men attacked me. Orpheus pulled the girl to face the wall and distracted her.

With a thwack I managed to throw one of them off and he fell to the ground with a thud. His neck was broken and he lay where he fell.

"You are so fired," Orpheus said to him.

The man recovered, leaping up with supernatural speed and struck me in the stomach, winding me.

"Or perhaps not," Orpheus said, allowing the eager girl to watch the fray.

His men shoved me up against the wall, securing my hands within shackles, fastening them tight. Another punch, this time to my chest. I struggled for air.

Orpheus watched on, obviously amused, while the young girl rested on a high-backed chair calmly observing the activity as if she had seen it all before.

"Gillian Stewart, allow me to introduce a dear old friend of mine, Jade." Orpheus lowered his voice. "Isn't it amazing what turns some men on?"

I was horrified, realizing the young girl thought that I was in the club for this.

"I will kill you, Orpheus!" I shouted. I had to get out of here.

"Someone needs to be punished?" he teased.

"Fuck you!" I said.

"Now we're talking."

"Where is she?"

"Two hundred years. Doesn't time fly when you're having fun? Though I dare say it probably dragged for you." Orpheus turned again to the young female and winked. "The punters love the fantasy. We just play along and fulfill their every desire."

I pulled on the restraints, struggling against the shackles. "Get out!" I screamed at the girl. "He's not who you think he is."

She stared back at me.

"You are in grave danger," I warned her.

"Shush," Orpheus said. He pressed up against me, turning my head to expose my neck. He nuzzled in and bit.

Not this.

My blood poured into his mouth.

I swooned, angry that I had allowed him to play me again. Dizziness came in waves. My head fell back, my jaw dropped. Orpheus sucked furiously, his body now rocking against mine.

"No." My words had no strength.

Leisurely he savored the pleasure of the drink. He quenched his thirst. Eventually he pulled away, wiping the blood from his mouth so as not to alarm the girl.

"Wow! How much bloody drug did you use?" Orpheus glared at Marcus.

No air in the room.

Orpheus closed his eyes, relishing the rush of my drug-laced blood. He forced his hand over my mouth and whispered, "Jadeon, I drank a little too much. You'll have to forgive my rudeness, but if it wasn't for my willpower I would have drained every last drop. So you have something to be grateful for."

"No." My legs gave way and I hung from the shackles. Despite the high-pitched ringing, it was imperative I stay alert.

Orpheus stepped back. "You're right. We need to replace that blood loss. I wonder if I know anyone who would volunteer?" He clicked his fingers.

Responding quickly, the young girl stood up out of the chair, waiting for further direction.

"My dear Gill, I have a small present for you." Orpheus removed a small clear plastic bag from his shirt pocket.

Gillian's eyes widened. He waved it before her and she recognized the familiar white powder within it. She pulled the packet from his hand.

"Don't snatch! It is a present from our grateful client here. Now go sit down and have a little. It's very good. Perhaps you would like to share? No?"

Taking a seat in the corner of the room again, she emptied a small portion of the powder into the palm of her hand, glancing up possessively. Pacing the room, Orpheus waited for her to imbibe.

He instructed his minions to leave.

Orpheus knelt beside the girl. "Here, let me help you." He pried the packet from her hand, pouring a large amount of the white powder onto his wrist. "There," he offered.

Gill frowned.

"Don't take it," I warned her.

"Looks like he wants his stuff back," Orpheus said.

The girl glared at me.

"It will kill you," I said.

"Would I ever let anything happen to my princess?" He smiled.

Gill leaned toward his arm and sniffed the cocaine. Her eyelids fluttered and she flopped back into the chair.

"Well, if you thought the answer was yes, you'd be right. That amount of drug is far too much for your little feeble human body, but that is the least of your worries. Now be a good girl and don't die just yet."

Her head fell back and she lay still.

Orpheus unlocked my shackles. He wrapped his arms around me and lay me upon the cold stone floor. He could see me weakening.

He slapped my face. "I need you to focus. Now remember, give my regards to Alex, though I will probably see him before you do. *Bon appétit*, Jadeon!"

Orpheus withdrew, locking the door on his way out.

I staggered to my feet and tried the door handle. I was trapped and reeled from the blood loss.

The dazed girl moaned in the corner.

"I will not do it." My cries echoed into the silence. "You cannot make me drink from her." I turned and stared at the girl, resisting the drag of my primal need.

XXVI

⊕RPHEUS

ALEX HAD FED. Replete, he returned to the castle. His victim had been a twenty-four-year-old rapist whom Alex considered fair game—hunting the hunter. Alex still tried to shake the man's thoughts from his own. He sat now in the reading room playing the music that Jadeon had bought him for his new stereo. Cacophonous noise blared through the speakers. Making himself comfortable in one of the large leather chairs, Alex enjoyed the many books and magazines he had purchased.

"Alexander!" I said.

Alex leapt up.

My skin glowed, indicating I too had enjoyed a recent feed.

"Daumia?" Alex looked me up and down, having never seen me in modern attire. He was struck at how well the fashions of leather trousers and white shirt suited me.

"It's been . . . too long," I said.

God, he was beautiful. I had almost forgotten how perfect he was. I'd missed him.

"Where did you come from?" Alex was terrified.

"The underworld. Care to join me?"

He stepped back.

"Alex, you know me better than that. Open your mind to me."

He glared. "Get out!"

"So much for hello."

"You are not welcome."

"I promised I would come back for you," I said.

"Yeah, right."

"Don't get pissy with me."

"I said get out!"

I shoved him against the wall. "If I wanted to kill you I would have, but I don't."

Alex could feel my breath on his mouth. "What do you want from me?"

"Why so afraid?"

"Take a guess."

"I've missed you. I had to see you."

"You chose this life for me," he began. "You tricked and lied. You murdered my father."

"Your father all but murdered you."

"He thought I was—"

"You would have bled to death."

"Let me go."

"I transformed Jadeon so that you wouldn't mourn him."

"You lie."

"I just see things through a different perspective, that's all."

"Is that how you justify all that you do?"

"Look, Alex, I know that sometimes my moral compass can be a little off," I said.

"You're kidding, right?"

I smiled. "Do you remember when we spent that evening in that Marazion Inn, when I arranged that whore for you? Alex, you were so innocent then. You should have seen your face when you realized why she was in the room."

Alex blushed.

I leaned in to kiss him. Alex closed his eyes, expecting my lips. He reopened his eyes to see me smiling at him.

Alex turned his head, abashed. "Why do you torment me?"

"Because it gives me so much pleasure."

"No."

"Shush." I leaned in again.

He pushed at me. "I try to understand this hold you have on me," he said.

Our lips touched. I lulled him with a full sensuous kiss. Alex faltered. I drew back and Alex rested his head against me.

"Come back to me," I said.

Breathless, Alex leaned his head back against the wall, uncertain.

"Say it. I want to hear you say it," I said.

"And I want to hear where Catherine is," Alex replied.

We stared at one another

"She's in London," I said.

"Where in London?"

I let go of Alex's arms and groped for his shirt buttons, undoing them one at a time.

"Tell me please, Orpheus, and I will tell you what you want to hear. But first, where is she?"

"How long have you waited for this? For me?"

"Catherine, where is she?" he pressed.

"Catherine lives with me, and she came willingly. She wanted to leave that dark, dreary convent that your brother chased her into. She is happy and just wants to be left alone. Now, take off your clothes. This conversation is getting tedious."

"I need to see her," Alex said.

His shirt completely open, I reached for his zipper. Alex pushed my hand away.

"I have told you where she is. Now you are mine," I said.

"Not so fast."

"You dare to defy—"

"Yes, I love you. But I love my brother more. Please go."

I leaned against him again. "I like it that you have grown strong. You are like a fine wine, like the wine we used to drink together on those long cold nights. Remember?"

"You mean the wine you weren't really drinking?" Alex turned his head.

"Okay, I'll go." I stepped back. "I think I owe you—"

"An apology?"

"I wish to share with you my artful method of feeding. You see Catherine, when she first joined me, refused to drink from living creatures. Always has. From the moment I conceived her she would only ever drink from me. After a couple of centuries, as you can imagine, it was becoming rather a drag. There is a solution. Now listen carefully. There is a place where blood is stored and tested. It is of the highest quality, refrigerated within laboratories in hospitals. Humans donate their blood willingly for other weak mortals. It is transfused into their body to prolong life. They actually call them blood banks, and I'm giving you the credit card, as it were. There are no guards. And they would never miss the occasional unit or so. Just think, Alex, you need never kill again. Wouldn't that be something?"

"I don't believe you."

"Look into it. Alex, over the next few weeks you'll think of me.

You will find you will be unable to resist coming to me, and you will seek me out. I will be in your every waking thought. You will become obsessed with seeing me. I'll await you in my club in Belgravia called Belshazzar's.

"Join us and enjoy the company of others like you. Then you shall know what true pleasure really is. Or perhaps you would rather spend another two hundred years alone in this dreary castle?"

I left him to ponder my words.

XXVII

JADEON

DELIRIOUS.

I had lost all track of time lying in the corner of the room, weakening.

The girl's sobs echoed around the chamber.

I tried to reassure her that she was safe but having just sucked blood from her neck, she was hard to convince. My body ached and my flesh crawled. Symptoms I assumed I sustained from the tainted drink. My head felt like it was going to explode. Covering my ears again I tried to block out her shrills.

She banged furiously upon the door begging to be let out. In my confusion I was tempted to finish her off, just to have some quiet. Both of us welcomed the sound of the key turning in the door. Orpheus entered.

She ran to him. "Why the hell did you lock me in here with him? He actually thinks he is a vampire," she slurred.

"For real?" Orpheus said.

"Yes!"

"Gill, you're pretty stoned right now."

Gill freaked. "I'm not. Don't you pull that shit on me."

"You mean he really thinks he's a . . ."

"That's what I'm fucking saying."

"No, you see if he were a real vampire, you'd be dead."

"Look what he did to my neck." She pulled back her hair revealing two deep fang marks. "He's insane."

Orpheus reached for Gill's locks and held them away from her pale neck just long enough for me to catch a glimpse of her veins.

Torture.

"Well I do believe we are making progress," Orpheus said.

Gill staggered. "What the fuck are you talking—"

"Enough with the cursing. Can't you see we have a lord in our company?"

Gill watched him approach me. He knelt close and leaned in. "Jade, you have lost far too much blood. Come on, why deny what you are?"

I struggled. "I will not."

"I understand your conflict," he whispered. "Perhaps if you were to consider drinking from me?"

Orpheus turned his attention once more to Gill, who stood at the doorway ready to bolt.

"Gill, come here," Orpheus said.

She approached, taking the key he offered her.

"Go and lock the door. I can't have him thinking this is normal."

"What are you going to do?" She swayed uneasily.

"A lesson is required, to ensure that . . ."

"He can't attack people for real."

"Good point, well presented."

"Fuck you, Orpheus." Gill peered down at the large key.

I rallied my fading strength. "Gillian, you must leave this room now."

"What? And miss all the fun?" Orpheus glared at her. "I'm waiting."

Nervously she did as he requested.

Orpheus pulled the hair away from Gill's throat. "Good girl. Let me see your neck again. I really cannot believe—"

"Orpheus, you left me in here with a complete psycho."

"Did you finish the coke I gave you?"

"I had to have something to keep me sane," she said.

"So right now your blood is laced with . . ."

"Yeah, so?"

"Come closer." He ran his fingers over the puncture wounds. "You have such beautiful skin, it's a shame. Still, your friends will be impressed."

She pushed his hand away. "I just hope it doesn't leave a fucking scar!"

"Oh, those marks won't. Jadeon's far too much of a gentleman, but that's where he and I differ. I am his polar opposite, and my bite always leaves a mark."

Helpless, I witnessed her shocking attack.

Orpheus possessed her. Gill's gaze locked with mine, a pleading stare that went unanswered. My tears welled and blurred the vision of her slipping to the floor, dead.

Orpheus overpowered me. He bit his wrist and pressed it against my lips. The taste of blood offered no comfort. Instinctively I sucked, lost in needed rapture. I shared Orpheus's thoughts of Catherine. Unwilling to let her go I grasped his wrist. Together we lay on the stone floor, panting as our hearts pounded.

The cocaine's unforgiving hold ravaged on and took me with it.

* * * *

I awoke in blackness.

Where the bloody hell am I?

The deafening noise of a television roused me, the channels changing frantically. I pried my eyes open and was startled to see Alex holding the remote control. I was back in my suite at the Savoy with no recollection how I had gotten there.

"I didn't know you ordered takeout," Alex said.

I pulled the sheet covers up and over my thumping head. I had failed. I had to go back.

Alex tugged on the bed sheet. "Oh good, you're awake. Look. Jadeon, see how amazing this is."

I peeked over the bed covers. Alex was mesmerized with the television. It was wise not to tell him just yet. I wondered how long before I would find the strength to return.

Pain everywhere, which settled in my head. "If you turn it off right now we'll get one for every room in the castle," I said.

"You don't look too good."

"Alex, the TV."

He turned it off. "What happened to you?"

"I drank bad blood."

"How so?"

"Drugs," I said simply.

"What kind?"

"Too many questions, Alex."

"I read in *Cosmopolitan* that it's easy to become addicted."

"Thank you for your comforting words. And that's a girl's magazine. You cannot read that stuff. You have to read *GQ*. You'll be the death of me."

Alex laughed.

"Do you hear that?" I jumped out of bed and pulled on my robe. "I told you there's a guest waiting for you in the lounge."

"Takeout? That's not funny. Who is it?"

"Some girl." Alex opened the door. "Hey, come in."

I quickly gestured to him. "Wait."

Ingrid appeared at the door. "Hello, Jadeon, I . . . didn't know you had company." She stepped into the room and squinted. "It's pretty dark in here."

"Ingrid, how wonderful to see you!" I forced out.

She was as lovely as I had remembered her and she was wearing that familiar perfume. She was dressed in blue jeans, white shirt, and a black leather jacket, her hair tied up behind her head.

Coco Chanel, Alex conveyed telepathically.

How the hell do you know that? I replied in kind. On the other hand, please don't tell me.

I had to guard my thoughts more carefully.

Heavy-lined curtains omitted most of the light. I reached over to the table lamp and flicked it on. Ingrid glanced at the ruffled sheets on the four-poster bed which not so long ago she had slept in herself.

She blushed, self-conscious that Alex stared at her. "Is this is a bad time?" she asked.

"No." I read her suspicious mind as she eyed Alex. "He's my brother. I mean, Ingrid, this is Alex, my younger brother. We grew up together."

Alex smiled.

"Hello Alex, I am pleased to meet you. I've heard such wonderful things about you."

"All bad, I hope. May I offer you something?" He ignored my glare.

"No thank you. I can't stay long. I wanted to drop this off for you, Jadeon. It's a small gesture to thank you for dinner and of course the dress, and the wonderful evening." Pulling a small box of chocolates and a card from her bag, she handed it to me.

"Thank you, Ingrid, Cadbury's chocolate. It's our favorite." My stomach growled in response to the aroma of the rich chocolate. "You really shouldn't have. Would you like one?"

She declined.

I shoved the chocolates in a drawer in the writing table. In response to her subtle reaction, I fibbed. "Alex will only go and eat them all."

"Yummy," Alex said.

"Alex, will you give us a moment, please?" I gestured to the large couch.

He sat and pretended to scan the limited reading material on the coffee table. I guided Ingrid through the arched wall and into the lounge.

"Are you not feeling well?" she asked. "You look a little rough."

"I . . . drank too much last night. My own fault."

"Hair of the dog often helps."

"Excuse me?"

"Another drink," she said.

"Yes, of course. No, it's better I stay away from . . ."

I was disturbed to pick up more of Alex's thoughts. He was considering a visit to Belshazzar's and I had no idea he even knew the place even existed.

"Water is probably a better idea," Ingrid said.

"Yes, right."

Alex appeared at the archway. "You were at Belshazzar's last night? Why didn't you tell me you saw him?"

I glanced at Ingrid. "Alex, this is not a good time."

"Catherine?" Alex said.

"We'll discuss this later, Alex. When did he come to you?" I was shocked to sense this. I responded to Ingrid's quizzical expression. "It's brother stuff."

"Belshazzar's. That's that club Mr. Teddington mentioned in the gallery."

"It's members only." I hoped this would put her off.

"Sounds alluring," she said.

"It's not. I highly recommend avoiding the place."

"Why?"

I thought carefully. "Because—"

"I was going to tell you, eventually," Alex said. "When were you going to tell me?"

"Alex, this is hardly the time," I said.

Alex frowned.

I sighed. "Alex, I had every intention . . ."

"Where is it again?" Ingrid said.

"It's a very seedy place. The crowd is sinister and the food is . . ."

"I specialize in sinister." She studied me.

"Ingrid, I'm not asking you to stay away from Belshazzar's, I'm telling you."

The last thing I needed was the thought of her snooping around Orpheus's stomping ground.

Ingrid rested her hands on her hips.

"Oh, you're a policewoman," Alex said.

"She's a police inspector." I threw an intense stare at my brother.

"Like Sherlock Holmes?" Alex said.

"I wish." Ingrid smiled. "I could always Google it?"

"You what?" Alex said.

"Belshazzar's. I'll find out more about the places your brother Jadeon here likes to hang out in. It'll tell me more about him. In my job it's the food people eat, the places they go, the clothes they wear, and the friends they share that speak volumes."

"Sounds creepy," Alex said.

"How reassuring to know we have such dedicated people protecting us." I tried to keep the sarcasm from my voice.

Ingrid smiled. "Look, I can't stay. I have to get back to this course I'm taking."

"That forensic course you mentioned at dinner?" I said.

"Yes. Actually, the other reason I'm here is that an old friend of mine has arranged a party, and I was encouraged to bring a guest. I know they won't mind if you come too, Alex."

"He's busy," I burst out.

"No, I'm not. I haven't been to a party since . . ." Alex appeared thoughtful.

Ingrid beamed. "Then it's set. It's my crazy friends getting together. It should be fun."

"Will there be music?" Alex asked.

Ingrid nodded with a smile. "Alex, you are so cute. And great food."

"It will be our pleasure to attend," I said, still considering the invite. It was obvious that it meant the world to Alex.

"Very well, I'll give you the address and instructions on how to get there." Ingrid proceeded to look in her bag for a piece of paper.

I offered her the hotel notepad next to the bed. While Ingrid wrote, I glared at Alex.

He gave me a bashful smile.

I melted.

The throb in my head soon receded, one of the few benefits of being supernatural. Not ready to go back to the club just yet, I reasoned Ingrid's invitation would be the distraction I needed.

* * * *

Outside the party I changed my mind.

Alex detected this and rang the doorbell. "What?" He avoided my glare. From the noise coming from inside the apartment, the party was in full swing.

The door opened. "Now which one's the art dealer?" James Lemont welcomed us into his luxuriously furnished home. "Ingrid's told me all about you. She's over there trapped in the corner by one of my other guests. I know she'll be relieved that you're here to save her."

James was obviously well educated, wealthy, and traveled. His taste was somewhat eccentric, and the eclectic artwork seemed out of place in the modern bachelor residence. He made us feel welcome, and my feeling of wanting to bolt soon wore off.

Thirty or so guests mingled comfortably.

An attractive young woman approached us. "Hi guys! You must be Jadeon. Ingrid will be jazzed to know you made it. I'm Belle."

I detected her soft Cape Town accent. "May I introduce my brother, Alex?" I said.

She laughed at me. "You may."

"Have you eaten anything?" James said. "Food's over there. Do make yourselves at home." He pointed to a table strewn with assorted plates.

James returned to mingle with his other guests.

Belle screwed up her nose. "The food's vegan. He's going through this health kick right now. Last month, it was Macrobiotics."

Alex and I stared at her.

"I'll get Ingrid then." Belle withdrew to find her.

Alex and I scanned the room. We both noticed the lines between the sexes were almost erased. The closeness between male and female was as blurred as the indifference of their clothes. With the growing awareness of numerous admiring eyes, Alex's self-consciousness increased. He still captivated those around him.

"You're doing great," I reassured him.

"Hey, you made it!" Ingrid greeted me with a kiss on my cheek.

Her subtle perfume rose up. She wore the black halter-neck dress I'd bought for her.

"You look . . . beautiful," I said.

Ingrid beamed. "Thank you, Jadeon."

"We wouldn't have missed your party for the world," I said.

Alex gave a subtle smirk that only I noticed.

"Let me introduce you to one of my dearest friends," she said.

James Lemont approached us. "We've already had the pleasure."

"I first met James when he was working on a case in Salisbury,"

Ingrid said. "He's a lawyer and was defending a man I had arrested for car theft."

"Alleged car theft, darling," James laughed.

"He got two years," Ingrid said.

"Paroled in six months." James hugged Ingrid.

I studied them both to ascertain any romantic involvement. James was in love with her though Ingrid was oblivious to the fact.

"Well, we hit it off immediately," Ingrid said, "and here I am, scoffing his delicious food. James makes the best chocolate roll."

"Chocolate roulade." James rolled his eyes.

"That's what I said, chocolate roll." Ingrid winked at me.

James shook his head, remonstrating his disapproval. "Incorrigible. So, Jadeon, tell me more about your work."

"Well," I began, "I am passionate about art."

"Do you have a gallery?" James said.

"No, but I am considering opening one." This was not far from the truth, but I had things to settle before I could.

"I have some interesting pieces that I'd love to show you," James said. "What style of art do you prefer?"

"The old masters," I replied. "But I'm also open to contemporary."

"How wonderful. Have you sold any recently?"

"Yes, I sold a Joseph Turner."

"No, seriously, have you?"

"I hated it," Alex said.

"No bloody way!" Belle said.

James stared at us, unsure. "Are you for real?"

"Quite real," I said.

"Jadeon currently has a painting on show at the National," Ingrid said.

"Really?" James was impressed.

I nodded. "Raphael's St. Catherine."

"Super!" James responded.

"And you, Alex," James said. "What do you do?"

"I just look after the castle, pretty much," Alex replied.

"You guys are a riot." Belle laughed.

"No, seriously, do you work?" James asked again, amused.

Alex looked at the many faces now staring at him awaiting his answer.

"My brother Alex and I are very lucky to have inherited our father's estate in Cornwall. Alex spends a lot of time ensuring that it's maintained in keeping with its original style," I said.

"You really live in a castle?" Belle asked.

"It's very cold," Alex said.

"Wow. Ingrid, don't your relatives come from down there?" Belle said.

Ingrid nodded.

"Which castle?" Belle asked.

"Marazion," I said.

"St. Michael's Mount," Alex said.

"I know the one," James said. "It's beautiful, surrounded by water."

I smiled. "That's the one."

"Really?" Belle grinned at Ingrid.

Silence . . .

"So let me show you one of my newest paintings, come on." James guided us to the back of the apartment where on the far wall a modern large painting hung—the scene of a naked man and woman, their limbs entwined, their heads leaning back unnaturally.

I sensed Ingrid staring at me, trying to figure me out.

I threw her a wide smile.

"It's by Augusta Nadam!" James announced proudly.

"Well, Jadeon," Ingrid said. "What do you think? Now be honest."

I recognized the work by the Portuguese artist. Augusta had displayed several of his paintings in a small gallery in SoHo and had received rave reviews. Alex had been with me at the time, though he had spent the hour we'd been in the gallery avoiding the man. Augusta had pursued Alex to the point of stalking. I could not help but enjoy Alex's wide-eyed glare as if Augusta might leap from the painting itself.

"Well?" James pushed.

I chose my words carefully. "Nadam is expressive and fresh, but . . ."

"But what?" James said.

"But from the strokes of the brush he appears distracted, unfocused. See here." I pointed to the canvas. "And yet it works. His desire to rush ahead compliments the piece and allows us to gauge his desire to connect with us."

"You get all that from this painting?" Belle asked.

"I kind of cheated. I've met the artist," I said. "He's a tormented man."

"How so?" Ingrid asked.

"Augusta is a recluse," I said. "Apart from when he's presenting his work, he doesn't go out."

Alex peered at me with his intense baby blues.

"It's a good investment, James. You'll be happy with it," I said.

James beamed. "And Ingrid told me it looked like a druggie had painted it."

"She's right, James," I answered. "Augusta is a heroin addict."

"Bloody hell," Belle said.

James sighed.

Ingrid patted James's arm affectionately. "Well, I've rather grown fond of it. Come on Jadeon, let's get you a drink." Ingrid guided me toward the refreshments. "Do you really know Augusto?"

"Augusta Nadam," I corrected her. "I only met him once."

I sensed James studying me and turned to fend off his glare. James quickly headed to the other side of the room.

"You know, Jadeon," Ingrid said, "I'm pretty good with figuring people out, but there's something about you that I can't put my finger on."

Perhaps it's because I am a vampire. No, that would not be funny. "I'm a southerner, so maybe..."

"I'm going to keep prodding until I put my finger on it," Ingrid said.

Amused, I smiled at her. Ingrid blushed. The sound of her laughter was contagious.

"Are you spontaneous, Ingrid?" I checked my watch.

"What do you mean?" she said.

Music emanated from James's piano and caught Ingrid's attention. She realized that it was Alex who was performing the ethereal music.

Conversations ceased as other guests now listened in awe.

"Do you ever do things on the spur of the moment?" I asked Ingrid.

"Sure. Why?"

"How would you like to be standing in St. Michael's Mount by morning?"

* * * *

Ingrid, Alex, and I arrived in Marazion just after three o'clock in the morning, having driven down in my new silver Jaguar. At Ingrid's request we had stopped off at her hotel, the Hilton Trafalgar located in Trafalgar Square, so that she could gather some overnight belongings. It was here she was staying while attending the course at Scotland Yard.

Ingrid had settled back into the leather car seat and had not minded when I occasionally broke the speed limit. If anyone could talk us out of a speeding ticket, she could. It was reassuring that she had hit if off with Alex. They both shared a love of modern music, their tastes it seemed almost identical.

Ingrid hung on my every word when I talked about my passion for art and I found her profession extraordinary, enjoying the insights she revealed when discussing the law. Even though her petite frame made her seem an unlikely opponent, her quick mind and confident nature were a match for any criminal. Her ability to lull you into a sense of comfort then slowly extract what she wanted to know was uncanny. I had to make a point of staying one step ahead of her. My growing fascination with Ingrid proved a challenge. Despite my reasoning that this was just a fleeting distraction, my desires told me otherwise.

On our arrival I parked the car in a small alley in the center of Marazion.

"This is where we walk." I held open the car door for Ingrid and escorted her toward the causeway, carrying her small overnight bag for her.

As we turned the street corner, Ingrid was struck by the vision before her—the magnificent castle looming in the distance. Despite her weariness she soon woke up. Ingrid peered at the resplendent château. The tide was out.

"This way," I said.

We guided her down onto the pathway.

I smiled. "I hope you're a good swimmer, in case we don't make it before the tide turns."

"That's not funny, Jadeon." She picked up her pace.

"When we get inside it's quite cozy," I reassured her.

We trekked over the gravel, all three of us excited to reach St. Michael's Mount. Ingrid was thrilled to be seeing the castle for the first time, and we were happy to be home.

I unlocked the original large wooden doors and gestured to Ingrid to enter. She stepped inside. She gazed in awe at the enormous low-hung chandelier.

Alex and I smiled at one another. We knew we had taken our home for granted and now through Ingrid's eyes we were able to rekindle our perspective. She sighed in wonder at the sweeping staircase in front of us. Two armored knights stood on guard at the base of the stairwell, presented as in battle.

"Wow!" she said.

I checked my watch. "Come on. I'll get you a drink."

With little time left with her until Alex and I would be forced down into the dungeons to sleep, I was determined to savor her.

We lingered in the kitchen where I poured Ingrid a glass of water, aware that after her journey she would be thirsty.

"Thing is," I said, "I have invited you down here and now I have to dash off for a meeting. Will you forgive me?"

"I don't want to cause any trouble," Ingrid said.

"No trouble. Come on, I'll show you to your room," I said.

I escorted her up the sweeping staircase and along the corridor to our father's large bedroom.

"It's another four-poster bed!" Ingrid said.

"So it is." I smiled. "Alex and I have business in Marazion pretty much all day. Just a boring old art deal. How about we join you for dinner in the evening? Ingrid, you have the run of the castle."

I held her hand to my chest and felt her frailty. Her alluring presence threw me and I felt an uncommon need to get close to her.

"You're cold," she said.

"I'm fine." I closed my eyes, melting into the moment.

Ingrid seemed to sense what I needed and stood quietly. I leant forward and kissed her cheek. Ingrid moved her mouth against mine and our lips touched. Her scent ignited my senses.

I wanted to stay but with sunrise imminent, judging by the sting of my flesh, I had to pull away. "Later then?" I said, and stepped back.

"Hurry back," Ingrid replied and glanced out the window. She took in the exquisite colors of the morning as a burst of light flooded the room. She turned to face me.

She was alone in the room.

Ingrid looked about for me. She stepped out of the room and peered both ways down the corridor. "Where did you go?"

From within my place of rest down in the lower depths of the castle, I telepathically followed Ingrid on her tour. She headed down the corridor, eager to begin her adventure. She strolled down the imposing corridors retracing her steps from when she had first been guided to her room.

The dimly lit passageways provided meager light causing her to consider for a moment whether she should wait for my return before she ventured any further. Intrigue drove her on and she descended the sweeping staircase, holding onto the carved banisters for support, admiring the many paintings hanging upon the walls of the stairway.

She stopped momentarily, distracted by a painting that caught her attention. It was of Alex and me, captured on canvas as boys. Ingrid admired how the artist had represented our features so perfectly, recognizing that familiar glint in Alex's eye. But examining it more closely and reading the name of the painter in the lower right hand corner of the portrait, she realized she must be wrong. It was dated 1791, the artist Sir Thomas Lawrence. Though surprised, she realized this must be a portrait of our ancestors and continued to walk down the stairs, pondering on its familiarity and marveling at how uncanny it was.

She stood in the main foyer, looking in wonder at the chandelier again and considering which direction she should go. Turning right she headed down yet another dimly lit corridor until she reached a grand oak door. Curious, she opened it and peered in at the huge library, admiring the large mahogany table in the center and the thousands of books that completely covered the four walls. Walking over to one of the shelves she noticed a book lying flat, not part of the perfectly placed collection. Ingrid appreciated how we had maintained this library in its original form. She picked up the leather-bound book, blowing the dust away. On the first page she observed an inscription. She read the words written in italics:

To Lady Anna Beth Artimas, my darling wife, on the occasion of your 21st birthday.

The book's subject focused on both British and foreign flowers with what appeared to be hand-drawn pictures. Turning to the next page she read the date, and realizing it was over two hundred years old, she quickly placed it back upon the shelf. Ingrid took one more look at the room, deciding she would return here again later.

On entering the armory she explored, carefully running her fingers along the ornate swords, avoiding their sharpened blades. She admired the fencing equipment, noticing how the weapons appeared like new and well cared for. Ingrid walked over to the extensive collection of antique guns in the corner. They looked strangely out of place, as if stored in a hurry and not in keeping with the organization of the rest of the armory. A large wooden chest pushed up against the far wall fascinated her.

She froze, wondering if she had heard someone outside in the corridor. Ingrid decided she should go and investigate, but before she left this room she wanted to first take a peek inside the chest that reminded her of an old pirate's trunk. Raising the heavy lid, she peered inside. It contained numerous silver cups and silver-plated awards. Taking one of the antiquated goblets out, she noticed its inscription. Brushing off the dust, she read the engraving:

Presented to Lord Jadeon Artimas – Cornwall's fencing Champion. The year of our Lord 1798.

"No bloody way!"

She assumed it was obviously one of my ancestors again. She closed the trunk and left the room to investigate the noise. Ingrid lingered outside the armory, listening. On hearing nothing, she decided to continue. She was peckish, and checking her watch, realized it was now 0830. Ingrid decided she would search for the kitchen. We had insisted she make herself at home and she felt comfortable doing so. She soon discovered the old-fashioned kitchen, recently renovated in keeping with the castle's history and style. Opening the fridge she found nothing within it, though within the freezer she found ice cream.

"Typical bachelor pad," she remarked.

After Ingrid had eaten she returned to where the bedrooms were situated, looking for my room. She soon found it, just a few doors down from the room in which she was staying. She recognized my tailored suits hanging in the wardrobe. For a moment she felt a little guilty intruding in such a way, but then something caught her eye—an old book resting on my secretaire.

Upon closer inspection she discovered it was a book of poetry. It looked as old as the ones in the library. Gently she picked it up, opening the front page. Inside she found a letter, written on what appeared to be very worn paper. Carefully she unraveled it, noticing some of the edges crumble away as she did so. Placing the book back down on the secretaire, she read the words:

The year of our Lord 1797

My darling Jadeon, as you know, the decision I have made has not been easy. To become a bride of Christ is something I have given much thought to over the years. I am aware of your feelings for me. Know that I share the same love for you, but I have made a promise to God and cannot break it. I know that you understand, or will come to, as God will guide you to your destiny. Know this, I will always love you and will pray for you every morning when I awake and in the evening when I go to sleep. You are my brother and will be forever safe within my heart.

Yours forever and in God,
Catherine

"Now that's what I call romantic." Ingrid then realized there were two pages. They were almost stuck together but she could not resist peeking to see what was written on the other letter. As she pried the other piece of paper away from the first, she realized it was not a letter but a drawing. She gasped. The sketch on the page was of a likeness to me that was again uncanny. It was my face looking up at her, drawn beside the image of a beautiful young girl. The drawing was signed *Alex, 1796*.

Gently sliding the letter and drawing back into the book, Ingrid placed it again on the writing desk as she had found it. She climbed onto the comfy four-poster bed.

Ingrid laughed. "I have solved the mystery. Jadeon is over two hundred years old." She snuggled into the soft blankets.

She fell asleep.

Reassured that Ingrid had settled into my room, I too allowed myself the luxury of sleep and soon drifted off.

XXVIII

⊕RPHEUS

I LOOMED OVER HER.

Ingrid awoke with a start.

Taking in her surroundings, she reoriented herself. She was alone. Ingrid checked her watch—1630 hours. She had slept the day away, not surprising as she had slept little during her journey down from London.

Stepping out of Jadeon's bedroom, Ingrid called out his name. On hearing nothing but an unearthly silence she headed off to look for him. Walking to the top of the central stairway she paused for a moment, listening. A noise caught her attention, rising up from the lower chambers. Descending the stairs, she again passed by that familiar painting with its uncanny likeness to Jadeon and Alex. She shuddered in response to the freezing breeze. It felt as though someone had just opened a door.

She continued into the main foyer of the castle. Hearing the noise again she walked in its direction, discovering a clandestine doorway leading down a dark stone stairwell. The light in the corridor dimmed. She descended, and shivered. She found it difficult to distinguish whether it was through the lowering of the castle's temperature or her wariness. Goose bumps rose up on her skin.

"Hello?" she called out.

She continued down, arriving at yet another corridor leading to what appeared to be a long line of cells at the end of it. Intrigued, she was keen to view the ancient prisons. On approaching the bastilles she detected an unpleasant damp mustiness. Peering in at each of the cells, all similar, Ingrid was enthralled.

Reaching the end of the hallway she touched the stone wall, running her fingers over its cold rough surface then turning, headed back the way she had come. She observed how it appeared even scarier at this end of the long passageway.

Ingrid reflected for a moment how frightened those imprisoned here must have felt. She glanced again into one of the cells, noticing the rusty shackles upon the wall. Fascinated, she entered the cell, eager to view them.

She examined the shackle. A noise of grating stone in the darkness startled her.

She froze. "Hello?" Ingrid listened. Only quietness now. Sensing a presence again, she called out. "Jadeon?"

"No," I replied from the blackness.

"Alex?"

"No."

"Oh, come on guys, please stop playing with me. I'm not enjoying this. This is so not funny."

My tall silhouette loomed. "My name is Daumia, but my friends call me Orpheus."

Ingrid's eyes adjusted.

I peered between the bars. My gaze penetrated hers. She had a sense of familiarity with my regal stature and chiseled features.

My accent, with its deep unearthly resonance, increased her nervousness. Squinting, she studied me as shadows danced on my face.

"Oh, hello," she said. "I'm a guest of Jadeon's. I was just having a look around."

"My timing is usually impeccable." I neared her. "But this time I've outdone myself, Ingrid."

"Do I know you?"

"Perhaps," I said.

She sensed danger.

I took another teasingly sinister step toward her and leant against the doorframe of the cell, gauging her reaction.

"Please, if you don't mind I would appreciate it if you would keep your distance," she said.

"Oh, but where's the fun in that?"

"Jadeon!" she called out.

I retreated from the doorway.

Ingrid sighed with relief and watched me saunter back up the corridor and disappear.

She pounced forward, slamming the rusting door to the jail with an echoing clang, safely locking herself in and her dark assailant out. Looking out into the passageway she scanned the empty corridor left, then right, and sighed. Shaken, she took a moment to catch her breath. An eerie silence descended into the dusky chambers once again. Her goose bumps returning, her heart racing, she sensed me behind her.

Ingrid spun round.

I smiled at her.

"How the hell . . . ?"

I took several steps forward and pushed her back against the hard bars of the jail cell. "Completely trapped, helpless, powerless, and humanly frail. Does that sound like anyone you know?" I clutched her wrists.

"So you're a friend of Jadeon's then?" Thinking quickly, Ingrid attempted to control the situation with some small talk.

"Don't be boring, Ingrid. I was beginning to enjoy myself."

Ingrid pushed at me. "I'm a police detective, and this is assault. If you don't let me go right now, I'm going to arrest you. You'll get two to three years in a prison much like this one."

"Promises, promises." I stared deeply into her eyes.

Ingrid froze, reluctant to anger me. She looked up, attempting to get a good look at my face. She was struck at how my eyes fixed upon hers, making her feel a little light-headed, and wondered if this was due to her panic. We were now breathing together, in unison, and she could feel my heart beating, my chest against hers..

"Surrender to me," I whispered.

She could feel my breath against her face, my lips close to hers. Her breathing became rapid. Ingrid closed her eyes, swooning in response. She felt my kiss upon her neck now, my teeth grazing her skin, my lips moving over hers.

Dismayed, she resigned to her desires, feeling my mouth hard against hers. Passion exploded and she surrendered to my deep, sensuous kiss. It was too much. Breathless, she tried to fathom her uncharacteristic response. As I nuzzled into Ingrid's neck, her head fell backwards and banged against the rough bars.

She staggered.

Regaining her footing, she blushed, her stare incredulous.

"It was quite wonderful to meet with you, Ingrid," I said. "I hope to see you again very soon." I opened the cell gate and disappeared.

XXIX

JADEON

I FLEW INTO THE dungeons. "Ingrid! Are you all right? Let me see your . . . You look fine. You're okay."

I was horrified Orpheus had been able to get into the castle undetected, and I cursed myself for letting my guard down. After sensing him I had almost tripped over myself trying to get to Ingrid.

"Jadeon, who the hell was that?" Ingrid asked.

"What are you doing down here?" I lifted her into my arms. She was badly shaken. We made our way up the stone stairway, through the foyer, quickly ascending the sweeping staircase. When we reached my bedroom I placed her down upon my old bed, covering her with a blanket.

"He said he knew me, but I don't recall . . ."

"He's an old acquaintance."

I tried to grasp what Orpheus wanted with Ingrid. The knot in my stomach distracted me. I pulled Ingrid toward me and hugged her, attempting to put thoughts of Orpheus out of my mind and hoping she would too.

Alex appeared at the door and stared at me wide-eyed.

"He's gone," I said to him.

"What did he want?" Alex asked.

I looked at Ingrid and tried to answer that question.

"What did he say?" Alex asked.

Ingrid sighed and pushed off the blanket. "It didn't make any sense."

"He's gone now," I said.

"He moved so fast, I mean he came out of nowhere," Ingrid said.

"It's dark down there," I said. "Things can appear . . . different."

"I thought it was you or Alex," Ingrid said, "so I followed you down. But it was—"

"When I said make yourself at home I wasn't referring to the dungeons, Ingrid." I sighed.

"How embarrassing. Who the hell is he?" she asked.

"Orpheus," Alex said.

I glared at him—a warning not to reveal anything else. "He is an acquaintance of ours. He's a little . . . unruly."

"In what way?"

"He's a little crazy," Alex said.

"Does he have a criminal record?" Ingrid asked.

"Not exactly," I said.

"What's that supposed to mean?" Ingrid snapped.

"It means no. A drink. Alex, bring wine. No, something stronger," I said.

Ingrid's face flushed. "I'm so embarrassed."

"It wasn't your fault," I reassured her. "Come on, we'll go to the drawing room. I will make it up to you. I promise."

"I'm fine, I'll bounce back." Ingrid sighed.

I guided her out of the room. "Come on, let's go and get ourselves a stiff drink," I said.

"Perhaps some tea?" Alex offered, following.

I studied Alex, concerned that he too was shaken. He closed his thoughts to me before I could examine them.

I turned my attention back on to Ingrid. "I do hope this hasn't ruined your visit."

"Goodness, no," Ingrid said. "Before all this I was thoroughly enjoying myself. You have a lovely home. This place is huge. So many exquisite antiques. I adore antiques."

"Perhaps that's why we get on so well," I jested.

Ingrid did well to bluff her decorum. But I wasn't fooled. I was determined to extinguish Orpheus's dark spark.

We settled within the anteroom. I uncorked a bottle of Chateau Leoville-Loire 1972, pouring Ingrid a large glass, and watched her sip from the dark red vintage. Both Alex and I appeared to sip at ours and attempted to recall the taste.

Alex had purchased takeout. We both prodded our Chinese food as Ingrid, with her healthy appetite, devoured hers. As the evening progressed Ingrid relaxed, lulled by Alex's beautiful piano playing which he performed with his usual mastery. Alex even persuaded me to play several duets with him much to Ingrid's delight.

Soon the aged wine took its effect and she was lost in the semblance of the room, warmed by both the fine wine and the roaring fireplace. She sat on the luxurious leather couch, crystal glass in hand, absorbed in the music. Conversation flowed as we naturally wooed her.

As the midnight hour approached Alex made his excuses to retire to bed.

"Alex, you and I, we need to talk," I said.

Alex stared off.

"Later then?" I pushed for a response from him.

Alex nodded then left the room.

Conceding to Ingrid's request we headed out on another tour. On arriving within the armory I reached up and took down one of my old fencing sabers, easing it from its casing, and proceeded to provide Ingrid with a demonstration. I swung the fine epee this way and that as if masterfully dueling with an invisible opponent, moving forward with assured expertise, impressing Ingrid with my obvious skill.

Next we made our way toward the library. I took my time carefully selecting then removing from the tall shelves, one book and then another, using the stairs when needed to reach some of my most cherished. The leather-bound books were the oldest and most valuable within the collection, and most of them Ingrid noted were first additions and out of print. We fervently viewed the many pages, admiring the bindings and fine font, agreeing that books were no longer produced in such a unique fashion.

"I have a great collection of originals," I said. "Do you like Shakespeare?"

On seeing Ingrid's expression, I pretended I was joking.

Ingrid was drawn to me, her attraction as clear as mine was to her. She studied me, fascinated. Years of pretending to be human were paying off. This was a dangerous game I played and I questioned my motives for allowing her to get so close and see so much. However, my desire to be both accepted and feel affection was undeniable.

She reminisced about her encounter with the stranger in the dungeons. Orpheus's recondite effect upon her was no different from how it influenced anyone. His seductive ability had deeply affected her. Orpheus would draw his victims in, seducing them and then push them away, leaving them wanting. In order to protect Ingrid, I knew what I had to do—inflict such an indelible impression upon her that thoughts of me would push out all traces of Orpheus.

Taking her firmly by the hand, I led Ingrid down the stone

stairway to the lower chambers of the castle and into the darkest room. It had been many things—once a torture chamber and more recently a bedroom for Alex. Now it was just a clandestine four-walled chamber. Despite its darkness and chilly temperature, I hoped Ingrid would feel safe with me and nudged her inside. I lingered at the open doorway, pausing for a moment, reconsidering.

Take Ingrid home and then forget her.

I followed her in. "This room was used by my ancestors to subjugate witches and the like," I explained. "The accused were brought here to be tortured, part of a soul-cleansing ceremony. They were then taken to another place, one far from here, to be offered up in sacrifice."

Ingrid's eyes adjusted to what little light was in the room. "Where were they taken?"

"Stonehenge."

"They must have been terrified," she said.

"They were."

Ingrid explored. She noted the heavy wooden door, the only exit from the dark chamber, admiring its design. Carried by her imagination Ingrid observed me lighting the candles upon the altar and within the sconces. Flickering flames threw shadows. The arcane light danced on the central table.

"Look at this." She rubbed dust from the wall.

"What is it?" I asked.

"An inscription, see. Haven't you seen it before?" she asked.

"No, I've never noticed it. What does it say?" I wondered if Alex had written it as I did not recall seeing it.

Ingrid read the faded letters. "The truth will out."

"The truth will come out?" I repeated.

"It's a Northern expression, it means that . . . well I suppose it speaks for itself," she said.

I rubbed my fingers over the painted stone. "It's signed."

Ingrid and I studied the scribe.

"Fabian Snowstrom!" I read.

"Do you know him?"

"Yes, I know of him. But I . . ."

"What?"

"Nothing. It's nothing." It was not so much the fact that Fabian Snowstrom had written on the wall. It was the fact that the signature was dated last May. "Alex must have written it," I reasoned.

Ingrid peered down at the worn table positioned in the center of the room. The ancient ominous markings and deep scratches upon it indicated its age, its once-sinister use made obvious by the original chain shackles still hanging down from it. The room's eerie presence was intensified and heightened by the peeling paint on its walls and the low dark beams. I forced out thoughts of Snowstrom and focused once again on Ingrid. I stared at her, watching, waiting.

Ingrid strolled around the chamber, aware that something was looming. She ran her hands over the objects and furniture. When she was ready, I locked the door. I approached and kissed her passionately, embracing her firm, wanting nothing more than for this moment to last. Her taste was sweet, her softness soothing.

She is perfect.

Taking my time, I undressed her. Her pale naked body appeared so vulnerable and it made me want her more. Ingrid was shaking.

I hugged her again, kissing her until she softened into me. Her female scent arose and fired my senses. I undressed. Taking her hand I guided her to the central table and lifted her onto it, laying her down upon it. I caressed her nakedness, exploring her body with a gentle touch until her soft skin blushed.

Her gasps echoed . . .

I took her, crushing against her, responding to her every desire. She surrendered to my whispers as our bodies intertwined and immortal flesh embraced mortal skin.

* * * *

As I lay next to Ingrid, both of us spooned in my four-poster bed, I knew this was the last time I would ever see her. This relationship, whatever it was or whatever it had become, could not continue. Though fate had brought us together and I had relished the brief time I had spent with her, I had to let her go.

Anyone close to me would become a target for Orpheus and I was not prepared to let another woman be his victim. The last hour of darkness faded. I caressed Ingrid, kissing her tenderly, attempting to rebalance my previous domination of her.

Ingrid roused. "What time is it?"

"Go back to sleep. It's early." I kissed her shoulder.

Ingrid sighed and snuggled into me. "I'm so glad I got that postcard," she said. "I never did find out who sent it, but it led me to you, so—"

"What postcard?"

"The postcard of St. Catherine of Alexandria. Someone sent it to me anonymously."

"When?" My heart raced.

"The day I met you at the gallery. All it had was my name and a time on it." She yawned.

"It was probably sent by the gallery. They do that sometimes to tweak your interest," I lied.

I lulled Ingrid back to sleep and eased myself away from her side, careful not to awaken her. Once again I returned to the lower chambers with a knot in my stomach. Orpheus would be coming back for her. I had to get to him first.

✖✖✖

⊕RPHEUS

RAYS OF MORNING LIGHT gradually moved across Jadeon's bedroom and fell upon Ingrid's face. She recalled her time with him. He had revealed to her secret pleasures that still left her breathless. She snuggled under the covers, smelling his masculine scent on the bed linen. Reaching over for him, her heart sank when she realized Jadeon was no longer lying beside her.

She sat up and looked for him. She could not deny that it was... such a nocturnal life. Surely art could be discussed, bought, and sold during the day. Indeed the daylight would be more natural and appropriate for such things, but he was not here. A sound alien to this place distracted her. She recognized the loud beeping noise. Her pager was going off. She jumped out of bed and rummaged through her handbag. Ingrid peered at the number on her pager. Work had contacted her. Glancing around the room, she soon noticed the antique phone on a side table next to the bed and wondered if it actually worked.

"Hello sir, this is Jansen." She greeted her boss Detective Chief Inspector Vanderbilt.

"Jansen, I apologize for bothering you on your weekend off but we have a situation. We have a double homicide. Initially I assigned Bradford to the case but his health has taken a turn. I need you back in the office."

"I'm on my way. I'm in Cornwall, but I'll leave now and should be with you in four hours or so."

"I'll send a car," he said.

"Sounds perfect. The victims?"

"So far, two single females. It appears they didn't know each other from what we can tell, but we're still following up leads. It's nasty, Ingrid. Their bodies were discovered one night apart. One at Avebury, the other at Stonehenge, both tied to the stones."

"*The* Stonehenge?" Ingrid asked.

"There's only one Stonehenge, Ingrid."

Ingrid thought it uncanny she had just been speaking to Jadeon about rituals performed at the site.

"You still there?" Vanderbilt said.

* * * *

The police car sped along, blue light flashing. With little or no Sunday traffic at such an hour it easily reached the dizzying speed of over 110 mph on the clear motorway. Ingrid focused upon the first murder case, perusing the file intently.

Vanderbilt had emailed the case details to the squad car's onboard computer which he had arranged for her. The first victim, no older than twenty, had been tied to one of the stones and stripped completely naked. The girl's arms had been artfully restrained with what appeared to be white silk.

Such positioning reminded Ingrid of a painting by the old masters, one where females were portrayed as saints. Ingrid noted that the corpse was particularly pale. Opening the other file she recalled her conversation with Jadeon in reference to the witch's persecution. She was sure he had stated the women had been murdered in a sacrificial ceremony. Perhaps, she pondered, someone who believed in something similar caused these murders.

The second girl, whose photographs had been taken not twenty minutes ago, had been scanned from her boss directly from the crime scene. The victim had been strewn upon the large sandstone alter at the center of the tall pillars of Stonehenge. She, like the first girl, was bound as if in sacrifice and was similar in age and pallor.

Ingrid considered calling Jadeon but realized she had forgotten to take his phone number and wondered how she could contact him and apologize for her rapid exit. It would have to wait.

* * * *

The sanitized aroma of the morgue caused Ingrid to shudder. She hated this place. Ingrid had helped herself to a cup of coffee and a bagel placed in the communal staff room. Despite its staleness—probably left over from the previous morning—it tasted good.

Still eating her breakfast, coffee in hand, she headed toward the autopsy of the Stonehenge victim. Ingrid passed along the line of laboratories, pausing briefly at the desk directly outside the coroner's office and recognizing Zara, the pathologist's assistant. The young girl rested her legs up on the desk, totally engrossed in a magazine.

"I'm not allowed to start yet," Zara said.

"What's the delay?" Ingrid asked.

"We're waiting for you. Ellison's in there now working on his preliminaries. Oh and FYI, there's five rookie-student policemen who have come to view their first *post mortem*."

"Deep joy," Ingrid said dryly. "Who sanctioned that?"

"Your boss, Vanderbilt," Zara said.

Ingrid threw the remainder of her bagel in the waste bin and entered the chilly examination room, coffee in hand. A female corpse rested on the cold, stark central table. The five graduates were dressed in theatre scrubs. They viewed Ingrid wearily. Ingrid approached Dr. Ellison, the fifty-two year old short and stocky coroner.

"What have you got for me?" Ingrid did her best to avoid the gazes of the eager students.

"Coffee!" Ellison snapped his fingers, taking Ingrid's drink from her. He gulped it down, handing the empty cup back to her. "Ingrid, you'll be bringing your lunch in next." Ellison smiled and placed his small round glasses on.

"It's just that the smell of the coffee beans helps to . . ."

"Sterility has its disadvantages," Ellison said and pulled on his exam gloves. He leaned over the corpse and moved the girl's limbs this way and that, viewing her body carefully.

"Fingerprints have confirmed her identity," Ingrid began. She faced the police students and addressed them. "Purple highlights are unusual. Such a marker may help with tracking her movements." Ingrid pulled out her writing pad.

Ellison peered over his glasses. "So my Jane Doe is really a . . . ?"

"Gillian Stewart," Ingrid said. "Her fingerprints are in the system."

"What's her prior?"

"Arrested on a drug possession violation."

"Figures. Her prelim tox screen was positive for narcotics."

"T.O.D?" Ingrid asked.

"Judging by lividity and rigor mortis, she died approximately thirty or so hours before we even found her at Stonehenge."

"So two nights ago?"

"Approximately. With no primary crime scene and no witnesses, it's an educated guess, I'm afraid."

Ingrid made a notation.

"Her parents?" Ellison asked.

"Blake's there now," she said.

Ellison sighed. "Worst part of the job."

Ingrid shrugged.

"Look." Ellison pointed out to the eager crowd. "Track marks on both arms. She was into the hard stuff. Looks like she frequently mainlined. This girl moved in dangerous circles."

"Are those what I think they are?" Ingrid leaned in to the victim's neck area.

Ellison reexamined the four deep pinpoint puncture marks on the dead girl's neck. "And a Goth to boot."

Ingrid addressed the crowd again. "She's got what appears to be vampire bite marks, so she's possibly into role play."

"And it looks as if it may have been a big factor in her death," Ellison said. "From what I can tell, it looks like she's lost a lot of blood. We'll have more of an idea when I open her up and run a few more tests. There is a slim possibility her blood was drained from these marks. We'll take some specimen swabs and a wound cast to see if it gives us an indication of the weapon. I doubt they're fang marks, but they certainly look like that. I'll keep an open mind for now. No sign of sexual abuse."

"What instrument would you need to do this?" Ingrid asked, eyeing the punctures.

"Well perhaps . . . surgical in design, but blood clots quickly in a healthy person so it's unlikely."

"Is a drug addict compromised?"

"His or her clotting factor could be off, but . . ."

"Where else could she have lost the blood from if there are no other external puncture wounds other than these?"

"Time will tell. Science is our victim's advocate," Ellison said. "Ingrid, as soon as I have something substantial I'll call you." He pushed his round-rimmed glasses back up his nose.

"I wish I hadn't eaten that bagel now," Ingrid said.

"I brought those in for the staff two days ago."

She screwed up her nose.

Ellison placed his sharp knife to Gillian's chest and cut into her pale flesh.

Ingrid was amused by Zara, who stood close by and revved a

small powerful chain saw.

Two of the police officers fainted.

* * * *

Sipping on her third mug of coffee Ingrid scanned the reports once more, readying herself for the Salisbury Police Unit briefing. A provisional psychological profile had been completed and would be imminently presented.

"Everyone's here, ma'am," Sgt. Blake said.

"How's Inspector Bradford holding up?" Ingrid asked.

"He's in ICU. Apparently he's lost a lot of blood and they're trying to determine from where," Sgt. Blake said.

"Oh my goodness. What happened?"

"Well he has all sorts of health problems," Blake said. "So it's probably his ulcer, but they're running more tests and he's scheduled for an MRI this afternoon."

"Send my regards to his family, will you?"

"Will do, ma'am. Looks like you're the it-girl. I hear the case is all yours."

Detective Chief Inspector Vanderbilt began the briefing. Ingrid looked around, confirming the criminal forensic team, the senior forensic psychologist, and her other police colleagues were present.

"So far," Ingrid raised her voice for the benefit of the crowd, "Dr. Ellison's findings indicate that both girls were drained of blood. We're awaiting test results to ascertain more. Excessive blood loss is the confirmed cause of death. We have primary sites, still unknown as place of death, and secondary, where the girls were dumped after death.

"As you are aware, the first girl found at Avebury was nineteen-year-old Tabitha Web. Tabitha left home at seventeen, and as far as we can tell spent most of her time in London staying with friends until she disappeared from a friend's flat in Notting Hill three days before her murder.

"She had a history of drug abuse. The drug use is the only connection we have between the two girls. Gillian Stewart is our second victim, twenty-one years in age with one prior for dealing and using. Similar story—left home, went to live in London, and then disappeared off the face of the earth until she turned up dead at Stonehenge today.

"Neither girl was sexually assaulted though they were sexually active. The blood test results also indicated they both took the pill, so we know that they probably visited a doctor's clinic.

"The blood tests confirm death by hemorrhage. Their hemoglobin had dropped to untraceable, bearing in mind the average female hemoglobin is 12-16 mg/dl. We are looking for small instruments used to make minute puncture marks. We have no other leads, no other clues, no fingerprints at the scene or on the bodies. Whoever committed these crimes is astute at covering up their tracks. Any questions?"

"Yes, ma'am," Sgt. Blake said. "Were there really no footprints at Stonehenge?"

"Blake, I'm as baffled as you all are considering there is so much mud at Stonehenge. It's difficult to comprehend, but forensics insist."

Ingrid nodded to Dr. Agatha Wright and invited her to the front of the room.

Dr. Wright, with laptop prepared, began her presentation. "Hi, everyone. I think I know everyone here—a few new faces. So for your benefit, I'm your assigned forensic psychologist. I look forward to working with many of you again and some of you for the first time. Right, down to business shall we?

"To recap, in the last two nights we have had two murders at two separate sacred sites. Two innocent looking—but not—girls drained of their blood. The first strung up, the second laid down, both posed in respectful, somewhat sexual positions, naked."

She flicked on the computer projector switch, throwing a wall-sized image of the first dead girl tied to the stone. "If you look carefully she is positioned so that she appears asleep, not dead—her features calm, her long hair covering her body, staged as if in a painting or as an object of art.

"We are presented with images of beauty, possibly indicating the killer's intelligence. Second image, again an ancient monument is chosen, the girl now lying down, perhaps reflecting the first. Positioned arms down by her sides, legs together indicating dignity, but again her nakedness proves her vulnerability.

"These are complex and contradictory images. They appear as messages but they are difficult to decipher. We believe we are looking for two, perhaps three young males working together. A female's involvement is possible. Their ages probably range from early twenties to late thirties. They are educated, possibly employed, and have a creative background—someone involved with art.

"Chances are they have no priors. We are looking for individuals with egos. These are high-profile murders, so the culprits crave the spotlight. I wonder if this is a cult killing, these sites indicating sacrifices to the gods, or God. Let us first review Avebury, a Neolithic monument, a large prehistoric tomb on the highest man-made hill in Europe, and with the most extensive hedge enclosure.

"Are the criminals sending us a message, perhaps of both human frailty but at the same time indicating the worth of that human? Now we move to Stonehenge. This monument predicts the dates of the lunar eclipse. The principal axis of the monument is oriented in order to take advantage of the direction of the sunrise at summer solstice.

"Incidentally this falls on or around June 20 and 21. See a pattern here? The first girl was killed on the 19th at Avebury, the second at Stonehenge on the 20th, and tomorrow, June the 21st, there may well be another murder on or close to these sites. In approximately ten hours, thousands will be gathered at Stonehenge for the summer solstice. As always, time is an issue.

"Interestingly enough, bloodletting was used in rituals up until the early twentieth century. We saw this with the fossilized remains of humans found in the bogs all over Europe. We believe that the draining of their blood is also linked to their locations. Therefore, we are looking for a group of men or women who are perhaps copying these ancient rituals. They may even practice satanic worship or a form of witchcraft.

"So as you see, I am offering very little in the way of a refined lead. All I can say is I'm sure they will strike again and the victim will be another young girl, bled out and placed at one of our many places of heritage. My only suggestions are to place guards on these areas and hope that we get a lead this way. We can also investigate, as Jansen has suggested, the locations where the young Goths and pseudo-vampires hang out."

Ingrid stepped forward. "Blake's all over the web and Smith is working with the Metropolitan police. I will handle the press. We are starting with the girls' last whereabouts. As it's London, the Met police are on it. We believe we are looking for a club or group of individuals from London. Satanic rituals, however, are practiced predominantly in Scotland and Cornwall, so we are sending limited resources to local covens."

"Witchcraft is heavily-practiced in these areas," Sgt. Blake offered. "They tend to be more peaceful in nature though they may have important information that may assist us."

"Thanks Blake," Ingrid said. "There is another possible lead. We've had reports from two local hospitals that units of blood were stolen from their laboratories. The first, the local hospital in Avebury; the second—and just before the second murder—a break in at Salisbury

General. Only blood was taken, blood used in patient transfusions.

"We believe there is a possible connection. Staff have been alerted and hospital security heightened. We are also going to expend some resources investigating these activities. We meet back tomorrow unless something pressing arises."

Sgt. Blake raised his hand. "Perhaps if we installed security cameras in the blood banks? Who knows, the cult members may be using the blood as part of their ritual."

"Great idea, Blake, make it happen," Ingrid said.

XXXI

JADEON

DEEP IN THOUGHT, hands in pockets, I loomed in the shadowy alley opposite Belshazzar's, waiting for Alex. We had arranged to meet just outside the club at midnight. That way we could watch out for each other. After several long discussions, I had deemed Alex ready. However, having no need for time keeping, Alex was not particularly good at it. And after thirty minutes of observing the club's regulars arriving I doubted he would show up. Perhaps the thought of seeing Orpheus again had put him off the idea.

Someone lingered behind me. I spun round to face Marcus and several of his minions.

"It's addictive, isn't it?" he said.

"If you're referring to the club, then no," I said.

"Orpheus sends his regards."

"What is it that you want, Marcus?"

"I have a message for you."

"What is it this time?" I asked.

"He's paying her a visit. He was wondering whether—"

"Ingrid!"

Marcus peered past me and stared over my shoulder. "Snowstrom?" he said.

I spun round and followed his gaze. In the shadows at the end of the alley was a tall man, dressed in a priest's attire, who stared back at us with piercing blue eyes.

"Who is that?" I asked and turned to face Marcus again.

Marcus and his men were gone.

I stared back to view the priest.

He too was gone.

"Fabian?" I echoed into the night.

Whoever he was he had rattled Marcus.

With no time to search for the mysterious priest I flew toward Ingrid's flat, fearing for her safety. With concentrated thoughts my mind studied Ingrid's home. I viewed the apartment with clarity.

Orpheus watched over Ingrid while she slept. He had been tracking her. If unable to follow her himself during daylight hours, he arranged for his mortal devotees to.

Orpheus closed his mind to me.

Waves of anxiety threw me into a panic. I shot through Ingrid's sitting room window toward her. Hearing me enter, Ingrid awoke. I skidded and caught myself seconds before stumbling into her bedroom. She leapt out of bed and peered into the sitting room. Orpheus had disappeared before Ingrid had even caught sight of him.

Upside down I clung from the light fixture suspended from her ceiling, staring down at Ingrid as she walked about the room.

Do not look up.

Ingrid checked both the kitchen and her front door, reassured not to find anything out of place. The phone's shrill ring almost sent me hurtling. Ingrid answered the call and spoke rapidly into the handset, her expression stressed.

"Where is he now?" Ingrid asked the caller. "Keep him locked up until I get there." She headed into her bedroom to get dressed.

She was talking about Alex and my grip loosened on overhearing that he was imprisoned back in Ingrid's station. With sweaty palms my grasp slipped and I swayed on the fixture. Where the light was secured into the wall, cracks appeared in the ceiling. Dust fell into my eyes, hinting that the light was about to give way. A jolt confirmed my fear.

Ingrid passed beneath me and a sprinkle of dust trailed behind her. Without noticing she headed out of the apartment.

I did a back flip and landed on the floor. I hesitated at the window, moments before exiting, astonished by the book titles strewn on Ingrid's coffee table and disconcerted that all referred to vampires. Several beige folders lay nearby and I peeked inside those too, dismayed by the content of the police files. Ingrid was investigating vampire-style murders.

Within minutes I had followed Ingrid to Salisbury Police Divisional Headquarters on Wilton Road. I flew past the guards, making a discreet leap toward Alex's jail undetected and tapped on his door. The place was awful, and it was terrible to bear the thought he was in here.

"Jadeon!" Alex jumped off the prison bunk and peered through the door's grate.

"Shush." I checked for the guards. "What the hell happened?"

"I couldn't do it anymore. I can't bear their thoughts," Alex said.

"You're not making any sense," I snapped.

"I heard it was possible to get blood."

"Alex?"

"The hospitals, they extract it for humans. And they—"

"Who told you about such a thing?"

He peered sheepishly through the bars.

"Alex, haven't you learnt by now . . . ?"

"Get me out of here."

I subdued my fury. "I'm working on it. What happened?"

"I was taking a unit of blood from the—"

"Dear God!"

"I got attacked by this burly security man. He had this taser thing and zapped me."

"Are you hurt?"

"No, please don't be angry," he said.

"Sometimes, you just need to—"

"What's the time?"

"I'll get you out of here before dawn, okay?"

"Your word?"

I nodded. "Look, you need to know that Ingrid is working on a murder case. It's connected somehow to the blood you stole."

"How?"

I turned to see Ingrid advancing toward me.

"Jadeon?" she called out. "How did you get in here past the guards?"

"Ingrid, there's been some mistake. Alex—"

"You didn't answer my question," she said.

"Perhaps that's a question for your men," I said.

She rested her hands on her hips. "Look, I need to interview him. I know this is difficult for you. It's difficult for me. I'm seriously considering handing him over to a colleague to interview because of our . . ."

"Relationship?"

"Friendship," she said.

"There's been a mistake," I said, "but let him out and I won't take this any further."

"No mistake has been made." Ingrid frowned.

"Ingrid, you must listen to me."

"He's a suspect in a murder case. I could get into a lot of trouble for just talking with you. Look, I'm sure this is some huge misunderstanding and we're going to sort it all out. However, you have to let me do my job. Okay?"

"Ingrid," I whispered, "surely after everything that you and I—"

"Don't you go there, Jadeon."

I lowered my voice. "Perhaps if I could invite you back to—"

"You're trying my patience now."

I was shocked at her response. "I need to get my brother out of this place. How do I do that?"

"Step away from the cell and come with me."

"Ingrid, I'm not negotiating with you. I am telling you that my brother—"

"He's part of a bigger investigation. Alex is not going anywhere tonight."

"No."

"Unless the murderer himself turns up and confesses tonight with corroborating evidence, your brother—"

"There must be something else?"

"Look, I know this is difficult for you." She softened. "Here's what I'm going to do. I'll start the process with the paperwork for Alex's bail and as soon as I can legally release him, I will."

"It's not enough, I need to do . . ."

"Get Alex a lawyer. I'm sorry I can't do more. I've probably said too much already."

* * * *

I was panicked. It was hard to think straight but I had to move fast.

I lingered in the dark alley in the center of the old Salisbury town, not caring who she would be. I just needed a body. The tipsy girl walked alone, her provocative appearance confirming her prostitution and her drugged-out face gave away her death wish.

I followed her.

Covering her mouth I dragged her into the dark passageway, pulling her along, giving her no time to react. The alcohol deadened her senses and made it easy to penetrate her mind.

She was seventeen.

With shame I let her go and pushed her back into the street. Stunned, she staggered off, not quite sure what had just happened. I withdrew into the shadows and leant against the wall of a house, feeling monstrous. With no time to feel sorry for myself, I mustered the strength to return to the police station on Wilton Road.

I leapt onto the police station's roof in order to gather my thoughts. It would be easy to break down Alex's cell door and expedite his release, but not only would we both be on England's most-wanted list, we would lose the castle. It was imperative we did not arouse any more suspicion then we already had.

Was it too late for that now?

From my position the police mortuary was within easy view. With a leap I made it onto the side of the building. I yanked at the surveillance camera's wires, disabling them. Checking to see the place was deserted I headed into the parking lot and quickly found Ingrid's black Honda Civic parked in her personal space. I pulled up the hood and ripped at the engine wiring. Moving swiftly, I proceeded toward the coroner's green Range Rover and did the same to his. With that accomplished I scaled the wall of the coroner's building.

Halfway up the five-story building, I spotted a window ajar and scurried up the wall until I rested at the window ledge. With a shove the glass frame gave, enabling me to climb through. Following the deathly scent down the stairs, I was soon standing in the macabre presence of the cold storage room where layer upon layer of closed shelves housed the recently deceased.

Thanks, Alex.

Searching the contents of the huge mortuary fridge, opening the long drawers one by one, I found her—Gillian Stewart, her flock of purple hair a harsh reminder of when I had been trapped with her in that room back at Belshazzar's. I slid her corpse out of the chamber and wrapped her cold limp body in a white linen gown, disturbed by the deep incision marks—the telltale signature of the coroner. I lifted her onto my shoulder and returned with my find to the window, cringing in response to her head pounding against my back.

Ingrid wanted another body, so I would give her one.

On arriving at Stonehenge I hid amongst the trees and lay the dead girl down, noting the several police officers guarding the site.

Relying on my unearthly nature to see me through I took out the guards one by one, leaving them to sleep where they fell, reassured with the knowledge they would awaken with no recollection of tonight's events. At the center of the stones I placed Gill's body onto the stony altar. It was strange to imagine she would not leap up and start cursing me as she had done back at the club. I hated Orpheus for doing this to her. Taking advantage of her desperate need, seducing her in with empty promises. He was evil incarnate.

I found one of the guard's radios and made a call. My thoughts wandered in the fractured stillness.

Sirens blaring signaled their arrival. Following protocol, the first police officers on the scene covered Gill's corpse with a sterile plastic covering.

Ingrid soon followed. I could see her clearly, despite her distance. With her usual self-assurance she climbed out of the police car. I winced, aware that the woman I had grown so fond of would soon be standing over the dead girl. Despite the fact that it was her job, it felt wrong. I considered myself Ingrid's friend, but now she was close to discovering my secret. I was heavyhearted at having failed her.

She headed toward the stones, her oversized boots slugging in the deep black mud. Turning on her flashlight, she stopped at the perimeter. Her colleagues had sealed off the area with a yellow strip of tape around the periphery of the stones. She gazed past this in awe at the megalithic monument.

Ingrid flashed her ID to a young police officer who stood guard.

"It's her," he said.

"Who?" Ingrid said.

"Hey, Ingrid, wait up!" A short, tubby, out-of-breath man hurried toward her, pulling on a white forensic suit with 'Coroner' stamped on the back in bold letters. He had arrived just behind Ingrid. "Is it true you had car trouble, too?"

"Hi, Ellison. Yes I did. I hitched a lift with Blake," Ingrid answered with a quizzical expression. "*And* you had a car problem, as well? That's a freaky coincidence?"

Together they ducked under the tape, joining the other officers and lingering a few feet away from the central stone.

"This shouldn't have happened," Ingrid said. "Blake's searching for the guards we posted. Where the hell are they?"

"Good point." Ellison pulled his surgical gloves onto his hands. "This town doesn't get a murder for years, then three young women murdered this week. I wonder if she's been bled out like the others. Looks like the same positioning as the other girl."

"I thought we had the suspect, but now I'm not so sure. He's been in lock-up back at the station so his alibi is solid," Ingrid said.

Ellison stared at the stone structure. "Truly remarkable."

Ingrid followed his gaze. "Is it true that they still don't know how they got those larger stones to lie on top of the others?"

"Lintels. Yep, still a mystery," Ellison said.

"I'm ready." Ingrid took the examination gloves Ellison offered, handing him her flashlight before pulling the gloves onto each hand. They both huddled over the body, barely protected from the rain by the umbrella held by the nervous young police officer at their side. Ingrid eased back the plastic covering placed over the corpse.

They jolted back.

"Bloody hell!" Ellison dropped the flashlight. "Ingrid, this is—"

"Yes, I recognize her. But how the hell did she get back here?" Ingrid glanced at the left side of the girl's neck.

"Well, she didn't bloody walk here!" Ellison snapped.

Ingrid looked around for the police officer who had tried to warn her. "Why did they bring her back here?"

"How and who?" Ellison fumbled for the dropped flashlight.

"These are sick minds."

"Shameful." Ellison ran his gloved fingers over the girl's face.

"Who placed her in the mortuary fridge?"

"That'll be me," Ellison said. "So far, I'm seeing no indication of further injury."

"What motivates someone to do this?"

"Good luck with that one."

"She's positioned identically to when we found her before. Where are the bloody guards?" Ingrid searched the horizon. "Heads will roll."

"We'll have to work fast before the elements compromise our evidence."

"Let's hope forensics gets something this time." Ingrid frowned. "My men had strict orders: Do not leave your post. Do not take your eyes off the stones."

"This is a first for me."

"What? Guards going AWOL?" Ingrid asked.

"No. Well, yes, and someone snatching a body."

"What a mess." Ingrid studied the female and surveyed the surrounding area. "As soon as forensics have worked their magic we'll get her straight back to the morgue." Ingrid removed her gloves. "I'm hoping your second post mortem will give us something. I'll have our cars fingerprinted, and then we're going to have a good look at your mortuary."

Ellison wiped the rain off his glasses. "The good news is we're back down to two bodies. The bad news . . ."

"Go on."

"The press will have a bloody field day!"

Ingrid backed away from the body, deep in thought. She stopped in her tracks. "Oh, my God!" She dialed her mobile phone. "Do not let Alex Artimas out. What? What are you talking about? What just happened?" She slammed her phone shut. "I'm going to need more men." Ingrid stomped through the rain.

Something had gone wrong.

I turned toward Salisbury, heading for Alex.

Unseen and unheard, they descended upon me, my capture fast and furious. A black hood was shoved over my head, rendering me incapable of fighting back. Through muffled screams, I yelled for Alex.

XXXII

⊕RPHEUS

THE MAGNIFICENT SALISBURY CATHEDRAL tower loomed crookedly in the sky. An entourage entered via the front, unlocked as it always was, guarded at night by one lone vampire. They dragged Jadeon to the rear of the church and down to the lower catacombs. Once inside the dark secret chamber they removed his hood. Jadeon recognized the room. He had hidden here just after I had transformed him.

"*Deja vu*, Jadeon," I said and checked my watch.

"Orpheus, Alex, you must listen."

"Ah, I doubt even I could make such a flight now."

He struggled frantically. "I promised him . . ."

"You have murdered him."

"No!"

My men held him.

"I share your pain," I said.

"No. Not this time, not this way."

"Choose. Catherine or Alex," I said.

"What?"

"Who do you choose to live, Catherine or Alex? Time is of the essence, so—"

"No!" he screamed.

"Sorry, so much noise in the room I didn't hear you. Say again?"

"Why? Why do you . . . ?"

"Habit, I suppose. Now which one?"

"Let me go to him."

"I see," I said. "Wait." I placed my hand to my temple and closed my eyes. "No, I fear the worst. Prepare yourself. Your brother Alex is . . . dead. Yes, not so much a snapping of his mortal coil. More like a disintegration of it."

Jadeon fell forward, glaring at me, shattered. "You lie to me again. I don't believe—"

"Who was it, Jadeon, who asked him to wait? Who was it who promised to return to free him? He trusted you. Go back to your bleak castle. It's over, and you're once again the cause of your own grief."

"I beg of you," he said.

"If you want to join me, if the loneliness becomes too great, come to me."

"Never!"

"The time for mortals is running out. It's now time for us to take our rightful place. We will no longer hide within the shadows."

"What are you planning?"

"Members only," I said.

"I could never be part of any of your dark schemes, and I will do everything within my power to stop you. You are Satanic."

"Satan had his chance but failed. I'm something altogether different."

"I will kill you!"

"Catherine. She'll be interested to hear that you chose Alex over her."

Jadeon was thrown into a corner. I strolled through the open doorway, my immortals trailing closely, and the door was slammed shut. We headed into the darkened vehicle that awaited us. Jadeon pulled himself to his feet and banged at the door. It was locked. He turned and slid down the wall.

* * * *

Patient though anxious, Alex paced. He had promised Jadeon that he would not do anything untoward but await his brother's return. He had almost succeeded with his venture to steal the blood, actually holding the plastic container within his hands. The scent of it had first stirred his appetite when removed from the fridge but the coldness of it had suppressed his desire. He had lingered in the hospital basement looking down at the unappetizing blood. So engrossed with his thoughts on whether to abandon his venture he hardly noticed the uniformed mortals until they had descended upon him. They had attacked him using an electric device, sending waves of excruciating pain through his body and rendering him unconscious.

I sent in my finest. Three well-dressed gentlemen entered the police station at 0355, all distinguished lawyers familiar with the environment in which they now stood. The senior of the three spoke to the police receptionist.

"We represent Lord Alexander Artimas. We believe he is to be released within the hour. We have come to complete the paperwork and ensure his bail. Who is the officer in charge of this case?"

"Hello, sir," the young intimidated police officer answered. "That would be Inspector Jansen, but I'm afraid she's not here. Sergeant Rutledge is in charge of the holding cells. I'll get him for you."

The lawyer backed away from the reception desk, whispering to his colleagues, causing the police officer to feel even more worried. She phoned down to Sergeant Rutledge, asking for his presence at the reception desk immediately.

The lawyers were guided down the steps toward the department where their client was held. Expediting all paperwork they ensured his immediate release. They could hear him within, frantically struggling to break down the door.

Approaching Alex's cell the senior lawyer spoke again, his colleagues at his side. "Calm yourself, Alex," he whispered. "We are here to take you home. All is well now. A car awaits you outside."

The door was unlocked and opened.

Alex burst out of the cell toward them. "Where is Jadeon?"

Alex was guided through the police station to the waiting car parked outside the front of the building. He leapt into the long limousine, avoiding the rising of the sun by a fraction. Swiftly, too afraid to use caution in movement, not caring if he was seen or not, he jumped into the long black coffin that lay within the limousine and shut down the lid, blocking all light. Alex was safe.

The three lawyers joined him within the car, sitting comfortably upon the leather seats, resting their feet on the lid of the coffin, their client secured within it.

*****

After her third cup of coffee, Ingrid made her way to face her boss's inquisition in his office—question after question about why their only suspect had been released. Her first warning had been given. One more bad decision and she would be suspended. Though she believed mitigating circumstances had led to the confusion, she was reluctant to relay such information. She took full responsibility for the error that she promised to put right.

Ingrid left his office deeply troubled. It was now 0645, and she was exhausted. She had been unable to fathom why the second murdered girl would have been replaced at Stonehenge. With most cases she had been able to at least grasp some reason, some underlying influence that made a criminal act in such a way—hate, anger, self-defense, or just plain evil.

However, this case left her bewildered. She could see no motivation or sense how the criminal's mind worked. She would have to completely rely on the forensic psychologists. Ingrid's beeping pager pulled her out of her harried state. The forensic scientists working on her case were requesting her presence.

Ingrid entered the laboratory, struck immediately by that old familiar sterility. She was directed toward the lab's darkroom where she found Andrew, the department's senior technician, peering through a microscope, engrossed. Ingrid tapped him on the shoulder and he looked up.

"What have you got for me?" Ingrid said. "Fingerprints?"

"No, ma'am."

"Footprints?"

"Err . . . no."

"Andrew! A strand of hair? Blood?"

"Nope."

"And why are you working in here?" she asked him.

"Look at this." Andrew directed Ingrid's attention to two slides, one placed under the microscope, the other by its side. "These are some of the cells taken from both the girls' neck areas, the wound or puncture sites where we believe their blood was drained from their bodies. They are like nothing we have ever seen. They're human but they've mutated in some way. Take a look yourself."

"So, Andrew, what have you found?" Ingrid closed her left eye, peering down the long microscope with her right. She could make out what appeared to be cells. She watched in amazement their frantic movement upon the slide. "They're still alive! That's not possible, is it?"

"Yes, ma'am. I mean, no. I've never seen anything like this before. We'll give you a demonstration. That's the only way we can explain it. Now, with no support system—i.e. the human body—cells die within minutes. But these cells, which have an abnormal molecular structure, are still alive without a support system. You're not going to believe what kills them," Andrew said, his two colleagues gathering around, waiting for Ingrid's reaction.

"Okay, give it to me. What kills them?" Ingrid attempted to look enthusiastic for his sake. Andrew had obviously been working hard all night.

"Well, Laura and I used everything. We isolated a few and tried anything and everything that would kill cells instantly, or at least change their structure. Then—and this is the spooky bit—when daylight flooded the lab, all of the cells on the slide died."

"What are you saying?" she asked. "Light?"

"We believe so."

"Ultraviolet?" she asked.

"Yep."

"You're saying daylight alone killed these cells?"

"Yes, the only thing," he replied, looking excited.

"Hence you're working in here."

He nodded.

"So what you're saying is that whatever these cells came from can only live at night? The moment daylight comes around they have to avoid the light or they'll die. Oh, bloody hell, you complete bastards! You know this is a vampire-style murder. I am too exhausted for such crap."

"Ingrid, we know how this looks. That's why we called you here. Now these are the same cells but taken from the second girl. Again they were found in the wound on the neck. The cells are an exact match to the first ones gathered the night before from the first victim. They haven't been exposed to the light yet."

"If you're pissing with me, I'll be so mad." Ingrid studied his expression.

"There is a condition called porphyria cutanea—PCT, for short," Andrew said. "It's a genetic disease resulting in abnormal pigments in the skin. Those who suffer with this condition are extra-sensitive to light. If the sunlight touches them, their skin blisters terribly. They usually are anemic. Therefore, their bodies crave iron, even blood. In fact, theorists believe it's what the vampire myth is based on.

"Perhaps this is somehow related to that, maybe it's a more serious strain. There may even be some evidence of cerebral damage, leading to delirium. Who knows? Of course, we'll know more when you catch the murderer."

"But Andrew, surely if our guy was delirious he wouldn't have the sense not to leave evidence. I mean, no fingerprints, footprints, or any other forensic evidence other than this?"

"It's not within the norm."

"Do these porphyria cells react in the same way until struck by light?"

"Um, no. In fact, they're a lot more fragile."

"Back to square one."

"Maybe it's a similar condition," he said.

"Okay. I suppose we could contact doctors in the Salisbury area to find out if any of them have ever treated anyone with this disease or another similar one. Perhaps it's a mutant strain or something. Now show me the cells' reaction to light."

"Take a seat and keep your eye on the screen up there," Andrew said.

Ingrid sat on the stool positioned at the workbench, watching as Andrew worked around her. He extracted the cells from the small glass tube and with detailed precision placed them upon the slide. Ingrid stared up at the screen watching the perfectly formed oscillating cells. They quivered on the glass slide. Andrew opened the door and light flooded in.

Ingrid watched the screen carefully. The cells, which had first appeared so vibrant, now withered. One by one, their matter became almost invisible under the microscopic lens.

Ingrid was astonished. "What the . . . ?"

"Something out there is an anomaly. We are wary of professional ridicule as much as the next person, but off the record," Andrew pointed to the specimen, "if you told me those blood cells came from a vampire, I would believe you."

* * * *

Ingrid's head spun. She left the lab and headed back over to the library. She gathered all the books they had on cults, vampires, Stonehenge, and Avebury, receiving strange looks from the librarian. She had to smile at the librarian's remarks about her being a closet Goth.

Ingrid hoped this reading material would provide her with insight into how an individual believing himself to be a vampire would behave. She was desperate. After a phone call, Sgt. Blake picked her up from outside the library, glancing wearily at her collection of books but saying nothing. They headed south.

The journey to Cornwall was uneventful. The police car's blue light flashed, warning other drivers to move out of the way, allowing them to get there quickly. Ingrid slept a little. She had closed her eyes, sunglasses on in the front passenger seat, navigating only when nudged. The journey was somber, so different from when she had ridden this road only a few days before. She was determined to return to Salisbury with Alex, and it troubled her he would be restrained in handcuffs.

XXXIII

JADEON

CONSIDERING WAYS IN WHICH to kill myself, I tried to imagine which would be least painful. Without Alex, life would be unbearable. A familiar presence distracted me from my suicidal thoughts.

Ingrid was here.

Upon arrival at the castle she had found the tide still out and guided Sergeant Blake along the path on the causeway. She instructed him to search around the castle walls giving her the opportunity to enter the castle alone.

Ingrid had easily picked the antique lock, a skill she had learned at the academy. She began her search with the bedrooms, looking for any sign we were home. Making her way up the sweeping staircase, she remembered how she had been in awe during her first visit. Even now she gazed in wonder at the many paintings and perfectly preserved antiquities. Ingrid entered my bedroom, looking for any evidence to suggest I had recently been here.

Hold me.

Everything appeared to be in its place. The bed had not been slept in since she rested there. Leaving my room, she walked toward my father's old bedroom where she had stayed. Ingrid noticed the light within the castle was dimming with the setting sun. Making her way down the stairway to the dungeons, she had mixed memories from when she last explored this part of the castle.

Flickering candle flames beckoned her. Ingrid walked away from the cells, following another smaller passageway toward the shadowy light. Squinting, she attempted to see. Aware of an eerie presence, she realized the danger she was placing herself in.

She kept close to the wall, trying to blend in at the end of the arcane corridor. Ingrid continued, impatient to find what was on the other side of the door. As her fingers touched the handle . . .

I pulled open the door.

She screamed and leapt back.

"Bloody hell! You shouldn't creep up on people like that," she said.

"Excuse me?" I snapped. "This is my home. I'll creep around in it all I want."

She followed me into the darkened room, maintaining a little distance.

I hunched in the shadows.

Ingrid's eyes adjusted. "Why are you hiding in here?"

Silence.

"Jadeon?" she said.

"Get out, please."

"We need to discuss—"

"I can't talk."

"What happened?"

I glared at her. "I warned you to let him go."

"Jadeon?"

"Alex." His name caught in my throat.

"Where is he?" she said.

"What?"

"Alex?"

I studied her. "What happened last night?"

"I know your lawyers expedited his release."

"What lawyers?"

"Are you telling me those lawyers weren't sent by . . . ?"

I sprang to my feet. "Who are you talking about?"

"Alex was released from the holding cell about an hour after you left. Three men, all lawyers, took him out of the police station. I thought you knew about it."

"Did Alex leave before dawn?"

"Why, yes."

"Orpheus!" I kissed her and then vanished.

XXXIV

⊕RPHEUS

I POSITIONED ALEX'S coffin in the corner of the lavishly decorated room within Belshazzar's.

He climbed out disoriented and stumbled around, looking for clues that would reveal his whereabouts. Alex heard the faint beat of music. He detected other vampires looming and caught the subtle aroma of blood. Unsurprised to find the door locked, he searched for another exit but found none. He heard a key turn in the lock.

I entered.

Alex glared at me. "Your ruse almost got me killed."

"Now why would I trap you then free you? What sense is there in that?" I gestured sincerely.

"Where is Jadeon?"

"With Ingrid." I reached for the blood-filled decanter and poured us both a drink. I handed one of them to Alex.

He was hungry.

Alex sniffed the glass. Tentatively, he sipped. His eyes fixed on me. "How long do you intend to keep me here?"

"Is that the thanks I get?"

"Yes."

"And to think there used to be a time when you couldn't wait to see me."

"Two hundred years ago," Alex snapped.

"I brought you here so that you will not be alone."

"I'm not."

"He has transformed Ingrid. She is now one of us."

"You lie."

"I will not allow you to lock yourself up in that dark place, alone again while he wanders the world."

"I do not believe—"

"Alex, I admit I have at times been a little harsh but you have always known my feelings for you. I would never hurt you. I adore you. You are everything in this world that is good and right. Perfection itself. There is a change in your circumstances and I wish to extend to you my friendship, a home here with me."

"Why should I want to be with you? You have killed my father, tormented—"

"It's time you knew the truth. Your brother does not always tell you everything. He keeps you in the dark on many things. Remember how as young men he failed to tell you how he had become your father's apprentice and how he was chosen over you? He came to you a vampire and left you alone and vulnerable in order to find Catherine. He still considered himself to be a Stone Master. He visits Stonehenge and drinks from the innocent, reveling in the pleasure of slaughtering mortals. He drinks from the pure and perfect—from angels—and you drink from the damned. Do you see a pattern emerging here? Do you want proof?"

"Jadeon has never drunk from the innocent," Alex said, attempting to interpret my mind's messages. "Jadeon will explain."

"While your brother travels the world, explores the pleasures and revels within them, I offer you the life you've always wanted. Let me take away your loneliness and fill you up with passion. We are powerful allies."

Alex gazed at me. His world was falling apart. The fear of being alone terrified him.

"He never once returned to the castle in two hundred years. Does that not strike you as strange?"

"He was searching for—"

"Please, don't let that old lie ruin another two hundred years of your life."

"What?"

"Must I be the one to tell you?" I said.

"Tell me what?"

"Catherine told Jadeon that she . . ."

"He spoke with her? No, these are more lies and—"

"Dear God, he never told you?" I said.

"Told me what?"

"That he was so saddened she rejected him he slept for one hundred of those years. All the time you were waiting for him, he slept comfortably in an ancient tomb. Oblivious to you or your needs."

"No, he never . . ."

"If I had not sent my men, you would be ash."

"I can't think straight."

"And I don't expect you to. I want you to rest here. You are free to go anytime you want. See, the door is unlocked."

"Daumia, I . . ."

"It's a cruel twist that you get arrested for the murders your brother committed."

"I will never trust you."

"Consider this. In my world, the pleasures will overwhelm you. Every day you will live in a vampiric bliss and you will finally be rewarded for everything you are. No longer ridiculed by your brother, you will stand proudly alongside me."

Alex closed his eyes.

"Jadeon will be fine. He will live as he plans to, making a new life with Ingrid while you make a new one with me."

Alex stared off.

"Now come, I have a gift," I said. "Let me show it to you."

"I'm not going anywhere with you."

"Catherine wishes to speak with you," I offered.

"Where are we going?"

"Down," I said and guided him out of the room along a whitewashed corridor and toward the open elevator. I stepped into it and waited.

He hesitated. I pulled him in.

Alex leaned against the elevator wall nervously rubbing his hands together.

I placed my hands over his to calm him. "Yes, I can hear your every thought," I said. "So be careful what you wish for, as I may just go ahead and give it to you."

"Haven't you become bored of me yet, Daumia?" he said.

"No, and I never will."

The lift stopped and we strolled down another dimly lit corridor. We passed room after room, stopping finally at one of the many identical doors. We entered. Alex cringed at the young female sitting in the corner. The well-dressed woman appeared calm.

"No," Alex said.

"No, she's not for that," I whispered. "I thought you might be thirsty. I feel your need and I'm concerned."

Alex lowered his voice, self-conscious. "I don't feed like this. I never drink from . . . Daumia, why is she so calm?"

The woman responded to my gesture and drew toward Alex, gazing at him, smiling. In a seductive gesture she pulled her hair back, revealing her neck, offering. He stared longingly at her perfect skin, her golden locks framing her carotid. He was captivated, the blood thirst thinking for him.

"Get out," he warned her.

"He's just shy," I said.

Alex covered his face.

"I'm tempted to take her for myself." I gestured to the chair and she sat down.

"Ah, succumb to it. Trust me. She is for you. Why would I offer you something dark? I think more of you than that. This way is so much more natural. It is more pleasurable. Do as your brother does. Her dreams and fantasies will become yours. Savoring her blood will be more than you ever imagined. Now drink slowly. She is fragile. See how she gives herself willingly."

"She has no idea," Alex said.

"Well, if I told her, she wouldn't stay in the room."

"I can't."

"She will never grow old, never suffer disappointment or pain. What a gift you give to her. A human form of immortality. Now do it."

"Where is Catherine?" Alex said.

"She wants you strong first."

"Catherine would never want me to . . ."

"She's changed, as have you. It's time to evolve, Alex." I patted his arm.

He gazed at the girl with hungry eyes.

"Gently," I said.

I brought my hand up to Alex's eyes and held it there.

Alex's senses filled with her scent. The moment was perfect. All three of us stood as if in a theatrical performance, waiting for the other. The young female glanced at me questioningly. I smiled at her placing a finger over my mouth, instructing her to be quiet and admiring the vulnerable mortal who would soon be bled dry. Another life extinguished in a moment.

The blood thirst drove Alex on, his instincts lost to logic. My hand rested on his arm and he opened his eyes. I pressed my body against his, savoring the mood, fascinated by Alex who was mesmerized. He leaned against me, his breathing fast.

Alex oozed sensuality, but the fact that he was oblivious to this was part of his charm. I sighed.

A knock at the door broke the spell. Alex turned, facing the wall, crouching in the corner. Head in hands, he sobbed.

"Yes?" I snapped to the ill-timed intrusion.

The door opened and Marcus appeared. "Sorry to disturb you, sir."

"What is it?" I said.

"May I have a word?"

"What?"

Marcus scowled. "He's upstairs."

"Jadeon is here?" Alex stood. "I must see him."

"Soon, Alex, soon," I said. "First though, you must eat." I shooed Marcus away.

Alex shook his head.

"Get out," I ordered the girl.

I turned to Alex. "I will not tolerate your—" I calmed myself. "Let me teach you how to appreciate this life I gave you."

Alex followed me back to the elevator. The doors closed and the cart jolted. We descended into the depths of Belshazzar's. Alex concentrated, attempting to read my mind.

"By the end of this night, you will never defy me again. If I am to teach you, then you must be willing to learn. You must trust me. I know what is best for you."

We stood before the dark wooden door finely engraved with Nepalese carvings. I opened the door, pushing Alex into the room. He made out three individuals dressed in black attire.

Alex realized the two women and one man had been waiting for him. He detected immediately they were vampires, and though attractive, their outfits provided them with a sinister appearance. He assessed the mood, taking in the décor. A few candles provided some meager light. The only furniture within the room was a bench. Alex noticed the metal shackles secured upon the walls.

Alex stood his ground.

Swiftly they shoved him into the corner. I offered him no reassurance.

I addressed my leather-donned workers. "See to it by the time he leaves this room he is broken in."

Alex made a break for the door. They overpowered him and dragged him back.

"Inform me when it is done," I said. "Alex, the next time I command you to drink—or, for that matter, do anything—you will do it."

I withdrew.

XXXV

JADEON

I WAS READY TO kill Orpheus.

Marching through Belshazzar's I headed straight for the lift. I was going to get Catherine and Alex out. Scanning the club's many guests, I ignored their stares.

Marcus approached me. "He's expecting you."

"Is he now?" I asked.

Marcus pushed the elevator button and we stepped inside. We headed into the heart of Belshazzar's.

"We better be going toward Alex," I said.

"Sure."

The lift jerked to a stop and the doors opened. I followed Marcus down the dark corridor, studying his every move and memorizing every twist and turn that we took. Stopping abruptly, my chaperone opened a door to our right and quickly entered. The door was left open in wait for me to follow. Peering into the empty room, cautious and ready for trouble, Marcus moved swiftly toward the far wall, waiting at yet another doorway.

A girl's sobs echoed from within the next room.

I scanned her thoughts to see if it were Catherine. Marcus's bearing was intent as he gestured for me to follow. Despite my better judgment warning me otherwise, I stepped forward into the center of the room, cautioned by his dark eyes.

The trapdoor flew open beneath me.

I hurtled through it, grappling to slow my momentum. My

shoulder banged against one of the shaft walls and bounced me against the sides, thwarting my ability to rise. Plummeting and battling with gravity, my head struck the hard stone. With a loud thud I hit the ground.

Gradually, afraid of what I might feel, I ran my hands down my torso and back up to my head, reassured to still be in once piece, though bruised and in pain. I scrambled to my feet, looking down at my bloody hands and again checking myself. My blood clotted and my wounds healed.

I took in my surroundings. The ground was dry, but this was part of the sewage system to judge by the reeking odor. Three corridors led off in different directions.

A noise startled me.

They descended upon me without a moment's pause, a dozen vampires hungry for blood. They pinned me down, shoving ferociously. The pain was unbearable.

Catherine!

Their fangs sank into my flesh.

I had to survive this, had to get to Alex and Catherine.

Their moans of pleasure resounded. Dizziness came in waves, the blood loss draining my strength until consciousness lost its hold.

XXXVI

⊕RPHEUS

MANY HOURS HAD PASSED, and Alex wondered if the melding of intense pleasure and pain would ever cease. His hands, tied tightly behind his back, ached with the strain of their bindings. He was strung up helplessly and begged to be freed.

They ignored him.

He now regretted he had not drunk from the girl as I had asked him to. His captors appeared to take pleasure in their work, disregarding his sobs. They judged both his reaction to the pleasure and his tolerance to the pain.

Pushing him over the edge, they held him there, masterfully bringing him back again to that familiar dark place. Alex sensed something within his soul dissolving. He wondered if he would ever feel the same again. His torturers probed his every want and fear and responded accordingly.

He relinquished.

Alex was permitted to rest upon the wooden bench. I settled next to him and ran my fingers through his hair.

He shuddered.

Alex's emotions of shame were twined with his calm. He reacted to my fingers caressing his sore flesh, gently stroking his skin, my firm touch decreasing the incessant sting.

"Again," I said. "He's not ready. Again."

XXXVII

JADEON

IT WAS IRONIC THAT my once-suicidal thoughts had now turned to those of survival. With my eyes closed it was easy to pick up the rich aroma of blood permeating the air. My blood.

The drag of frustration nagged at me. I was always in such a hurry that my ability to use sound judgment was impaired. This was something I had to bear in mind. If I failed to learn from this lesson I would be doomed to repeat it.

As quickly as the vampires had appeared, they left, commanded by the female who lingered behind me. She pressed her wrist against my lips. Unable to resist the offer, I grasped her hand and suckled. Death's taste soon dissolved.

I opened my eyes and turned awkwardly.

"Catherine!" I drew back, wiping the blood away from my lips and sat up.

Are you real?

"Jadeon. I won't let them hurt you again."

My heart leapt. Looking around, I checked that we were alone.

"We don't have much time," she said.

Reeling with emotions, blown away, I reached out and touched her. "I never gave up."

Catherine had not changed at all. She offered her wrist again as tears fell.

I grasped her hand and held it in mine. "Why did you not come to me before?"

"Impossible."

"I'm so happy to see you." I sighed. "Are you all right? Has he harmed you in any way?"

Catherine shook her head.

"I let him take you. I should have known . . ."

"Jadeon." Catherine sobbed. Her hands roamed my face, moving over my lips. "Orpheus is too quick for all of us. I should not have gone with him in the first place when he came for me at the convent, but he told me you were in danger. I was so naive."

"Where did he take you?"

"France, a château in Marseille. I knew that you followed us. He threatened me that he would kill both you and Alex if I ever left him. I kept you safe by staying with him."

"Why did you not contact me. I . . ."

"He watches my every move."

"But no message?"

"Impossible. He has me constantly guarded."

"I have you now," I said.

Catherine glanced into the darkness. "You have to stop him. He vowed that he would break you, destroy your will. I became his to protect you, but not a day has gone by that I have not yearned for you. Jadeon, you are not strong enough right now. You must go to the ancient one, the Alchemist."

"Who?"

A noise startled her. "He's an immortal who will guide you to the truth and then you will return to free us and, indeed, Orpheus from himself."

"I am not leaving you here."

"You have no choice," she said. "He has Alex."

"We'll find him."

"I can't leave just yet."

"No. I'm not letting you out of my sight."

"I know it seems hard."

"Catherine, you are my everything."

"Then trust me. Find the Alchemist." Catherine kissed me. All thoughts melted away.

"How do I find him?"

She fumbled with the engraved ring on her middle finger.

"Well isn't this cozy?" Orpheus stepped out of the shadows.

I rose to my feet, still weak, determined to stay focused.

"Catherine," he said, "we talked about this, remember?"

"Orpheus, they would have killed him," she said.

Orpheus folded his arms. "What's your point exactly?"

Catherine caught a sob.

"You know I hate seeing you this way," he said. "Jadeon, you've upset her enough. Oh, and by the way, if Catherine's your 'everything,' what exactly were you doing with Ingrid Jansen?"

I cringed.

Catherine reassured me with a gesture.

"She's so forgiving," Orpheus said. "Jadeon, how about we see how your brother is?"

Catherine followed him and I limped after them. Orpheus led us down the darkest of the three corridors. It would only be a matter of time before he got bored and would finally attempt to kill me.

Orpheus turned and stared. He had picked up on my scrambled thoughts. We ascended a stairway leading to the first floor. At the top of the stairs his men waited.

"Take him," Orpheus said and faced me. "I'm bored with playing you."

As Orpheus's men dragged me away, Catherine's sobs echoed behind me.

XXXVII

⊕RPHEUS

ALEX HUNG FROM the shackles. He stared off into space, unaware that both Catherine and I had entered.

Catherine ran to him, freeing his wrists from the harsh binds. Taking his full weight easily she led him to the corner of the room, assisting him to lie down on the long wooden bench. She wiped away his tears. Taking the leopard skin blanket heaped on the floor, she pulled it over him.

"Was this really necessary?" She glared at me.

She sat beside Alex.

"Careful," I warned her. "Don't go and undo all my hard work."

Alex was dazed, unaware of her presence.

I smiled at her. "My dear, it's all part of the master plan. Be part of it or be a victim of it."

"Your cruelty never fails to amaze me," she said.

I shoved her off the bench and pulled Alex toward me, placing my arm around him. "Now, Alex, how are you feeling?"

Alex buried his face in my chest. He opened his eyes and saw her. "Catherine!"

"Yes," she reassured him.

Alex averted his gaze. "Please."

"Alex," I said, "You've learnt your first lesson in obedience." I gleamed at Catherine, aware of her scorn and enjoying it. "Thirsty?"

"Yes," Alex said.

"Let's get something appropriate to celebrate our new and

improved Alex." I helped him to his feet. "No, Catherine," I said. "Stay here. I'll call you when you are needed."

She protested, but this was futile. She drew close toward Alex, taking his hand affectionately, embracing him. His flesh was hot, sticky from perspiration, and she could smell his familiar aroma, his sweetness. She had missed him. What passed between them was not for my eyes. Catherine kissed his cheek. Passively, she retreated.

Within my private chambers Alex showered and was provided with fresh clothes—clothes specifically purchased for him, a white shirt and blue denim jeans, his usual attire. I hoped he would feel like himself once again.

"It's time to test your readiness," I said.

We headed toward the center of Belshazzar's, always thriving and pulsating. Alex followed faithfully, staying close. His limbs ached and though confused, he knew one thing—never to anger me again. He staggered and I caught his fall.

Alex recoiled as a ring fell from his trouser pocket, rolling out on the floor in front of us. It circled several times before coming to stop at my feet. I peered at it then back at Alex before picking it up and carefully examining the small round object, recognizing the foreign inscription engraved upon its round surface.

"Where did you get this?" I asked him.

"I found it," he said.

"These markings? What do they mean?" I asked, studying the strange shapes that encircled the ring.

"I . . ."

"You may keep it." With a wry smile, I handed it back to him. "Fascinating."

Alex tucked it carefully into his trouser pocket and judged my response.

"Better the devil you know," I said.

"What does that mean?" Alex said.

"The path that ring leads to is an empty one."

The elevator ascended.

"I know you're hungry. I have something special for you."

We were in the club now and a party was in full swing. Alex detected mostly vampires with only a few humans within the room. He realized the mortals were unaware of whose presence they were in. Although there for the party they were blissfully ignorant of the part they played. With me in the lead both Alex and I pushed through the heaving crowd. Bodies rubbed against bodies, moving and dancing to the mesmerizing music, stirring the appetites of the immortals.

Together we made our way to the bar where the bartender prepared our drinks. Alex sipped the thick red liquid and gazed off. He stared in the direction of the doorway, thirstily gulping his beverage. He was going to bolt. I leaned toward him, squeezing his arm in an ironclad grip. Clicking my fingers, two men responded to my signal and locked the door. Such a gesture was a warning to Alex. He stared into my hazel eyes, realizing he was not going anywhere. The drug-laced beverage took effect and soothed his nerves. When he finished it he was handed another.

"Ah, calmer already. It will make it easier for you to choose which one." I looked out into the crowd, indicating for Alex to do the same. "Choose."

Alex peered into the throng, admiring the dancers. He was enticed into the hypnotic mood. The liquid enhanced the ambiance. He wanted to join them. Neon lights jumped and pulsed to the thumping bass.

Alex was seduced by the music. The poison raced within him, inflaming his every desire. A handsome mortal stepped before him, staring at him. Reading his mind, Alex detected the man's intensions. Alex held his breath, glancing at me for permission, and on receiving a nod he stared back at the mortal.

Alex studied the man's form, his height and dress. The mortal enchanted him. Alex felt empowered and reveled to be found exquisite, beholder of an ethereal beauty. He glanced again at me. The blood thirst overwhelmed him and he allowed the mortal to take his hand and guide him into the center of the gyrating crowd.

The mortal moved seductively, perfectly in time with the base. Alex judged him to be no older than twenty-four. Any previous doubt he had disappeared. Alex could no longer resist. Led on by obsession, he leaned in and placed his bared teeth against the balmy neck. The gullible man snuggled in close, embracing him.

I placed a distracting hand upon Alex's shoulder and drew him back.

Alex caught my gesture of disapproval.

"Not here. We'll go into the private part of the club," I shouted over the noise.

On entering the lavish room I nudged them to the furthest corner. The music thumped through the walls.

"This is more like it." I sighed. "Now remember, slowly. Enjoy it, and not too rough."

"What the fuck are you talking about?" the mortal snapped. "You can piss off." He headed back into the club.

"I am Orpheus," I said.

He hesitated and turned. "It's your club?"

"It is," I replied.

"I . . . well, I'm just not into this kind of scene," he said.

"Funny, that's not what I heard, Edward," I said.

"Have we met before?" Edward asked.

"No."

Edward was confused. "Then how do you . . . ?"

"Let him go, Daumia," Alex said.

"Excuse me?" I glared at Alex.

"What I meant was . . ."

"I'm waiting," I said.

"Waiting for what?" Edward said.

I checked my watch. "Perhaps, Alex, you would rather return to the basement and have a third round?"

Alex reeled. "Daumia."

"This is a form of torture, Alex. Put him out of his misery."

Alex wavered.

"Right then," I said, "back to the basement, now."

"What the . . . ?" Edward staggered back, horrified.

Alex clung to him. He punctured Edward's neck and sucked.

I placed my hand on the back of Alex's head, holding him against the man, sharing in the thrill of the assault. Edward's jaw dropped. Alex submerged himself in the feed. He rocked, his hunger subsiding. Alex was enraptured.

"Alex, he's begging to be let go. Don't kill him!" I said.

Alex pulled back. He wiped blood from his mouth. Dazed, he stared at the young man whom I supported. I turned Edward toward me and bit into his neck, drinking what was left. Edward's mortal coil quivered, then snapped. I dropped him to the ground, dead.

"Now bring me another. You have exactly two minutes," I said.

Alex stared at me.

"Well?" I said.

Alex withdrew, heading back through the doors to the dance area of the club. Pushing through the crowd he searched the room, scanning for the one who would please me. Vampires glanced in his direction, fascinated. Alex ignored them and looked around for our next victim. He wondered for a moment if this was his perfect opportunity to attempt an escape. He admitted he was actually beginning to enjoy himself. Perhaps, he considered, for the first time that he could remember. This game was exhilarating. He looked for the most attractive victim to present.

Alex's eyes fell upon him. He approached the tall dark-haired man, his raw arrogance discernable. The stranger offered him one of his cigarettes. Alex declined, taking his hand and leading him away from the dance area. Alex was relieved to see I had hidden Edward's body.

"Meet Matthew," Alex said.

"That was three minutes," I chastised. "But you're forgiven, as this one is an improvement on the first."

Matthew sensed danger. "I'm out of cigarettes. I'm going to get—"

"You know that stuff can kill you?" I said.

Matthew rolled his eyes. He turned to go.

Alex grabbed hold of Matthew's shirt, yanking him back.

"Careful, boy, the shirt's Armani!" Matthew joked and headed toward the doorway.

"Matthew, wait," I said.

He scowled. "I'm done."

"Yes, you are." I grabbed hold of him.

Alex watched in wonderment.

The music thumped on . . .

I sucked at Matthew's sweaty neck, controlling his head by grasping his scalp, savoring his weak tussle. With each beat of his heart blood was forced into my mouth.

Alex and I locked gazes.

The man fell to his knees in shock, unable to move from the loss of blood, his expression one of horror. His eyes glazed over.

I gestured to Alex to drink. "Mind the shirt. It's Armani!"

Alex gave me a wry smile. He knelt down beside him and nuzzled in.

Stepping back, it was my turn to watch.

Matthew neared death. He was fading fast.

Alex dropped him to the floor with a thump.

"Oh, no! I think you killed him!" I laughed. "Are we having fun yet?"

Alex nodded.

"Come here then." I opened my arms to him.

Alex ran into them.

He followed me toward the private rooms. With a shove, he landed on the richly engraved wooden four-poster bed.

"Welcome back," I said.

XXXIX

JADEON

IT WAS MY HUNDREDTH attempt to break down the door. I franticly beat it with my fists, leaving bloody smudges and scraping the skin off my knuckles, furious with myself for ending up here.

Use sound judgment. Yeah, right.

Just when I had almost given up hope of leaving this dreary room, a key turned in the lock. To my relief Alex entered, closely followed by Orpheus. I was so relieved to see Alex. I flew at him, wrapping my arms around him. When he failed to return my hug I pulled back and studied his expression. Alex stared at the floor, refusing to make eye contact.

I tried to work out why he stood so quiet. "Alex?" I said.

Orpheus raised his hand, gesturing for me to keep my distance.

"Orpheus, what have you done to him?"

"Where would you like me to start?" he said.

I will kill you for what you have done.

"Empty threats, Jadeon."

"Alex, come on. We're going home."

Alex was quiet, occasionally glancing up.

"Alex, talk to me." I had a sinking feeling in the pit of my stomach. "Orpheus, if you have harmed him in any way, I swear . . ."

"On the contrary, it was I who removed Alex from that awful police cell that you left him in, if that's what you mean."

"Alex, you know that I meant to return for you."

"You left it too late," Orpheus said.

I shook my head. "I placed the girl back on the stones to make them think . . ."

"And you participated in her death?" Orpheus said.

"Don't you dare!" I said.

"Dare to tell the truth for once?" he said.

"You have never been acquainted with truth."

Orpheus smiled. "Insults are all you have."

"Enough!" Alex said.

His outburst startled me. "Alex, his men captured me and locked me up."

"I saved you." Orpheus shook his head. "Had I not sent my men you would never have made it."

"Alex, we're going." I reached for him.

Alex stepped back. "No! I don't want to leave here. Not yet, anyway. I refuse to return to that dark castle, the one you left me in."

"Alex! What has he said to you?" I asked.

"You've turned Ingrid!" Alex said.

"No. Why would you think that?"

Tears rolled down Alex's cheek. "I waited for you outside Belshazzar's, and you were with her when we . . ."

"You were late."

"That's right, blame your brother *again*," Orpheus said.

"Alex, you know how manipulative he can be."

"Or you can blame me again," Orpheus said.

I stepped toward Alex. "Have you lost your mind?"

Somewhere far off a door slammed.

"Alex," I said, "I don't understand why you'd even consider staying here."

"As always Jadeon," Orpheus said, "you choose not to understand."

I sighed. "Alex, I'll give you anything you want."

"Too little too late." Orpheus shook his head.

"Alex, you will not stay here. I will not allow it."

"Alex, looks like you've been put in your place." Orpheus smiled.

Alex peered up at me. "I just need some time to . . ."

"I am not leaving without you!" I said.

"Deny that you have never drank from an innocent!" Alex said.

I glared at Orpheus. "You bastard, you—"

"All these years you forbade me to do it," Alex said. "You made me drink from evildoers and in doing so I have taken their dark thoughts into me. Now I know that you had something to do with that girl they found at Stonehenge, which I was blamed for!"

"Orpheus put her there!" I shouted.

Orpheus shrugged his shoulders. "Do you want to hear more, Alex? Surely you have heard enough."

I lunged for Orpheus.

Alex stepped in front of him, protecting Orpheus from me.

I drew back.

"Jadeon, get out," Orpheus said.

"I cannot bear it. Jadeon, leave!" Alex said. "Let me stay here, I just need . . ."

"Staying is not an option." I again tried to work out what had got into him.

"You cannot stop me," Alex said.

"I believe that's your cue to leave, Jadeon." Orpheus opened the door and gestured for me to exit.

"No, not like this. Not without you, Alex."

"Someone's not listening," Orpheus said.

"Alex, after everything we've been through, everything he's put us through?"

"You slept?" Alex asked.

"What?"

"For the longest time," Alex said, tears streaming. "You slept while I was alone at St. Michaels, fighting off pirates and other . . ."

"I slept by day, yes, but never longer than that."

"Too many lies, Jadeon," Orpheus said.

"And you spoke with Catherine?"

"I just saw her now for the first time."

"And yet you fail to tell me this?" Alex said.

I reeled. "I'm trying to get you out."

"And leave her behind? No, none of this makes any sense. You've spent years searching for her and now you just walk out like she is of no consequence."

"It's complicated," I said.

"I have a right to know."

"He has a point," Orpheus said.

"Then ask him." I gestured toward Orpheus.

Silence.

"Leave with me, now!" I yelled.

"No, Jadeon." Alex stepped toward me and we embraced. He pushed something into my hand and squeezed it tight. His glare indicated I was not to look down at the small round object.

"Reconsider," I said.

His expression conveyed he was impossible to persuade.

Then I will stay here with you.
"I don't want that," Alex said.
I stared at Orpheus and back at my brother. "I will come back for you, Alex."
"I'm sure that's another empty promise," Orpheus said.
I glared at Orpheus. "If you so much as harm him . . ."
"One thing's for sure," Orpheus said, "Alex is safer here than in one of Ingrid's police cells."
"You bastard."
"Get out before my men drag you out," he said.
I had no choice but to leave. I took one last glance at Alex. "Use caution," I said.
Marcus's words haunted me. I recalled when he'd trespassed into our castle, threatening us. *He will take your Queen and then he will take your King.* Apparently to Marcus, my struggle was nothing more than a game to Orpheus. Marcus had warned that Orpheus was after Alex. Before exiting I turned once again to take one more look at Alex, be sure that this was what he really wanted and that Orpheus had not trapped him.
Orpheus's lips mouthed, "Checkmate!"
I pulled myself up to my full height. "Mene Mene Tekel Upharsin."
Heavy-hearted, I withdrew.

* * * *

I wanted to burn Belshazzar's to the ground. Not an option.
I lingered on a nearby roof and examined the ring that Alex had secretly passed to me. Around the band were engraved strange symbols. Catherine had mentioned the Alchemist, but I had no time to explore her words. This ring, with its inscription, must be a message from Catherine via Alex. I placed it on my small finger, pleased with its snug fit.
I struggled to understand why he would remain. Although he had once been infatuated with Orpheus, his behavior now was out of character. Fraught at leaving him behind, I considered returning to drag Alex out of there. It would only make things worse if such a thing were even possible. Moreover, Alex was right. After all this time I had finally been reunited with Catherine and I had left without her. I faced Belshazzar's and considered returning.
I must find the Alchemist.
I needed a place of shelter, familiar and safe. I couldn't return to St. Michaels. I wanted to be closer to the club. I flew into the air and

headed toward the welcoming towers of Salisbury Cathedral.

On my arrival a sense of calm came over me, as though this place of God had an aura of healing. The magnificent church had sheltered me unquestioningly, protecting me as a fledgling vampire; it was here I would find the quiet to think. God had not left me, I was certain of it. I entered the hallowed ground, making my way up the grand aisle of the cathedral and admired the large ornate cross behind the altar, fascinated with the myth that vampires were fearful of such religious artifacts. Such a cross only provided comfort. I sat down, resting in the front wooden pew, and gazed up in awe at the elaborately decorated nave.

I buttoned my jacket concealing my crumpled shirt, the only indication of my recent tussle.

Splintered memories of my childhood flashed through my mind and I remembered my mother, her gentle nature and kind spirit. I recalled fondly my nightly swims with Catherine and Alex and my father's approval when I succeeded in my lessons. Such sacred ruminations helped me to cling to my humanity. My thoughts kept returning to Catherine whose beauty was still captivating. Thank God I had seen her and she was alive. I would return for her and Alex as soon as my strategy was refined.

"Good evening," a stranger's voice greeted me.

I had failed to notice the priest within the otherwise-empty cathedral. The aroma of incense was so potent that it had shrouded the scent of this mortal's blood, a man in his thirties, his skin a light brown indicating Middle Eastern descent. His familiar black priestly robes were creaseless and he wore the familiar sacerdotal white collar of the Christian order.

"I am sorry. Do you wish to be alone to pray?" he asked.

"Please join me," I said, desperate for spiritual solace.

"I'm Father Jake. How are you?"

I am in hell, but otherwise fine.

"Jadeon. I am well, thank you. And you?" I took in the full presence of the spiritual man, enjoying the serenity he emanated.

"Where are you from?" the priest asked.

"Cornwall."

"Ah, God's country."

"Yes, they do call it that." I smiled.

"Yes, but He is everywhere."

"I hope so," I said.

"You're troubled, I can tell. Perhaps if you were to talk about it..."

"It's a long story... a very—"

"I have the time."

"Father, you are too kind, but . . ."

"Why put a lit candle in an already-lit place?"

"It's easy to forget the light," I said.

"When you find yourself in darkness, consider that you are there to guide the others out!"

I contemplated his words. The priest, like me, was a man of philosophy and it was comforting to hear.

"That's an interesting ring you're wearing," he said.

I removed it and showed it to him.

He peered down at it. "Well, I haven't seen that for a while."

"You mean those symbols actually mean something?"

"Why yes, it's Sumerian, an ancient written language, cuneiform. It is actually the oldest form of writing known to man."

"But how?"

"It's ancient pre-biblical text," he replied.

"Have you any idea what it says?" I was hopeful.

"I'm afraid not. The symbols are complex."

"I see."

"And for a minute there, I thought the Stone Masons were alive and well."

"What did you just say?" I asked.

"That once-secret fraternity. They are one of the few who still use this writing to communicate, in code."

My heart pounded. "Stone Masons?"

"An ancient society. An interesting history, really. Hundreds, no thousands, of years ago, there was a band of men, men who called themselves Masters of the Stones."

I nodded. "Go on."

"Well, history books reflect an ancient heritage led by lords of vast areas of land, hundreds of miles. These men believed in what we understand as legends and myths today—witches, trolls, vampires, and the like.

"They burnt the suspected villains. Terrible way to die, don't you think? The rituals were carried out at Stonehenge. They were called blood rituals, sacrifices to God. They took these poor mortals and burned them. One day, they made a fatal mistake, around about 1700, I believe.

"They performed a blood ritual on the bride of one of their own—Jacob Roch, a newlywed and a seasoned member of the Keepers of the Stones. He was away, abroad on business. On his return he learned that his wife had been accused of witchcraft and taken to Stonehenge for her final punishment. He never forgave them and sought revenge. Their activities were documented and published by one F. A. Snowstorm."

"Snowstrom?" I corrected.

"Perhaps that was it. You're familiar with his writings?"

"Well, I—"

"Anyway, they reportedly had the most spectacular rituals and it was recorded in his memoirs how they separated the ashes of their victims and poured them into the tops of the stones. They held the belief that if the ashes of the evil ones were given time to merge—or should we say amalgamate—they would return to their former selves.

Jacob was sly, taking his revenge upon the secret society he had once been a loyal member of."

"What happened?"

"Apparently, Snowstrom offered Jacob shelter and helped him through his grief. Jacob Roch was rumored to have lived out the last part of his life at Leeds Castle. Eventually the secret order died out, their rulers taken by disease. With no one to succeed and inherit the legacy their extinction became inevitable."

"How did Jacob seek revenge?" I said.

"You'll have to buy the book. It's probably well out of print by now. Fascinating theory, offering an explanation for the construction of Stonehenge. The most likely motivator to drag those rocks over thousands of miles, a time-keeping structure, or even more compelling, as Snowstrom scribes it, 'a sacred circle' that ensures the demise of man's one true enemy."

I bowed my head.

"A splinter of the fraternity continues to flourish today," he said. "The Catholic Church has spoken out on how it disapproves of their activities, but this does not deter members or prevent others from joining. The society is made up of businessmen, men of law, doctors and the like. It's men only, you understand."

I was speechless.

"I am sorry. You are here to find solace, and all I've done is provide you with a history lesson."

"The truth will out," I said.

"What's that?" he asked.

"Nothing, just something . . ."

"I must admit I'm as excited by the ring as you are," Father Jake said. "Let me copy down the markings. I will be delighted to investigate it for you. You never know, this ring may actually be an antique. It's probably worth something."

"Thank you Father," I said.

"Come into the vestry. I'll copy down the inscription off the ring and you can give me your contact phone number and I can give you mine."

I followed the priest.

"How exciting," Father Jake said. "You never know where these things may lead."

* * * *

I left the church inspired.

All that I had hoped for was spiritual solace and I had gotten so much more. I reasoned that the splinter group might have knowledge pertaining to the Alchemist's whereabouts. The ring's inscription was significant and I was eager to know its meaning.

Father Jake had promised to contact me as soon as he had deciphered the cuneiform. With a few hours remaining before I would have to find shelter, my thoughts turned to Ingrid. I wanted to check up on her and ensure Orpheus was leaving her alone.

I lingered at her doorway, wondering if such a visit would be a welcome one. Sensing she was home, I knocked and waited patiently for her to appear. The security chain jangled then the door opened. Ingrid stood before me wearing jeans and a T-shirt. She looked even younger and more innocent, if such a thing were possible. For a brief moment she appeared pleased to see me. Ingrid stepped backwards into her flat, allowing me to follow her in.

I closed the door behind me.

"Where is he?" she asked.

"How are you, Ingrid?"

"Alex. I need to ask him a few more questions."

"Good to see you, too."

She glared at me.

I sensed her wariness. "Perhaps a cup of tea?"

"Perhaps, or perhaps you wouldn't actually drink it."

Her remark made me even more nervous. "Why, I—"

"Why are you here?"

I sighed. "To see you, to check up—"

"Check on the case, perhaps?" Her tone was accusing.

"I left you in the castle. I had to dash off."

"You believed your brother was dead. What's going on?"

"You misunderstood me," I said.

"No, I didn't. Where is Orpheus?"

"He is of no importance."

"Is Alex hiding with him?"

I stared at her, trying to figure out how much she knew.

"What was Alex planning on doing with that blood?" she asked.

"What blood?"

"Who are you? What are you?"

"What do you mean?" I asked.

"You're part of a cult, aren't you?"

I smiled. "Come on Ingrid, be real."

"Deny it!" she shouted.

"I just did."

"I don't believe you."

"I shouldn't have come," I said.

"But you did, so let's talk about the facts."

"The facts are you are way off."

"Stop screwing with me," she said.

"Ingrid, I stood in that art gallery, alone, wanting my life to stay that way. You approached me. What do you want me to say?"

"Tell me you had nothing to do with the murder of those girls. Tell me you're innocent. That you are not evil and unnatural," she shrieked.

"Evil and . . . what are these words you use for me? When have I ever given you any need to say such things?"

"Did you murder those women?"

"No."

"Tell me."

"I did not kill those girls. Neither did Alex."

"Do you know who did?"

"You have got to back off," I urged.

"In case you hadn't noticed, I'm a policewoman!"

"I'm trying to protect you."

"Then tell me the truth!"

"It's complicated."

"You seduced me," she said. "For what purpose, I haven't discovered yet."

"Ingrid, I—"

"No, don't come any closer."

"What evidence do you have that I am anything other than what I have shown you?"

"You sicken me, you bastard." Her lip quivered.

"Ingrid?"

No, I am not that which you think I am.

"I formed the puzzle, and all clues lead to you," she said.

"What clues?"

"Evidence that places you at the scene of the crimes."

"There is no such evidence," I said. "I'm going."

"You wait right there. Who is Orpheus? What kind of place is Belshazzar's?"

"You must forget I ever mentioned that name."

"Yeah, right. You want me to ignore where the truth leads?"

"If you value your life—"

"So you threaten me now."

"Protect you from things you should never have to face," I said, hoping she'd listen.

"Protect me from what?"

I lost it. "From vampires."

"Pseudo . . ."

"No, Ingrid. No." I unbuttoned my jacket and threw it over the back of a nearby chair.

Ingrid's eyes wandered over my crumpled shirt, not sure what to make of my scruffy appearance. "A cult?" Ingrid muttered.

"No."

"Are you doing drugs?"

"You crave honesty, but you can't comprehend it. You have seen proof of what I really am when I invited you into my home. I permitted you to wander our castle, with all its secrets that reveal who and what I am. Perhaps some part of me hoped to connect, or at least have a sense of belonging. I was made into this. I was changed. This transformation was done to me, and then to Alex. Do you think we would have asked for such a life?" I neared her.

"Stay back. Stay right there."

Ignoring her, I drew closer.

Ingrid backed away, still focused on me.

"Have you any idea what it is to be transformed into something like me? This is why I live an isolated life. What do you know of such things? At least you have a choice, and you choose to stay away, to hide yourself from mortals even though you are one."

"Immortal?" she scoffed.

"Of course I am."

"Please."

"I have lived for over two hundred years."

"Jadeon, I need you to sit down on my couch. I'll make us some tea, okay?"

"And let you phone your colleagues?"

"You have to trust me. For the sake of those girls, for the sake of other women who may be in danger."

"Not from me," I said.

"Please, after all you and I have been through."

"I am peaceful and kind and have witnessed things that you can only read about. I have seen things that even the history books cannot accurately convey. You have touched my life as I have touched yours. In your world, you would have me locked away or worse. And in my world, you are but nourishment.

"Orpheus brought us together for his own amusement and gain. He means to destroy me, after two hundred years of me chasing him. He has tired of the game. How do you think you can possibly challenge such a creature? He would easily kill you. Of that I am certain."

"What then? I just turn a blind eye and allow—"

"Go back to your world. Turn away from mine. I will leave here tonight, and you will never see or speak of me again. No one would believe you anyway."

A glint of something silver—a shiny object held at Ingrid's side—distracted me.

"Ingrid, what is that for?"

She waved the long blade at me and stepped forward, her confidence returned. She had regained control. "It's time to face justice, Jadeon. Or if you are innocent like you say, you'll be vindicated, and then you'll lead me to—"

I leapt forward and grabbed her hand in mine, grasping her fingers tightly around the knife's handle and thrust it into my abdomen. The sharp blade imbedded and I let out a howl.

Ingrid shrieked, her hand still clenched firmly.

Blood poured from my wound and onto her, seeping from around the gash onto my clothes. I removed the knife, dropping it to the floor.

"Oh, Jadeon, no! Please, no, what have you done?" she cried, pushing against the wound, stemming the bleeding. "I'll get an ambulance."

"Is this what you want for me, Ingrid, to see me dead?" I ignored the pain.

I grasped her shoulders, pulling her back. I lifted my blood-soaked shirt, placing her fingers where the knife had penetrated.

"Look," I said.

The wound healed, the blood seemingly drawn back into my body.

Ingrid's bloodstained hands fumbled over my stomach, probing the area. "But how?"

"I thought we'd already established that," I said.

"You can't really be a . . . vampire!"

"Did I miss something?" I wiped my bloody hands on my trousers.

"No!"

"Now, please, you're standing on my foot."

"Sorry." She drew back. Ingrid furrowed her brow.

"Don't ask me, you're the detective," I said.

"What?"

"You just wondered what you're meant to do next," I said. "I read your mind."

"Shit!"

I unbuttoned my shirt and removed it. "Can I wash this out? It's my favorite shirt . . . well, was."

"You have a favorite shirt! You're a vampire with a favorite shirt!" Ingrid said. She slumped down on her couch. "You can read my mind?"

"Yes."

She blushed. "That's how you knew what to say to me and when—"

"That does happen to be a vampire trait."

"No, I can't . . ."

"Sure. I'd be happy to provide a demonstration."

"I think you just did." Ingrid's eyes wandered.

"Chocolate flavor?" I said.

"Oh, bloody hell! Every thought?"

"Pretty much."

"Even those thoughts?"

"Particularly those!" I said with a wry smile.

"I hope you can't put thoughts in my mind as well. Can you?"

"No, those are your thoughts. Even I can't think that dirty!"

"That's how you seduced me, isn't it? You read my every desire. You scanned my mind so that you would know what would work on me?"

"Your desires are those of a normal woman."

"No one will ever believe me," she said.

"That's probably a good thing."

"This is freaking me out!"

"Me too at first time."

"This is such a mess."

"I never meant for any of this to happen. I will go now, and you need never see me again." I backed up, shirt in hand. "This . . . you, me . . . it's unnatural, not meant to be. I have to go, and you must forget me. I also beg you to forgive me."

"Jadeon, no! Not like this. You do not come into my life, turn it upside down, then say, *Sorry I must be going.*"

"We are an impossible match."

"I couldn't bear to think I'd never see you again."

I smiled. "You just stabbed me!"

"I'm ready to learn more about you, about what you are," she said. "I know that this is fundamental to my case. I must learn everything."

"Go and wash your hands. My blood's all over them." I followed her gaze to the table.

Ingrid saw me looking at the books. "I was hoping they'd help me with my investigation. Oh God, I need a drink!" Ingrid walked over to the cabinet and poured herself a large whiskey. "Would you like one?" she asked. "Of course not."

A book title caught my eye: *Necromancing the Stones.*

Ingrid carried her glass to the couch and sat down again.

"Orpheus will always be a threat to you," I said, "while you are in my world."

"It's a risk I'm willing to take," she said.

I sighed. "But one that I am not."

* * * *

I was getting close.

Father Jake had interpreted the inscription on the ring. I had phoned him just after leaving Ingrid, and Father Jake had relayed the ancient words he had deciphered. I immediately comprehended them: *"Fabian-eternal leads you."*

The immense castle loomed before me, situated on an island formed by the river Len—a harsh reminder of my own home. The gatehouse, with its barbican and drawbridge, was a worthy entrance to 'the loveliest castle in the world.'

Leeds Castle, six miles southeast of Maidstone, was cradled in the English countryside, a paradise of the past. I had known of this fortress since I was a child, though this was my first visit. It had earned the reputation of being the "ladies' castle" due to its numerous female royal residences. Catherine of Aragon had resided here, first wife of Henry VIII. Elizabeth I had walked the very path where I now stood. After she was freed, darkness had befallen the grand manor. Its reflection shimmered in the dark water of the river.

When Ingrid had finally fallen asleep I watched, fascinated

with her alcohol-induced dreams that provided a myriad of images, impossible to grasp or even interpret. Had I once dreamt in such a way? I could no longer remember. While she slept I read *Necromancing the Stone*, scribed by Fabian Snowstrom, shocked by what the words had relayed, and still reeled from his prose.

I scanned the pages of Fabian's book, looking for anything that would be a clue to the Alchemist's whereabouts. Then I stumbled on a paragraph so profound that I almost fell off Ingrid's couch. I recalled Fabian's words:

My friend, Jacob, had sought out the Servants of the Stones—the chosen ones tasked with assembling the ashes and pouring them into the stones. He had bribed them with vast sums of money, ensuring they would fulfill his wishes. He knew many of the noblemen from when he was a member of the Royal fraternity himself. They had no idea he was a vampire.

To be honest, many of them doubted the validity of the ceremony and believed that once the vampire had been stabbed or staked through the heart, they could no longer be revived.

In fact, it was assumed that this and not the light was what caused their demise. Burying them within the stones was considered passé, just part of the ritual, and deemed no longer necessary by the younger men. Though it was of course still carried out.

They envied the Stone Master, who obviously took pleasure from drinking the sacred blood. They coveted their master's role. They too wished to experience the rapture of the drink. Therefore, they obligingly gathered up the vampire's remains and delivered them to Jacob just as he had requested. More money paid for their silence. In the end, he had obtained quite a collection.

Looking back at those years, he realized his foolishness. For what use was such an endeavor? Yet at the time, outwitting Lord Archer Artimas and his descendants, who also held the title Masters of the Stones, had provided some solace for Jacob, some retribution for the loss of Lilly, his mortal bride.

I was stunned.

Would Fabian know where Jacob had stored the ashes, and could Sunaria's be amongst them? Perhaps, I considered, it would be possible to retrieve Sunaria's remains and make a deal with Orpheus—exchange her ashes for the safe return of both Catherine and Alex.

Could it be this easy?

I entered the castle with caution through an open window in the attic and silently descended the winding stairway until I found the huge library. On the many shelves was an assortment of books rivaling my own collection. The immense catalogue of novels and manuscripts were interspersed with a rich collection of compendiums. High arched windows with their richly stained glass obscured the night. Their colors would be exquisite in daylight. This was the room in which my search would begin. But where, I pondered, was my first clue?

At the center of the athenaeum stood a large antique oak table. Three leather-bound chairs were pushed up against it. Upon the table lay a book, out of place in this organized and catalogued room. I picked up the timeworn volume and read its title: *Mao Lou and His Insight into Inner Truths.*

From within the first page a small white card fell out and onto the floor. I picked it up, examining the writing, and noted the style of italic script written in fine black ink, though it was the words themselves that stole my attention. *What sleeps yet to be awakened.*

"Consciousness," I said. "The answer must be enlightenment." I understood this was a trial. If proven worthy, I would meet with Fabian. I wondered how many clues I was going to have to put together to find the elusive nightwalker who was toying with me. Studiously I walked by each bookshelf, scanning the titles until I found a book entitled *Enlightenment: A Seeker's Guide.*

I eased it off the shelf, prying open the dusty cover, delighted to see another white card, the familiar script written upon it. I read the words, fascinated: *The one who is able to still the water will see below and view his inner being.* I understood.

I was enthralled. Who was this Fabian? I was impatient to meet and converse with him. Looking around, another volume caught my eye, high upon one of the corner shelves, the title's relation to water a distinct clue: *Aquarius's Existential Effects.* I opened it quickly, pulling another familiar white card from the bindings and reading the inscription. *What distracts the searcher from the search?*

Speaking aloud to myself, it was easy to comprehend the philosophical notations. "Along the journey on which we search for the truth, we can be caught up within the journey itself." *Travel, A Life Well-Spent,* was the next book. My head spun. The letter within it was addressed to me.

Jadeon,

You have done well, but I knew that you would. I am Fabian, the one whom you seek. We shall meet soon, for I have much to teach you. I have lived for over three thousand years, traveling this strange earth. I was a shaman when I lived in the rhythm of the sun. I have been watching you for many years, and I want to share with you my knowledge.

We have nothing but time and love, and therefore it is with these words that I continue to guide you to me. Are you worthy? We shall see. There is a Zen expression fish weir. As we search for the experience, we must let go of the techniques and practices that lead us there. We must let go of the concepts and methods. It's a bit like getting out of our Jaguar, so to speak, and leaving it behind after we have arrived at our journey's end.

My head jerked up. I looked around the silent room. Was Fabian watching me even now? I was sure of it. I continued reading.

If we cling to our past and our former lessons, how can we truly appreciate the experience when we have arrived at our destination? We must make ourselves available to the reality of enlightenment.

The fish weir is there to catch the fish, but when we have caught it, we must keep the fish and let go of the weir. As Chuang-tzu explains so well, "Words are there to convey a profound meaning. We should keep the meaning and forget the words."

Jadeon, your next clue is as follows: "And lo, thou shall be seated at the king's table, and he shall serve you till the end of his days, and he shall call you master, as you will him." Good luck.

Yours Forever and Eternal,
Fabian Snowstrom.

I was overwhelmed, feeling my mind and spirit opening up to such a profound experience. I paced the room, pondering on all that had happened in the last few nights. My world of torment and my conflict with Orpheus now seemed a million miles away. I would have to return soon and take up the fight again with Orpheus, but it was here in this mysterious castle that I would learn the skills I would need to defeat him.

Would this two-hundred-year-old trial soon be over?

My thoughts wandered to Alex and Catherine, trapped within that awful building in London. Time was of the essence. I found my next book, *Man's Law of Equalization*. Written on the white card were instructions to read a paragraph within the text.

The most fundamental and basic law is that of equalization. Until you have accepted this, you cannot move on. Man, woman, and child are created equal. Indeed, race, color, and creed are but illusions. The physicality of form is nothing other than a facade. When one comes to view himself as equal to, not better or worse in any way to, others, then one has succeeded on this first stage along life's journey.

For we are one – not separate in any way, other than by our mind and thoughts. Nature does not separate itself in any way, except in our perception of it. Therefore, mankind does not separate in any way, except in our perception of it. We are all one. We come from the same and will return to the same. To discover the true essence of being is the way of truth. You are truth.

I read the inscription in the margin of the book, written in Fabian's handwriting. *What moves mountains and turns water into wine?* it read.

"Faith," I said and walked through the aisles, looking for the book most relevant to the question. I peered out the windows again, wondering how long I had spent in the library.

The large, richly bound Bible stood out amongst the many books that surrounded it. As I removed it from the shelf, a white card fell from between the pages. I picked it up, quickly reading the familiar florid.

Dearest Jadeon,

I know what it is that you fear the most. Have you the faith to face it? Do you have the faith to enter the light and become one with it? If so, when the dawn arrives, remain within the room until I come for you. I shall, of that you can have no doubt. I will not make you do anything you are not ready for. I will not take you anywhere where you are not prepared to go. Trust is all I ask. You must let go of the 'I,' Jadeon – your ego. You must examine your fears, move through them, face and embrace them. For they are but illusions. Give in to the truth and accept what is real. For only when you live in truth can you find the happiness and fulfillment you so desire.

Yours Forever and Eternal
Fabian Snowstrom

I was unsettled by the letter. Facing my fear would most certainly kill me. I was crestfallen, having gotten so close. And yet here was the final stage. How dare Fabian ask such a thing? This stranger was asking me to risk my life for an audience with him. A glint on the stained glass hinted that the morning sun neared. If I were going to back out, it would have to be soon.

Dispirited, I thought of Alex and Catherine imprisoned within Belshazzar's. I rallied myself, willing to do anything, even die if it bought their freedom. My faith was imperative. Resigned, I pulled one of the four leather-bound chairs back from the table and sat down, fighting my exhaustion. Fabian had promised to come for me. I chose to believe him.

XL

⊕RPHEUS

BLAKE AND INGRID STARED at the many files and books on Ingrid's coffee table. They sat back on her couch.

"Okay, so run it by me again," Blake said.

"What we have believed to be myth all this time is in fact real," Ingrid said.

"Ingrid, you know I always run with your ideas, but this time . . ."

"I've seen things when I visited St. Michael's. Jadeon Artimas had artifacts that pertained to him. I've never once seen him eat anything, and every time it gets light he's nowhere to be seen."

"Come on, Ingrid."

"And he's always one step ahead of me . . . me!"

"Maybe you've finally met your match," said Blake.

"Trust me on this, Artimas is . . . different."

"Different how?"

"Look, I—"

"What . . . are you holding out on me?'

"It's complicated," she said.

"Ingrid?"

"He hasn't got a birth certificate. He has no driving license."

"Well, we can get him in for questioning on that alone."

"He's too elusive."

Blake ran his fingers through his hair. "You said you've left the best for last. So go on then. Let's have it."

Ingrid opened the large beige folder and spread the contents on the table. "DNA," she said.

He studied the papers.

"As you know, it's possible to determine the sequence of base pairs in the DNA and thus identify . . ."

"We got a fingerprint?"

"Better, a blood sample." Ingrid smiled.

"Where from?"

"Jadeon Artimas."

"How did you . . . ?"

"I need you to keep an open mind."

"I'm listening."

"There was marked transmutation," she said.

"Okay. Wait, there was what?"

"Jadeon Artimas is over two hundred years old. And no, before you ask, there is no way it could be one of his ancestors."

"So you determined the age?"

"The results were run three times!"

"Impossible," Blake scoffed.

"Ellison verified it."

"Maybe—"

"They used cutting-edge technology."

"Okay, as always I'm seeing it through your eyes. And I know you have something else for me."

"I do."

"Do I need a drink?"

"Do you need a drink?"

"The suspense . . ."

"I am going to show you a photograph of Orpheus, otherwise known as Daumia Velde. See here."

Blake viewed the photograph. "Okay, a snapshot of one of our suspects on the opening of his club in Belgravia."

"And now this." Ingrid handed Blake the black-and-white newspaper cutting.

Blake leapt up. "No way! Tampered with?"

"The lab tells me it's authentic."

"That's the same man, but he's dressed in 1930s garb and standing next to—"

"Sir Winston Churchill."

Blake went pale. "Okay, I definitely need that drink now."

* * * *

Of what do mortals dream when vampiric blood races through their veins, quickening their souls and magnifying their senses?

Waiting for her colleague to leave, I had chosen my moment to enter Ingrid's flat. She slept deeply on her sofa, watched by me. "You're dreaming again," I said, waking her.

Ingrid sat up with a jolt. On seeing me she jumped up from the couch and headed for her bedroom. She banged her door shut.

"Are we safe now?" I whispered from behind.

Ingrid whirled around.

I bore down on her, my gaze threatening. "Déjà vu."

Ingrid pushed past me, running to the far side of her bedroom. She searched for something, anything that could be used as a weapon.

"Shall I help you look?" I said.

Ingrid tried to gain composure. "What the hell are you doing here? What do you want?"

"I'm here to wish you happy birthday!"

"It's not my birth—"

"Oh, but it is." I approached her, glaring.

"Get out."

"I'm offended. I thought there was an understanding between us. After all, we have shared such intimacy and—"

"I saw the photos of you," she said.

"Ah. Sometimes it's difficult to keep track and destroy that."

"I know that you are connected with these murdered girls."

"Damn, you're good," I laughed.

"Get out of my flat."

"What have I done to deserve such hostility?"

"You're—"

"Insane, no. Bad, yes."

"Tell me what it is you want, just so that we are clear."

"I don't plan to kill you. In fact, on the contrary, I have a rather special gift for you. It's the ultimate bestowal, Ingrid—the gift of immortality. We are connected, you and I. It was my lover Sunaria that bound us together. She had returned to Cornwall to find her relatives and observe how—"

"Wait."

"Ingrid, I'm talking. As I was saying, I found Sunaria's obsession with her lineage strangely amusing. She could not resist seeing them, and the more I told her not to go, the more she wanted to. Her stubbornness was to be her downfall." I nodded, remembering the way Sunaria used to frown when she was determined to do something.

"You are related to Catherine. You are descended from her younger sister. Sunaria's bloodline ends with you. You even look like her. After she was taken, I observed her descendants closely over the years, just as she had done.

"I chose you, my love. I lost her, but found you. My plan to make Jadeon fall in love with you has worked remarkably well. All this time, he thought I kept Catherine away, but it was she who kept me from him until now. Can you fathom it? In the meantime, I watched him suffer through his affection for you, which can never be realized." I leaned in close to Ingrid.

"Orpheus, you have to calm down."

"Don't I seem calm to you?" I said.

"I need you to step back and—"

"And I need you to listen. Catherine was never really mine. She gave her heart to God long before I met her. She has only stayed with me to protect Jadeon. However, it was never her that I wanted. It was you. I've watched and waited, biding my time until a female was born from Sunaria's lineage who resembled her in every way. I waited for you to ripen. I came into your bedroom every night and joined you in your dreams."

"No!"

"Yes, and I led you out of them again. You were born to be one of us."

"What are you talking about?" she asked.

"I can give you all that you have ever desired. I am one of the oldest vampires, and the most powerful. Now drink."

"There's no such thing."

"You said so yourself. The science is undeniable," I said.

Ingrid watched me bite into my forefinger. Blood trickled down my hand.

"You are dripping blood on my carpet."

I pressed my red-stained finger to her lips.

Ingrid turned her head away and pursed her lips.

"Always so controlled, aren't you?"

She glared at me.

"I will not offer you my blood again as a mortal." I forced my finger into her mouth. "Consider it a sedative."

Ingrid bit down hard onto it.

"What you call pain, I call pleasure," I said.

My blood flooded her mouth. Helpless to forestall her reflex, she swallowed.

"Enjoy your rightful inheritance," I whispered.

Unable to resist the urge, Ingrid sucked wide-eyed.

"Good girl, that's right."

Ingrid faltered.

I removed my finger and kissed her passionately. I nuzzled into her neck.

"What if," she gasped, "what if I don't want this?"

"Answer me again when my blood has done its work."

A tear fell. "This is not happening," she said.

"Be honest with yourself for once. You are bored with your life and fascinated with mine. You are intrigued with my strategies and fail at your own. Enjoy what I have to give you. Once a vampire all pleasures will be multiplied, sensations more intense."

"I don't want this."

"Don't fight it."

"You've drugged me." She groaned.

My words faded into the background. She buried her head into my chest, clinging to me. Ingrid opened her eyes and searched for my lips. Spellbound, she returned my kiss.

A firm hand tugged on the back of my shirt, pulling me away from Ingrid. I turned quickly. Ingrid slid to the floor.

"Alex!" I yanked my arm away from him, disgruntled with his ill-timed intrusion.

"What is this?" Alex asked.

"What does it look like?" I asked.

"What are you doing to her?"

I pointed to the door. "This is kind of a private moment, so if you don't mind . . ."

"Daumia!"

"What?"

"You said Jadeon had turned her!"

"Ah, I did, didn't I? Well . . . sometimes I can be wrong."

"You're scaring her," he said.

"No, you are," I snapped.

"Orpheus?"

"Since when have you called me that?"

Alex glared at me.

"You betrayed me, Alexander. Consider this as part of your . . . punishment." I knelt down to comfort Ingrid. She lay shaking, dazed upon the floor. "Now look what you've done. You know better then to startle her during the blood-sharing."

"Leave her alone."

"This has nothing to do with you."

"She's my friend," he said.

"She wants to put you in jail again. Some friend."

"She said that?"

"What do you think, Alex?"

"I think you're lying again."

"Like the lie you told me . . . about the ring?" I drew close to him. "You gave Jadeon the Sumerian ring, the one that Catherine gave to you. Don't look surprised."

"It was just a ring," he yelled.

"No, Alex, not just a ring. Its markings are meant to lead the wearer to an ancient. As we speak your brother is looking for Fabian Snowstrom. Well, there is no Fabian Snowstrom. He does not exist."

"What are you talking about?"

"This is hardly the time."

"Who is Jadeon meeting with?" Alex glanced down at Ingrid. "Why should I believe you?"

"Because of who I am."

"Please."

"I know that you and Catherine have conspired against me behind my back. All this time you thought you had the upper hand." I grasped Alex's arm. "You have no power over me."

"It was just a ring."

"It will lead Jadeon to his death."

He panicked. "We must warn him."

"I'll see what I can do. But you have to back off."

"Ingrid?"

"She'll be fine. Ingrid is in Nirvana. Don't you remember that feeling? Don't you want to feel that way again?" I let go of Alex's shirt and tugged on it, straightening it. "Now be a good boy and do exactly as I say."

"You have to let her go."

"You must understand. I am your master in all things."

"Help me to understand this." He pointed to Ingrid.

"I'd prefer it if you didn't question me."

"Then how can I trust you?"

"Look, all I'm doing is giving her a taste. You can see she's not transformed."

"Why?" he asked.

"To protect you. Once she's experienced the bliss, she'll be sympathetic to your foibles."

"I don't want this for her."

"It's not up to you."
"Orpheus."
"What?"
"I have to get to Jadeon."
"When I am done here, if you haven't pissed me off any more, I will help you."
Alex stared at me.
"Don't shield your thoughts from me," I said.
Alex sighed. "They make no sense."
"There is no sense in our world."
"It's madness."
"Chaos is inevitable," I said. "Don't fight it, or it will devour you."
"I don't understand any of it."
"And I don't expect you to."

XLI

JADEON

HOW TERRIBLE CAN *death be?*

Morning came with a shimmer of light, illuminating the vibrant stained-glass windows.

I had waited and observed the hands turn on my watch face—irrevocably, silently. An array of colors flowed through illuminating the dark, vibrant blues and reds in an exquisite ancient design.

Too late to run.

Painful welts appeared on my skin.

With that small drop of light came a foreign scrape as stone grated against stone and the fireplace shifted, disrupting my panic. With the secret passageway exposed I staggered through, fleeing the dawn into the dark corridor, shielded from the light. After several quick turns I descended the stairwell, stopping abruptly before a heavy wooden doorway with its 17th century baroque engravings. Behind me, I heard a grating as the fireplace settled back.

Blackness.

The door opened and I walked through, peering in. A tall figure stood silhouetted by the candlelight. I immediately recognized the priest from the cathedral.

"Father Jake!" I said.

"Jadeon, come in," he gestured.

Turning briefly I closed the door and took in the room, admiring the luxurious décor. Large tapestries depicting hunts and marriages hung fast on the walls. Lush carpet covered the entire floor and the

Victorian furniture offered up its generous hospitality. Father Jake guided me to an easy chair and invited me to sit. I was grateful to have a moment to rest, still reeling from both my recent attack and my tussle with Ingrid.

"Is he here?" I asked as I sunk into the soft seat.

"Catch your breath and then we'll talk," Father Jake replied.

"I have to get back to them."

"You are still weak, Jadeon. You've lost a lot of blood."

He was right. I had been fighting my fatigue, but it was fast catching up.

"The cuneiform," I said. "You didn't need to decipher it?"

"No," he said.

"You came for me," I said. "He sent you to find me."

"He's always watched over you," Father Jake said. "His way is not to interfere."

"Then why now?"

I have to fight this need to sleep.

"He will explain," Father Jake said.

I looked around, trying to keep my eyes open.

Gently, Jake placed his hands over my eyes and lulled me into a state of calm.

"When you awaken, you'll be ready."

The unsettling of my stinging flesh dragged me into unconsciousness.

* * * *

"He's ready for you," a voice whispered in the quiet.

I opened my eyes and jumped up out of the chair.

How much time had I wasted? My senses told me it was night, but it was difficult to gauge within the lower rooms of Leeds Castle. Father Jake stepped aside and another priest, thirty or so in appearance, stepped out from the shadows.

Father Jake withdrew from the room.

"Fabian?" I said.

"Welcome, Jadeon," Snowstrom said. "Now that you have rested you'll be able to think more clearly."

This was the man who had appeared to me outside Belshazzar's, the person whom Marcus and his minions had run from. Perhaps, I reasoned, they knew something that I did not.

Despite my disquiet I accepted the cup he offered and gratefully gulped down the red liquid, quenching my thirst. The potent drink was from an ancient and it quickly revived me.

Was I drinking his blood?

He smiled. "I am Fabian Snowstrom, but I'm also known by many other names."

"You're the Alchemist?" I said.

"I am."

"And Father Jake is Jacob Roch?" I asked.

Fabian nodded.

"Why such secrecy?" I asked.

"As I said in my letter," Fabian began, "I have lived for thousands of years. There are those who think that I am nothing but a myth, though others—those who believe in me—would come in droves for the ashes of their loved ones and the world would be awash with vampires."

Fabian's eyes were a vibrant blue and I could not help but stare. His very presence was startling.

"You know why I am here then?" I asked.

"I do."

"Alex and Catherine?"

"Down to business so quickly."

"I don't have much time."

"On the contrary," Fabian said.

"I didn't mean—"

"No offense taken."

"I just have to do something."

"You cannot control another's destiny."

"I disagree." I really did.

"But of course you do." He smiled.

"Who are you?"

"I was once a shaman. And now I watch over the nightwalkers. Waiting for when one of them needs to be reigned in."

"Orpheus?"

"And you."

"Me?" I asked.

"You."

"Why do I need to be reigned in?"

"Orpheus needs to be reigned in because of his dark. You need to be reigned in because of your potential."

"For what?"

"The Knowledge."

"Please explain."

"Powerful dormant forces lie within you because you have

opened the gateway of the soul," he said.

"I don't get you."

"As a seeker of the sacred knowledge, you have the ability to manifest."

"Obviously I need some practice."

"I agree," Fabian said.

"Why didn't you come to me sooner?"

"You weren't ready."

"How do I know I can trust you?"

"Can I trust you?"

"Of course."

"Then, of course," he said.

"There's something about you that's—"

"Age brings with it eccentricities." Fabian smiled. "After thousands of years, one is allowed an idiosyncrasy or two."

Teach me everything so that I can get them back.

"There is nothing that I can teach you that is not already within you." Fabian answered my thoughts.

"But I am here for you to show me how to kill Orpheus," I said.

"You are here because I brought you here."

My mind raced ahead and I sensed Fabian inside my head, weighing every rumination.

"You're wondering if I have them."

"Sunaria's ashes?"

Fabian indicated for me to sit, positioning his own chair opposite mine. Fabian took hold of my hands.

"I have so much to learn," I sighed and gazed at him in admiration, enjoying the sensation of Fabian's touch as he rubbed his thumb affectionately against the back of my hand. "How is it that we are eternal? That we have such—"

"Longevity?" Fabian said. "A time-worn question for all of us. We can only surmise that it is the way our blood transforms. It is highly concentrated with oxygen, therefore durable. Our cells regenerate quickly at the molecular level. We have evolved into timeless beings that exist outside spatial realms. We are unaffected."

"I want to feel that I am not an abomination."

"Nothing is," Fabian reassured me. "You are merely another facet of nature."

I considered his words. "I have Jacob's pendant, the one I found at the Mount."

"He'll be happy to have that back," Fabian said.

"It belonged to Lilly, his wife?"

Fabian nodded.

I cringed. "It must have fallen from her neck when the Stone Masters..."

"They believed they were doing the right thing."

"How did you come to be here, though, in this castle? I always believed there were no underground passageways beneath this château. No hidden vaults or secret dungeons."

"Yes, I started that rumor myself." He chuckled. "I designed these very rooms, furnished them with the help of my love—a mortal. However, that was many years ago. I fulfilled my promise and took her half-sister's life. She was dying, you understand. I just sped up the process. It was a feud between Catholics and Protestants. My lover then repaid her promise to me and secured a place for me beneath this castle where I could live in peace. Away from prying mortal eyes."

"This woman you talk of—"

"The very same. Elizabeth, daughter of King Henry VIII and Anne Boleyn, crowned Queen of England in 1558. We met while she was imprisoned here, betrayed by her lover. I sheltered here one winter night and heard her cries. No longer able to ignore her supplications I visited her in the guise of a priest. I was a mysterious guest, no doubt, but soon my social calls grew more frequent. She guarded her castle well, took care of her land by herself with no man to help her. We worshiped one another. She was a brilliant and radiant woman."

Fabian's face lit up.

"And you dress as a priest still?" I said.

"I am ordained."

"By the Church?"

"The Church," he said.

"Catholic?"

"Older." Fabian smiled.

"Then I believe you are the right person to help me."

"I am."

"Fabian, help me to get Catherine back. I must return to Belshazzar's and persuade Alex to leave."

"What I am about to tell you will unsettle you," Fabian said. "Orpheus has given you the greatest of all gifts."

I was shocked. "Orpheus has been my enemy for—"

"You misunderstand me. Orpheus has brought you closer to God."

"I'm going out of my mind!" I said.

At least I'll have company.

Fabian smiled patiently. "Our friends are wonderful to have

around. They make us laugh and bring us joy. However, our enemies shock us awake so that we look to God for answers. As such, our relationship with Him deepens. We awaken. Orpheus has brought you pain and you brought him pleasure. Such opposites are as light and darkness, illusions that we attempt to define and place into categories. But they are as one—undivided."

"Does this mean that I must let go of Catherine?" I asked. "It's just not going to happen. I won't allow her to stay with Orpheus."

Fabian leaned forward. "When we hold onto something or someone, whether it is a person, a memory or a passion, suffering arises. It's not enough to fall in love. We must become love."

"This isn't for me."

"In time, this will be your guide."

"Perhaps."

"Consider my words," he said.

"My head's spinning right now. Fabian, please give me the ashes."

"Patience."

Forgive me.

"No need," he said.

"Are you the oldest of us?"

"There is one older."

"Where is he?" I asked.

Fabian smiled.

"So many secrets," I said.

"And even more than that."

I desperately tried to fathom his words. "What does it all mean?" I said.

"Of one thing I am certain." Fabian's voice was firm. "That the truth lies within love. No greater love is there than one who gives his life for another."

I pulled back. "It's too much."

"Trust the process. You have proven yourself worthy." Fabian rose. "Wait here."

He withdrew.

I turned my gaze toward the tapestries with their stories frozen in time. I understood why Fabian had kept himself hidden away all these years, safe within the walls of this clandestine castle. Fabian was indeed correct in his assumption that immortals everywhere would beg him for the ashes of their loved ones.

I understood that not every vampire would take the ashes and use them wisely. Was I intending on using Sunaria's ashes wisely? I realized I would have to restore Sunaria to her full form, otherwise

Orpheus would not believe me that the ashes were hers. How, I wondered, did one rekindle the ashes of a dead vampire?

Fabian reappeared. "Like a phoenix, rising from the ashes!"

I jumped up and stared wide-eyed at the large urn that Fabian held, ornate with Egyptian drawings.

"Sunaria will arise," he said, "and once again walk upon this earth."

My heart beat so fast I feared it would burst out through my chest. "Did you know her?" I asked.

"I did. Inevitably she will return to her true love, Orpheus. He changed her name to Sunaria. Before that, she was known as the Sumerian. She was a princess. She was beautiful, and with her alluring gift she seduced Orpheus. Your father destroyed both Orpheus's maker and bride."

"How do we . . . ?"

"It takes the blood of two *vampir* to create the correct environment to resurrect such a being. We will offer up the spell with our blood and relight the spark of life that rekindles. Have you the stomach for it?"

"Just tell me what I must do." I approached Fabian, ready to follow his commands and for the incantation to be over with.

Fabian tipped the urn upside down allowing the gray ashes to fall onto the long walnut table.

I stood by Fabian's side, eager to assist. When the urn was empty Fabian placed it onto the floor. He removed a knife from his coat pocket and cut into his wrist. Blood poured from the gaping wound onto the center of the mound of cinders.

He smiled. "Right, now give me your wrist." Fabian placed the knife against my arm and cut deeply.

I closed my eyes, reluctant to see the knife penetrate. The incision stung. "Done?" I asked and opened one eye. My blood splashed onto Sunaria's remains.

"How long will it take for Sunaria to rise?" I stared at the table and cringed at the sight of our seething blood.

"Well, it's been a little while since I last performed this ceremony, and to be honest I didn't exactly have a timepiece then."

"Dear God." I sighed.

"Do you detect it?" Fabian said. "It's your friend, she has company. It appears she needs you."

"Ingrid?"

"Orpheus. He is with her. We must hurry with Sunaria before Orpheus does something rash."

"I can't leave without her." I stared again at Sunaria's ashes.

"Go. I will deal with her. When she is raised, I will send her to Orpheus. Hurry."

"Will you be all right here with her?"

"Quite safe. Sunaria will be well behaved with me. You know where to go?"

"Stonehenge," I said.

Fabian nodded. "I have enjoyed our time together and hope we will see each other soon. With all that said and done, I ask only one thing of you. I have lived here undisturbed for many years. Tell no one of my whereabouts. This I ask of you as a friend."

"You have my word," I promised.

"One more thing, Jadeon. When the storm hits, stay centered and you will prevail."

Great. Another cryptic message.

I headed out.

XLII

⊕RPHEUS

EAGER TO FINISH what I started, I checked to see that all was in place.

The towering pillars of Stonehenge offered up their silent prayers to the night. The moon's radiance reflected off their formidable shafts. The last time she had been here, Ingrid had gazed down at the very stone she now lay upon. Now she was the victim. I had brought her here, carried her through the air, tied and bound her.

Ingrid was terrified as she glimpsed the two uniformed figures slumped over, laying to her left at the base of one of the stones. She arched her neck, attempting to look behind her. Another female was tied to one of the pillars. The female, whom she judged to be no older than twenty, stood upright and was eerily calm, her long golden ringlets falling over her face.

Alex tugged at my shirt. "Let her go, please. Catherine has remained loyal."

"Shut up, Alex, you're distracting," I commanded and tightened Ingrid's leather straps.

"Let's talk about this," Ingrid said.

"It won't be long now. Just be patient."

She pulled on her restraints. "My guards are coming right now."

I pointed to the dead policemen. "Those were your guards." I turned to my consorts. "Remove these corpses. When the ceremony is over I'll need you again, but not until then."

My men complied.

I checked Catherine's bindings. "Catherine, all this time that you spent with me and you were never mine. Denounce Him. Choose me and I'll let you go."

Catherine turned her head away, giving her answer.

"So predictable." I approached Ingrid. My hand moved over her face, pushing her hair back. I readjusted her clothing, straightening out the cuffs of her sleeves. "I will bestow upon you the gift of immortality." I kissed her forehead. "Alex, it's time," I said.

"Time for what?"

"Novice, prove your loyalty," I said.

Alex froze, gathering his thoughts. He flew toward me and pushed me backwards, striking me against the large stone. Baring his teeth, Alex bit hard.

"You have made your decision then?" I grasped Alex's hair, using it as a lever to pull him away. "Have you not learned by now that I am all-powerful?"

I forced Alex against the stone. I wiped his tears. "So now you have forced my hand. A decision is to be made. I will let Catherine go after Ingrid is transformed."

"No!" he said.

"So when you are ready, you may begin."

"Begin what?" Alex said.

"Do I have to lay it out for you? I have no intention of turning Ingrid."

Alex shrunk back, realizing. "I will not."

I reached out for his arm and shoved him toward Ingrid.

Alex gazed at her. "Ingrid, I . . ."

"Less talk, more action," I said.

Alex was panicked.

Ingrid screamed. "Don't do this!"

I glared at Alex.

Alex begged me with his eyes.

I threw him a wide smile. "It'll be kinder if you do it. Me, I'm just too damn rough."

Alex held Ingrid's chin and with his other hand he covered her mouth. He turned her head toward him, exposing her neck.

"Alex!" I yelled, "For God sake, make it quick and put her out of her misery."

Alex steadied himself. Exposing his fangs, he kissed her neck.

Ingrid struggled.

"No, Alex," Catherine shouted.

I struck Catherine across her face and she slumped forward.

Ingrid's heart weakened. Alex reeled as she softened under him.

"Ingrid," I said, "let go. Let us bestow this gift. Surrender." I stroked her hair. "We are locked together by the sacred blood."

XLIII

JADEON

I FLEW THROUGH THE night, so fast that the air scarcely filled my lungs. My heart raced as I feared what Orpheus was doing with Ingrid at Stonehenge. Whatever it took, I was ready to face him. And with thoughts that had no time to settle I considered how to destroy him. Snowstrom had said that within me lay the power to change everything. With a sense of what had to be done, my heart was heavy.

The stones loomed up, obscuring the horror within. Fabian was correct sensing Ingrid's danger, but it was Alex, not Orpheus, who threatened her. Catherine was bound to one of the pillars. Orpheus had drained her, leaving her weak. Our gazes met.

I am here now.

"Alex!" I yelled.

Alex pulled away and stemmed Ingrid's blood with his fingers.

"I do believe you're gate-crashing," Orpheus said.

"Orpheus, what is this?" I was disgusted. "Don't make one more move."

"Alex, it will be more painful," Orpheus said, "if you don't finish what you started."

"It's over, Alex," I said.

Orpheus placed his hand on Alex's shoulder. "When all this is over, I will reward you for your loyalty."

I drew close to Ingrid and squeezed her hand. "I'm here now."

Ingrid shifted. She'd heard me.

"Get out of here," Orpheus said, "before I kill you."

"This ends here, now."

"How did you know we were here? Did she warn you?" Orpheus glanced at Catherine. "I thought she was incapable."

"Snowstrom," I said.

"Yeah, right," Orpheus said. "Go away, Jadeon."

"I have something you want," I said.

"I doubt that."

I glanced behind him and detected the impending sunrise. "I have Sunaria's ashes."

"Dangerous words, Stone Master," Orpheus said.

"One of the lords of the Stones collected the ashes after the ceremonies, and it was during the time Sunaria was here."

"Where is she then?" Orpheus said.

"She is reforming."

"You bastard," Orpheus shouted.

"This is what I offer you." I pointed to Alex, Catherine, and Ingrid. "In exchange for them."

Orpheus glared. "I should have killed you when I had the chance. Sunaria . . . lies in there." He gestured to the pillars.

"You must listen."

Orpheus lunged at me, throwing a punch.

I fell back.

Orpheus grabbed my throat, choking me. "I will pour Catherine's ashes into those stones and watch you wail at their base."

He threw me up and out of the circle. I landed with a thud. Orpheus leapt at me and thrust his foot onto my throat.

"Where is she then?" he said.

"With Fabian."

Orpheus's foot came down hard, smashing my cheekbone. Alex came to my defense and yanked Orpheus back. Orpheus threw him against a pillar.

I fought the pain and leapt up, swinging wide. My fist met Orpheus's jaw with a crack.

I pulled Alex to his feet and we untied Ingrid. I lifted her into Alex's arms. I turned toward Catherine.

Orpheus lunged, thrusting me against the altar.

My head crashed against the sandstone. "Alex, go." I fended off another blow. "Now!"

"Alex," Orpheus yelled. "Don't." He struggled against me.

I rammed Orpheus against the rock.

Alex untied Catherine and she fell against him. With Ingrid, they ascended and headed south.

You are safe now.

Orpheus threw another blow, knocking me to the ground. His foot struck my right arm. I staggered back and cringed at the fracture. Gasping for breath, I grappled for Orpheus's foot as he lunged toward me again. Pulling hard, I knocked him off balance.

Orpheus regained his poise and punched me. He struggled free. He threw me into the air and my spine cracked against a horizontal stone, causing the lintel to give way behind me, grating off its structure, spraying dust in its wake. Tumbling after it, I crashed onto the large oblong stone.

I lay still, shocked by the numbness in my limbs. Horrified, I flinched at the stark white light that stung my eyes and smarted my skin.

Orpheus rose into the air.

With supernatural force I willed my rapid recovery and sprang after him, unrelenting. I grabbed his legs again and yanked him down hard.

Whirling, we fell fast.

Sunlight melded flesh with light. Being and brightness intertwined.

Agony.

Sunaria called to him.

"No!" Orpheus screamed as the florescence blurred his vision.

We plummeted, staring at one another, disintegrating.

The sun gnawed hungrily away.

For you.

XLIV

Snowstrom

SILENT WITNESSES, the stones reflected the dawn's rays, mirroring light off their surface. Daylight thundered over the ground, illuminating the vampiric necropolis, rendering the immortals into ash as it announced its arrival in its predictable orgulous fashion.

Quiet befell Stonehenge.

And she had risen, reawakened, as if from a dream.

When darkness came Sunaria had flown toward the stones, her full form perfect and uncompromising. Orpheus had projected the images of his warring partner and she had recognized Jadeon's face. Sunaria had recalled the last time she had seen him. He had been younger. The mirage faded.

Sunaria approached Stonehenge with fear in her throat. She vividly remembered her last moments of persecution and drew nearer, anxious of what she would find. She scanned the horizon, confirming she was alone. On the very altar she had lain upon within the circle of pillars were mounds of ashes. Twelve hours had passed since she had seen the vision of Orpheus and Jadeon struggling to the death.

All day, Sunaria had paced my room, waiting until it was safe to travel. I had insisted she be blindfolded, so that she would have no way of returning, and had guided her out into the night, setting her free far from London.

Drawing close she scooped a handful of cinders, allowing them to fall through her fingers, rejoining the others. And then she saw it—Orpheus's signet ring, the one she had given him on the night of his rebirth. She picked up the band and slid it onto her left ring finger. Sunaria smiled. Soon they would be reunited.

She removed the cape that I had dressed her in and laid it down, spreading out the material. She lovingly gathered his ashes up and poured them into the center of the cloth. She worked fast, glancing about for fear of intruders. Her hunger pained her but she ignored it. She secured her find and bound them tightly within the cape.

She was an ancient and fully aware of how one would revive such remains. Her task complete, Sunaria looked about for Jadeon's ashes. She saw none. Before Orpheus's demise, he had also sent her a clear vision of St. Michael's Mount. Perhaps, she considered, a member of the Artimas family had come here and, like she, had recovered the remains of their loved one.

* * * *

Sunaria landed at the water's edge and gazed up at the silhouetted St. Michael's Mount. She followed the worn pathway. As she drew near the castle entrance she recalled her past. This was the place where she believed she'd been imprisoned. Had over two hundred years really passed since her demise? I had told her so. Yet gazing up at the familiar monument, surrounded by water, she could not help but sense that such time had not elapsed—at least not here.

Sunaria steadied herself and listened. Within the castle she detected a presence. She remembered my words, informing her how Jadeon had come for her ashes and how, until his death, Orpheus had believed her to be imprisoned within the ancient pillars. She had been furious with me and questioned why I had not returned her ashes to Orpheus sooner.

Refusing to discuss it, I had dressed her silently.

Dazed from her sudden revival, Sunaria had closed her thoughts, thinking me incapable of reading them. She would be the one to carry on Orpheus's work. She would complete Orpheus's desire to put an end to the House of Artimas.

Sunaria entered the castle. Listening, she heard quiet sobs. Two nightwalkers grieved for Jadeon—the one who had killed her beloved. It appeared they did not have Jadeon's remains. Sunaria's eyes widened. She detected the scent of a mortal, lurking in the upper rooms of the castle. Perhaps, Sunaria considered, the human was being held captive for a later feast.

She was hunting again, stalking as she once had. Soon she would be ready to perform the ancient ritual in order to hold Orpheus in her arms again. After her feed, she would be ready. She hurried up the stairs, reveling with excited anticipation.

* * * *

And so it was over.

Alex sheltered in the castle dungeons, doubled over on the floor. He sobbed pitifully. Inconsolable, Catherine lingered by his side. Neither spoke. Both were lost for words. Silence galvanized their pain. The mortal Ingrid was upstairs. She had locked herself in Jadeon's old room. Catherine and Alex were trying to rally themselves in order to find the strength to take her to a place of safety, where humans could tend to her. They had provided some food and water for her and now hoped she would rest quietly.

The darkened room bore down, its shadows falling over them. The candlelight flickered as Alex's shadow rocked against the wall. Catherine stared into space. A presence in the castle startled them. They sprung up, wiping their tears. They listened. Whatever had penetrated their domain was now heading for them.

The door burst open.

"I am Sunaria." She lingered, silhouetted in the doorway.

Alex drew toward her. "But how?"

"I have Jadeon's ashes," she said.

Catherine neared Alex.

"I am reborn. Jadeon persuaded Snowstrom to . . . revive me," Sunaria said.

"Snowstrom is real?" Alex asked.

"Of course, and he bid me to bring these to you. Snowstrom told me I may have Orpheus's ashes if I return Jadeon's to you."

"We will bury them," Catherine said.

Sunaria sighed. "Perform the ritual and he will be with you again. Your beloved is not dead." Sunaria placed the bound cape at their feet. She unraveled it, exposing the mound of dark cinders.

"What are you saying?" Alex said.

"That your blood will bring him back," Sunaria said.

"How do we know we can trust you?" Catherine asked.

Sunaria stepped toward the door. "I will go then."

"Wait," Alex said.

Sunaria hesitated.

Alex approached Sunaria. "Let us hear what she has to say, Catherine."

"Oh, have you not performed this ritual before?" Sunaria feigned surprise. "Must I perform it for you?"

"How do we know that those aren't the ashes of Orpheus?" Catherine asked.

"No matter," Sunaria said.

Alex leaned toward Catherine and pleaded. "I have to know."

Catherine was unsettled.

"Sunaria, what do I have to do?" Alex said.

"Watch me," Sunaria said. "I will pour my blood onto them, and then you must do the same." Sunaria bit into her left wrist.

Blood poured, flowing over and around the many ashes, moistening both them and the garment beneath.

"Now you, Catherine," Sunaria said.

Catherine shook her head and glared at Alex.

"Then you, Alex." Sunaria thrust up his shirtsleeve.

Alex squirmed.

"Hold still." Sunaria bit into Alex's wrist. "The wound must be deep." She bit again.

Alex flinched. His blood flowed readily.

"Alex, please," Catherine warned.

"See how the ashes react," Sunaria wiped her mouth. "It won't be long now."

Tears rolled down Alex's cheek. "And my brother?"

"Will be formed, like nothing ever happened," Sunaria said. "Though with the revival comes great hunger."

* * * *

I had to rein Sunaria in.

It was too late. I entered the dungeons and found her, Alex, and Catherine.

There in the corner, half-hidden in shadow, was the whirling ash.

A corporeal wail emanated.

Horrified, we were witnessing a violent birth.

"Snowstrom," Sunaria said, "you are not welcome here."

"This is work for the elders," I said. "You have overstepped your mark."

A mortal presence caused us to turn. Ingrid stood at the doorway. She had followed us down.

Ingrid entered.

Sunaria turned away and stared back at the ash.

I followed her gaze. "What have you done?"

All eyes fixed on the unfolding event . . .

A rapid evolution of bone and flesh formed into a masculine figure. Igniting life, veins pulsated along a taut sinewy torso and surged toward outstretched limbs. Hands with long fingers shaped, fumbling and grasping.

Facial features failed to settle.

Fighting for life he stumbled forward, jaw gaping in a silent scream. Dark eyes searched the chamber and locked on Alex.

Alex froze, holding his breath.

The being collapsed as if struck by an invisible force.

We watched . . . waited . . .

"Fabian?" Alex whispered. "Who . . . ?"

I stared into his eyes and gave my answer.

Alex fell to his knees.

XLV

Me

AWAKENING FROM OBLIVION I writhed, gasping for life. Opening my eyes I saw her at last, my beloved Sunaria, perfect in every way. Her exquisite face lit up and tears rolled down her pale cheeks. She was here, real, close.

I staggered.

Others stared on, but their faces faded into the background. Taking my time I studied my form, admiring my nakedness, delighting to see my limbs were perfectly-fashioned and my torso firm and masculine.

"Orpheus? Is it you?" Sunaria cried out.

"Yes," I bellowed.

Yet something internal dragged at me, held on hard and pulled me back. I took the deepest breath and filled my lungs. The pain struck me. I fell forward, doubling over. My vision blurred and I struggled to hold on.

Fragmented memories.

Flaying limbs calmed and I stood tall. With a startling awareness, my flesh transfigured. Beads of perspiration covered my body. My skin crawled.

I studied my arms; peering down at my large frame confirmed I was different. Catherine, Alex, Snowstrom, Ingrid and Sunaria stared at me aghast, their faces contorted with expressions that acknowledged the worst.

With my will, I fought the inner coercion.

The air was so thick, I panted, struggling to fill my lungs.

Silence.

I beheld my childhood sweetheart, Catherine, wanting to be near her.

Shocking emotions, waves of confusion, and scattered memories.
Impossible . . . not happening.
A sob caught in my throat.

Catherine drew forward. "Jadeon," she said, "is it you?"

I reached out. "Yes," I cried. "It is."

Book III
A Vampire's Dominion
Prologue

LIKE ALL NIGHTMARES, I wanted out.

Naked and barefoot, I sprinted along the uneven rain soaked pathway, my mouth dry and thirsting, terror constricting my throat and threatening to choke me. I tasted freedom as though for the first time.

Remembering nothing.

A cold salty sea mist hit my nostrils and I shook my head trying to repel nature's sting. Night wrapped her arms around me as I fled past the grey crumbling wall, bolting left under an ivy-covered archway, descending faster still down slippery stone steps.

Don't look back.

Taking two at a time, I landed on the grassy bank and ran onward, following the sound of crashing waves.

I struggled to recall this place and how I'd gotten here, my memories seemingly just out of reach and my rambling thoughts making no sense and threatening to sabotage my focus.

There was no time to question.

My gut insisted someone was closing in and dread shot up my spine forcing me to run faster. Rustling dead leaves swirled around my feet causing me to stumble. Quickly, I found my footing again. I crunched over a pebbled beach toward the vast ocean crashing six-foot waves onto a dappled-grey shoreline and rolling them into foam. The force with which I hit the icy water shoved my shoulders back and snatched my breath.

This was no dream.

Descending further, spiraling into the darkest depths, the ocean buffered against me and with outstretched arms I thrashed blindly to stay afloat, braving to glance back.

The towering rogue wave broke over my head, dragging me lower and delivering me into the path of a riptide that snatched me further into the blackness, sucking me into the swirling undercurrent and forcing seawater down my throat.

Drowning me . . .

Surrendering to the infinite darkness, I passed out.

Unsure of how much time had passed, my eyes opened to a blanket of white cloud revealing pockets of stars and a glimpse of the thumbnail moon, only for it to soon shy away. The night chilled my bones causing me to shiver and pebbles scratched my back.

Turning awkwardly, there was that same castle rising out of the granite, an intimidating symbol of supremacy conveying the gut wrenching realization.

I'd not made it.

A grinding pain in my right shoulder blade; I cradled my arm with the sudden awareness I'd dislocated it.

With mixed feelings that I failed to understand, I took in that dark silhouetted castle looming large on the horizon, trying to recall why it instilled such trepidation. My mind scrambled to piece together memories of having wandered along its sprawling corridors, losing hours within its age-old library, reading my way through its infinite collection of well-worn books, each one pulled from the antique mahogany shelves. With nothing but quiet for company.

More curious still was a faint recollection of whiling away endless days in there, waiting until sunset so I could return to the highest tower once more and paint my beloved nightscapes.

Daylight, that part of my life I'd long given up, exchanging her burning mortal kiss to become night's lover, surrendering to that endless promise of eternity.

As only a vampire can.

With an unsteady hand I stroked my clean shaven jaw and ran my fingers up and over the rest of my body, relieved to find that other than my arm there were no other injuries. Using my good arm, I staggered to my feet trying to distance myself from the waves spraying foam.

Across the shoreline Penzance lit up the night skyline, the sleepy town still, quiet, and desolate.

I turned and there, standing serenely staring back at me with dark brown eyes, was a tall young priest.

"Jadeon?" The stranger stepped closer.

I went to give an answer but had none to give and considered diving back in to get away from the one whom I assumed had been chasing me. He reflected an easy confidence that went beyond his thirty years. He still hadn't blinked.

Trying to judge if I could trust him, I struggled to hold onto the faintest memories that dissipated like cruel whispers clashing with each other, tightening my throat.

"You've hurt your arm," he said. "Let me help you."

Ignoring the pain, refusing to reveal any weakness I asked, "Who are you?"

"Father Jacob Roch." His fingers worked their way down each button of his long, brown coat and he slipped it off. "Here you are."

Cautiously I accepted his coat from him and pulled the left arm through, wrapping it over the shoulder of the right, unable to lift it.

He made a gesture to help.

"I'm fine." Though clearly I wasn't.

"You're adjusting, even now."

"To what?"

He went to answer but stopped himself as though unsure. Rubbing my forehead I tried to find the answers and not be influenced by the man who I had no reason to trust.

Far off lightening lit up the night sky, and a few seconds later came the crack of thunder.

The sound of footfalls signaled someone fast approaching. Over the ridge a young man appeared and skidded to a stop when he saw us.

"Steady, Alex." Jacob gestured for him not to come any further.

Alex's expression was one of horror and I tried to decipher whether it was disgust or hate. Lost in a fog of thoughts I tried to recall how I knew him.

"Let's go inside," Jacob said.

The rhythm of the ocean sounded like it was now inside my head and my legs weakened. My feet gave way.

My mind blurred, threatening to slide off. *"Who am I?"* My face struck the pebbles.

"That's what we're going to find out." Jacob's voice grew distant.